Let's Connect!

Goodreads: https://www.goodreads.com/author/show/5854923
Facebook: www.facebook.com/pgshriverwrites
Instagram: www.instagram.com/pgshriverwrites
Be sure to read the first book Paradise Rising before you continue this book: books2read.com/u/3Lg1JD

TIME OF DREAMS

BOOK

2

IN THE GIFTED ONES TRILOGY

PG SHRIVER

Time of Dreams by P.G. Shriver
Previously published as *The Dream* original copyright © 2014 by P. G. Shriver

ISBN: 978-1-952726-02-6
Paperback Edition

Address comments and inquiries to the author:

author@pgshriver.com
Internet URL: https://www.pgshriver.com

TIME OF DREAMS

BOOK 2

IN THE GIFTED ONES TRILOGY

PG SHRIVER

Time of Dreams by P.G. Shriver
Previously published as *The Dream* original copyright © 2014 by P. G. Shriver

ISBN: 978-1-952726-02-6
Paperback Edition

Address comments and inquiries to the author:

author@pgshriver.com
Internet URL: https://www.pgshriver.com

ACKNOWLEDGMENTS

Many deserve acknowledgement for their patience, understanding, support and never ending, unconditional love.

My Family

All who played a role in listening, advising, correcting and allowing me to complete this book. You know who you are.

My furry family who have so patiently awaited my return from within the writing cave to the great outdoors of my farm. They deserve a pat on the head and many strokes of the fur.

Thanks to fans of Cheater and Jaz who have been so patient with my delays in completing this trilogy. You will finally get your ending to the fairytale.

DEDICATION

As an author, presenter, and mentor, I'm often asked what part of writing a book is the most difficult. For me, the most difficult part of writing a book has nothing to do with writing the story itself. This—the dedication—is always the most difficult, especially with this trilogy. As I've mentioned previously, I began writing this trilogy in the year 2000. Spurred by the expected changes of the Y2K predictions—which, I add, never took place—this trilogy began with a simple idea of comparisons between modern day teens and twelve powerful and important figures from the past; I'll leave it to the reader to determine who those figures were, as it may differ for each reader. From that idea, the teens formed into unusual superheroes with unusual "gifts" in search of one charismatic villain. As time progressed, twenty years to be exact, the story of these twelve teens and their life changing villain also progressed. With progress comes signs and strange times of the type we live in now, with the threat of COVID-19 all around the world.

Like the teen superheroes in this trilogy, teens in the U.S. suffer today, though different from my characters. Today's teens lost precious memories with friends, precious times only a senior year in high school can offer. To provide a special moment—which I know won't make up for all they've missed—I hope to alleviate their sadness and stress by dedicating this book to...

THE SENIOR CLASS OF 2020

WITH HONORABLE MENTION OF MY ADOPTED SENIORS

CAMERON DIAZ
KENZIE FISHER
YULIANA GONZALEZ
ALEX J.P. HENDRICKSON
TANNER PACE
STELLA ROBERTS
BRANDON TRUJILLO

You are my superheroes.

1

First, Nathan noticed the blood on her hands.

He didn't have time for this. The last time he tried to help someone in trouble, he was thrown in juvenile hall, and he never saw his parents again.

"Get away from me! How many times I gotta tell ya'? Quit followin' me! Go home!" He spun around and pointed up the path. "What is wrong with you? You stupid or what? You can't go with me! Just go back where you came from!" The anger he'd felt for weeks released in a rush of spittle filled words.

For the third time since this problem arose—and by this problem he meant her—Nathan jabbed his finger in the direction from which he had just come, speaking as if to an unruly puppy. He could tell, even before their eyes briefly met, that the girl didn't have it all together upstairs. He didn't know what frustrated him more, that she wouldn't (or couldn't) talk or that she didn't seem to understand what he was telling her. In spite of his annoyance, deep inside guilt welled from the harsh tone in his words. He hadn't been raised to be rude to others, and never had he bullied anyone, especially a helpless girl.

She created a dilemma, though. *"It's a rock and*

hard place," his grandpa's voice urged. *"Figure it out, son."*

Maybe he could call the cops anonymously. Hope gleaned while he patted his empty pockets, yet he knew full well he had used all his money to fuel that monster, gas-guzzling boat his grandpa called a car. Inside his pockets, his fingers collected flat blue lint.

He should never have run away in the first place. He should have stayed and fought it out, found a way to protect what was rightfully his. What could he have done, though? After all, he was just a kid, a kid on a farm he loved and now missed. Thinking about the farm brought to mind the night he left.

"Nathan! Nathan!" The teen rolled to his stomach and pulled the covers over his head to smother the sound.

"Not yet, Mom! I'm so tired. I worked hard with Grandpa yesterday."

"No, Nathan, I'm not your mother. Wake up, Nathan. You have to wake up!"

Nathan squeezed the blankets in his fist and mashed them with his knuckles against the pillow. "No," he may have replied. A slight, sleepy smile turned the corners of his lips as a cute girl with long, brown hair filled his dreams. Her hair gently blew back from her face in a delicate breeze, just like the supermodels he'd seen briefly on TV. The girl's soulful eyes reached deep into his heart. He had the urge to hug her, comfort her, make her smile.

She looked so familiar, yet not.

Nathan's brows drew down in concern.

Why wasn't she smiling? She should smile.

The wind whipped tendrils of her hair around her face; stronger and warmer it grew, spiraling the long strands upward.

Her lips moved with fright, "Get up, Nathan! You have to leave now! You're in danger. Get up! Get your Grandpa and go!"

Grandpa? What about Grandma?

Her urgency confused him, and he rolled to the other side keeping his covering at his chin.

Why should he leave Grandma?

"Now, Nathan!" She yelled, her eyes turning angry. Then a fire erupted, the hot wind growing.

"No—no—no," Nathan mumbled in his sleep, tossing to the other side, "Not him. Not this, again."

The heat rose around him and Nathan began to sweat beneath his covers. He threw them off seeking cool air.

A loud noise downstairs jolted him from the damp sheets and jarred his body upright.

He listened.

Through his sub-conscious state, semi awake now, she tugged at his flight sense. "Now, Nathan! Leave, now!"

After what happened, that girl who interrupted the dream he'd had the night he left turned out to be right; it *had* been a matter of life and death and he chose to live.

But, his selfish desire to sleep brought more guilt as he thought of his grandparents.

He shook off the memory. There wasn't anything he could have done. It had been too late. He didn't even have time to try and save them before—

He pushed the thoughts away, again; his too long, wavy, hair swung side to side around his ears, and he scowled angrily at the girl who had been following him. He'd tried getting through to her with motions instead of words, but she continued to stare blankly someplace beyond him.

She would certainly bring him death.

For the first time since their encounter, he took a long look at her, at the stringy, unkempt golden hair, half still in a ponytail from the night before, half poking loose, looping wildly around its tie. Her filthy, thorn-torn pajamas covered her thin frame. House shoes, two sizes too big, donned her pale feet, and her thin hands dangled at her sides, long fair fingers smeared in deep red blood.

Nathan's eyes scanned her again, inching closer at the same time; her blank expression static while he searched for a source from which the smears had come, hoping to find a bleeding wound, but his instincts told him otherwise. A fleeting hope that the blood came from an animal dispersed with his intuition. It was never something that simple for him.

He knew.

A long, sighing circle around the girl only brought a curse to his lips, "Dang it!" This was a real problem—a not-right-in-the-head girl with blood on her hands who wouldn't let him leave her.

In his rock star dreams, he'd always found girls fawning over him and following him, but not like this.

What was he going to do?

How was he supposed to handle this situation?

How could he make her understand that he couldn't help her right now, and that she couldn't go with him? More importantly, how could he quell the desire to find out what had happened to her?

It was all about the timing, and no matter how much he wanted to help her, he didn't have the time.

"Rock and a hard place, boy," the gruff old voice echoed through his thoughts.

No, she would slow him down and he had to return to the farm, finish what those killers had started, and avenge his grandparents.

Contemplating, he turned and walked away from her again. His clenched fists bounced in front of him with each "No!" he uttered. Each step felt more like a trek through thick, sucking mud.

Taking her back to her house wasn't an option.

It would take too long.

He didn't know where she lived, and she couldn't tell him.

But... there is the blood on her hands. Momentarily curtailed by that thought, he stopped, then continued.

He stumbled over a stump, catching his balance before falling and injuring himself.

The blood...

A mystery it was, but he couldn't get involved in her problems. He had his own. Every time he'd involved himself in someone else's problems, or caught himself up in a mystery, or simply tried to help someone in the past, it turned out bad for him.

"Okay, okay..." He turned, taking a few steps toward her. "Listen. I need to go home, back to my grandf...? You have to stop following me and go home. Do you understand me? You have to go home. Somebody else will find you." His voice softened with empathy as he moved closer to her; her head tilted sideways. He gazed into the absent stare of her light blue eyes. His grandmother's motionless face replaced her image. *No!* He told himself. "Home. Go home. Do you understand?"

She issued no recognition of his request, no response to his compassion.

Standing inches from her, well within her personal space, his chest puffed in desperation for an answer or some kind of acknowledgment.

He waved a hand before her vacant stare. He smiled, "Hello? Anybody in there?"

Finally, she turned away shuffling her slipper

clad feet across the autumn dried grasses and leaves.

"Good. Thank you, God!" He spoke the words sarcastically spinning on his heels in the opposite direction. He needed to get out of this town and its weird happenings, back home to Paradise. Though content with the recent outcome, a vengeful scowl creased his forehead at the thought of his last night at the farm, of the killers.

The crunch of dead leaves behind him halted his steps, again.

How long did he have to play this ridiculous game until she understood?

His shoulders drooped in defeat as he turned, trying to hide his annoyance. She was following him again. His angry eyes flashed.

"Look, I thought we had this cleared up! You were going home! You can't go with me!" His voice held firm as he reduced the distance between them to less than two feet.

He wanted to grip her shoulders and shake her, make her understand. Before he could act on his urge, she turned away, moving down the same path where they had first bumped into each other.

"Good, good. Let's try this again. You go on home and I'll go home, t..." How could he refer to it as home, now? His grandparents were gone. He had to stop thinking about them. He didn't know what he would find when he returned to the farm, but a desperate need to return fueled his anger and he took it out on her.

He waited warily, watching her walk away until

she was twenty paces from him, then he spun and ran, but the dragging noise of her feet behind grew closer instead of farther away, shoocrunch... shoocrunch... shoocrunch.

"No!" He screamed in a whirl of rage.

Run, he told himself, but his body wouldn't respond. He dropped to his knees, his gaze falling to the leaves before him.

She couldn't fend for herself.

She'd get lost in this place and die, or worse, some out-of-town crazy, some perv would find her wandering the town in her torn pajamas.

"Please, keep going, please! You can't go with me!" He begged her.

On the verge of indecisive tears, he rose to his feet, charging toward her, attempting to scare her away by waving his arms like a lunatic. "Leave me alone!" His arms shook.

She turned calmly and walked away, not in the least frightened by his torrent of emotion. When he didn't follow this time, however, she stopped and turned back toward him, head never straying from its slightly cocked angle, the forever blank stare taking her thoughts somewhere in the distance behind him, the thin shoulders sagging the message, "Well, come on then."

He thought he saw a championed flicker buried deep in the calm sea of her gaze, the tiniest of taunting motion in her narrow hand.

His weariness played tricks on his vision, that was all.

No, that wasn't all.

In defeat, he caved to her request.

She wanted him to follow her, most likely to her house, where the source of all that blood on her hands lay waiting for help. Silently, and without much conviction, he prayed it was not human blood.

This disaster would get him in more trouble with the law, like all of the other incidents since his parents' deaths; the turned-over headstones, the vandalized school, the burglarized cars, all events he tried to prevent in his friend's life. He hadn't participated in any of them, hadn't even touched a can or slipped through a door with malice; he just wanted to help the only person he considered a friend, but it hadn't worked out like he planned.

His grandpa told him to let it go. *"Some people can't be fixed, son,"* the old man had warned. He didn't understand, though.

Nobody understood.

His parents were the only ones who knew anything about him, about his lack of trust because of his abilities, about his knack for turning people in the right direction. Now he was the only one who knew... well, except the girl in his dream.

He didn't have time to deal with this problem before him, but he would anyway; his conscience wouldn't allow him to leave this girl to herself. The blood, the way she waited for him to follow, the sense that she understood more than he gave her credit for, all left him no choice but to help her.

It was the right thing to do.

Regardless of the trouble it would bring him, he always did the right thing.

She needed help.

He would help.

He let her lead him head on into the trouble that would come.

From behind, he watched her closely as she stayed a precise distance in front of him, walking into the leafless, near winter brush without a thought for pushing it aside and protecting herself from cuts or scrapes. No wonder her clothes were so torn.

Before long, a small, white, wood frame house appeared at the end of a narrow driveway perpendicular to the lonely road they crossed. The girl moved straight into the front door, so he gulped air.

This was it.

She paused at the door, holding it open for him to enter, a statue, staring at the doorjamb opposite her face.

Trapped—that's how he felt. He knew for certain now that somebody in that house was hurt, but he didn't know how badly, didn't know what he could do to help them, or even if he could. After the last incident with his friend, he no longer believed in himself.

What if he couldn't help the person waiting in there? What if this was a trap? What if he couldn't help this girl?

Reluctantly, he stepped onto the porch and reached for the screen door. As his hand touched the cool metal, the girl pulled back her bloody hand—leaving no smears behind—and shuffled through the house.

Cautious eyes followed her into the gloom, all curtains and blinds closed tightly, all present rooms lightless. Other than the gaping triangle of light left behind by the door through which they had entered, there wasn't a beam of sunlight filtering through the house reminding Nathan of another dark building.

"Jake, what're you doin'? Get out of there! Come on!"

"Oh, don't be such a baby. The door's open. I just wanna look around, maybe see if the science lab is open, too."

"The door wasn't open, Jake. Come on; let's go to my house, hang out until my parents get home. It's really dark in there, and creepy."

"Yeah, schools are creepy at night..." His voice grew fainter as he moved farther into the dark halls. "Come on, Nate! Hey, the science lab is open! Come on."

The loud crash of breaking glass drew Nathan through the door, though he knew it was too late. He had to stop Jake from doing anything else foolish. He'd already been to Circle Court twice. This time Jake would go to Juvenile Hall.

"Jake! What are you doing, you idiot? Let's get out of here before the cops get here!" Nate surveyed the room of broken glass beakers, smashed computer monitors, toppled computers.

"Teach him to fail me," Jake mumbled as he bent, gripped the bottom of the teacher's desk, and straightened his legs, forcing the desk on its face.

"Man, Jake, you're already in enough trouble! Let's go!" He turned from the room and into the chest of a security guard just before the guard's flashlight blinded Nate.

"Run, Nate!" Jake said as he flipped the latch on the nearest window, pushed upward, and slipped through the opening.

"Too late." The security guard's downward grimace forced Nate's frightened features to pale.

2

Nathan cautiously flipped the switch on the wall, illuminating the living room, expecting a police officer to meet him. When his expectation didn't hold true, he followed the girl into the house, pushing the door closed behind him. In the kitchen, his right hand felt for the light switch and tipped it upward, lighting the scene before him.

It was exactly what he thought it would be.

Not a dog, cat or pet of any kind.

There, in the middle of the floor, lay an older woman, gray hair matted with congealed blood, face pale gray with death. He knew that look. His grandmother looked that way when he last saw her, the night he left, the night she was k...

He turned away, angrily shaking the thought of his grandparents from his mind.

After surveying the room, he deduced that the old woman had fallen off the tipped over chair that lay in front of one cabinet; she was probably trying to reach something. The girl knelt next to the woman, pushing on her as if to wake her up, patting her face stiffly with her blood caked hands. Then she stood and took her place at the kitchen table, an empty bowl set before her.

She sipped slightly warm milk through a straw,

waiting for her meal, dried blood flaking and sprinkling the table, the bowl, the spoon beneath her hand.

Nathan could see the handprints the girl had left earlier on the floor. They were outlined perfectly in the sticky pooled blood. When he thought about how many times she must have tried to wake up the woman, the rawness of his own haunting visions cut through him like the bitterest of Arctic winds, chilling the heat of fiery emotions raging through him.

A pot on the stove crackled and smoked, filling the room with a burnt food aroma, and Nathan stepped around the old woman, clunked the hot pan against the back of the range, turned off the burner, and knelt near the elderly woman. He felt for a pulse as he learned to do when his grandmother was sick. He knew there likely wouldn't be one, but he checked anyway.

Once he thought his grandmother had died and he felt around at her throat until the pulsing blood pushed against his fingertips, slow at first, then faster until normal.

He knew instantly, though, that he would find no pulse on the throat at his fingertips. She was already cool to the touch, her eyes glazed over.

With two fingers he slipped her eyelids over the sightless eyes, stood, and cast a sympathetic look at the girl who faced the opposite end of the table.

He didn't know this girl, but now they had a common bond.

He knew what he had to do.

It was the same he would have done for his own grandparents, had he had time before fleeing.

Stepping carefully around the bloodstained area of the floor, through the kitchen, and to the right of the living room, he entered a hallway ending in a bathroom. There he located a linen closet where he pulled a flowery sheet from the back and a neatly folded, pine-green, frayed washcloth from the front. After wetting the washcloth in the low sink, he returned with the sheet under his arm, his intention to cover the woman's body.

His eyes stung with tears when he found the girl kneeling beside the woman again, pushing gently on the cold shoulder as if to wake her, a sole tear streaking the girl's left cheek. He did the same that night.

Obviously, the girl wasn't stupid as he had so thoughtlessly assumed earlier.

And though *he* felt stupid at that moment, he wasn't either.

By the time she returned to her place at the table, he empathized with her state of denial and hunger. The sheet billowed as he fanned the corners above the woman, then it settled like a falling feather atop the still body and blood. He gently lifted the corner up and over her face, considering for a moment the possibility of moving her to the living room, but he knew he shouldn't disturb the scene further, just in case.

He was going to have to call the police. There was no other choice. They would know what to do with the girl.

Of course, he knew the police would not have reason to investigate the woman's death. Even to him, a fourteen-year-old, it appeared an accident. For a moment, the boy wondered what would happen to this girl, whether she had any other family to care for her, or if she was like him. If she was orphaned, when the cops came to investigate the death, they would take the girl to a home, and not a regular type children's home, he imagined. He cringed.

He shook away the thought. What if it were him? What if he'd been picked up after the murder of his grandparents? He would have been blamed for sure given his record.

Anger flowed freely through his limbs as he glanced around the kitchen and thought about the future of this girl. The authorities no longer cared about poor people. One look around this falling-down home—the tattered clothing both inhabitants wore—would be enough for them to close the case just on the basis that the two of them weren't worth the effort of investigation or a relative search.

He stepped around the sheet, stood before the girl and gently lifted one of her hands from her lap, but she pulled it away from his grasp. It took three attempts before she quit flapping her hands at his own and allowed him to wipe at the blood with the washcloth while she remained frozen, deep in her own mind, thoughts and grief.

Was she in shock? Nathan wondered.

Dried blood flaked onto her striped pajama

pants and smeared the delicate hands with each swipe of the cloth. He wished he could lead her to the sink, but she wouldn't budge from her seat no matter how he coaxed her.

After the last warm rinse in the sink, he watched the diluted blood swirl into the slow drain. The girl's hands were their normal pinkish beige color.

Wringing the cloth out once more, he wiped away the flakes on the table.

Tossing the wet balled cloth into the sink, he began his search for another can of soup, finding one in the cabinet above and to the right of the stove; he found another pot in the cabinet next to the sink, the can opener on the counter. He heated the chicken noodle soup on the burner he extinguished earlier until steam rolled from the opening and filled his stomach with pangs. Then he poured the hot soup into the girl's bowl.

Next, he opened the saltines on the table and placed them before her. His hunger twisted into nausea as he recalled having administered the duties of death, so he pulled a cracker free and nibbled it to calm his stomach. He found little relief as he watched the girl eat while he considered how best to handle her situation.

"You can't be bringin' home strays all the time, boy," his grandpa's words quenched the urge to take her along, save her from whatever horrible life awaited her outside these walls. *Would she be put out on the street?*

A brief memory tempted him as he thought of the two stray dogs he'd brought home. His grandfather had acquiesced to keeping them, but cut off further adoptions.

On the table to his right were two opened letters, laying beside their envelopes. The woman must have been reading them before the girl entered the kitchen for something to eat. He scanned the length of the corpse, the height of the fallen chair, and the soup cabinet.

She hadn't needed a chair to get a can of soup. So, why would she get up on a chair?

While the girl slurped soup from her spoon, his eyes skimmed the top row of cabinets. Many platters and items that were too large to fit inside the cabinets sat atop, sticking out over the shelves in the four-inch space below the ceiling.

A bare spot between two stacks of platters drew his eyes. In direct line with the chair was a book of some sort, the corner barely poking over the edge. He tipped the chair upright and stepped up on the seat.

Reaching upward, his fingers grasped the book and slid it from its hiding place. That was what the woman had been trying to reach when the chair tottered backward, spilling her to the floor, her head bouncing off the sharp corner of the heavy table that he now scanned for blood and hair.

There wasn't any.

Stepping down from the chair, he searched the counter edges.

Nothing.

"What happened to this woman?" His low words enticed his puzzle-solving mind, bringing a determined frown to his features.

The girl's spoon plunked into her bowl and movement from the corner of his eye startled him, but when he looked her way, she had picked up the spoon and resumed the task of eating.

Was she about to answer his question?

Did she know what happened?

If so then that could be bad for her, especially, if like him, she had seen the killer.

Returning to his seat across from the girl, he turned the leather book over in his deeply tanned hands.

It was larger than a sheet of notebook paper.

It was old, with a button clasp on the front cover, the kind that the owner wound string around to tie the front and back together, like the diaries he had seen neighborhood girls get for their birthdays when he was younger, except it revealed no pages on any edge all the way around.

He wondered whether he should open it; a sense of intrusion stopped him from unwinding the string, but then, the girl couldn't answer his questions, and he certainly wouldn't get answers from the old lady.

Perhaps there were no answers in this book, either.

Indecisively, his index finger twirled the slack string around its tip; his eyes turned to the letters on the table. Twice he read a phrase at the bottom of one of the letters before the words chipped away at his thoughts and comprehension filled his features. He never was much for reading.

But he read the words again:

> I told you, if you don't leave me alone and stop pressing the issue, I'm gonna drive over there and take care of the problem. Then you won't have to worry about takin' care of that idiot kid.

Idiot kid? He frowned at the girl across from him, the girl he had earlier called stupid.

Ashamed, he skimmed the words again.

Picking up the letter, he unfolded it the rest of the way and began reading from the top.

> I never did claim that stupid child. She's your daughter's child, not mine! And since your daughter's dead, that makes her yours. And you can stop using that officer of the law crap on me, cuz it ain't gonna make me feel guilty. I don't care about her or you or your dead daughter. Being a cop just

makes it easier for me to take care of the problem unnoticed if you get what I mean.

I ain't sendin' you any money, either. I never will, so quit askin'. That's it! She's not my kid! None of my kids would be stupid like that!

Nathan closed his eyes to dam the hurt, then shook his head and continued to search for answers.

His own father had been so good to him.

His own father would have stood up for this girl.

He scanned the letter, again, turned it over in his hand, and slapped it on the table in disgust. Running his fingers through his hair, frustration flared with the realization that there wasn't a name at the end of the letter, and nowhere in the letter did it mention the girl's name. If he could find her name, speak her name to her, maybe she would respond.

He opened the book; inside were letters just like the two on the table, filled with hateful words about the girl and her mother, written by the same man who called himself a cop.

Her mother was dead.

He looked down at the sheet covering her grandmother and squeezed his eyes shut to block the image of his own grandparents, the thought of his parents, the burning tears.

The boy's option to call 9-1-1 scratched off his mental list, and his mind raced with other possibilities for her.

Sadness overcame him as he watched the girl slurp her soup and nibble crackers. Did she even have a clue what this meant for her?

She had no one, just like him. They were alone in the world.

What now?

When the girl finished eating, she pushed away from the table, her chair scraping the faded linoleum.

She carefully scooted around the edge of the sheet and walked down the hall. He followed her curiously, stopping outside a bedroom door, a peeping-tom sense causing him to avert his eyes.

The girl removed clothes from a drawer, laid them over her arm, and then she slid past him and into the bathroom at the end of the hallway, pushing the door closed behind her.

Moments later, he heard the shower running and returned to the living room, pondering her predicament.

Perhaps old photos would provide some answers, if he could find some. He remembered his mother writing the names of the people in pictures on the back. Maybe he could find her name that way—although, he didn't know if it would actually do any good to have it. It probably wouldn't even help with her understanding him or communicating with him, but he searched anyway.

3

Instead of a photo, he found an old blue and grey backpack squeezed tightly between the front wall and the dirty, beige sofa.

Sinking into the worn cushions, springs popping beneath him, he unzipped the backpack and fingered through the contents. He discovered a used spiral notebook and pulled it free with thumb and forefinger. Flipping greedily through the pages, he searched for clues about her, some tidbit of information he could use to connect to her, bring her out of her shock.

The phone rang, startling him to his feet and off the worn sofa.

On the third ring, the girl's soft humming in the shower traveled through the paper-thin walls and calmed his nerves allowing him to ignore the sharp trill; he reseated himself and thumbed through pages searching for a name at the top inside of the cheap, tattered, cardboard cover.

Instead, he found the most beautiful pencil drawings he had ever seen on the pages within.

Even in school, his best friend, whose drawings he admired, had drawn nothing as wonderfully realistic as the sketches the boy's fingers traced now.

Birds of color, yet without, flew off a page;

wildflowers waved with absent breeze in a green-grey field, bringing scents apparent to only the viewer's nose; animals of multiple colors represented by shading of graphite, stared back innocence and hope.

As he turned the page to another drawing, a tremble charged throughout his body, and he threw the notebook to the carpet.

His eyes shifted nervously, while fear forced him up again, a strong desire to leave making him pace.

The shower of soft rain drumming in the bathroom down the hall faded beneath the vigorous beating of his heart while the faint, acoustical humming that previously calmed his nerves through the walls now initiated panic.

He must have been hallucinating.

It couldn't be possible.

He'd never seen this house before, been in this town—had he?

He had never met this girl, or the woman in the kitchen.

Nothing about the city of Godley was familiar to him.

What kind of gag was this?

He looked down into the eyes of a pencil sketch of himself so lifelike it prickled every nerve; a recent image, as if drawn this morning after first seeing the girl in the woods, a floating head in a sea of blue lines.

But that wasn't all.

Opposite his own face lay the image of the man

in his dreams, realistic in black, grey and white, staring back at him without clear features.

The faceless man!

A gentle breeze from the floor vent fluttered the pages, slowly and carefully turning them; with that motion the faceless man was replaced by her, that girl... the girl that told him to run the night before his grandparents were murdered—and beside her, a boy, older, darker, angrier.

Who was he?

Who was she?

And who was that girl who brought dreams to life on the page?

4

Dread dredged Nate's mind; he paced faster.

Unlike most people, panicky in danger, he regained control quickly, thought sharper, more dynamic, even reasonably.

Seeing his picture on the thinly lined page, opposite his biggest fear, drawn by a girl he didn't even know, was another piece of the puzzle he had to solve.

How is she connected to that man in my dream?

Where has she seen me before?

Who is this girl?

Who are those others?

Questions thrummed through his mind, migrating birds in harried flight leaving a web of question marks instead of facts. His gaze fell on the flapping notebook pages, the image of the man again looking back at him from the lined page threatening interference.

Maybe that guy's her father, or the one who claims to not be her father? The police officer. Wait, no, he would have a face. Unless she's never seen him?

Her mother is dead.

Her grandmother is dead.

Her father is...nonexistent.

Could she be... like him?

He bent toward the notebook, page corners flittering as he closed it, carefully flipping open the front cover. On the inside cover, her name—Rebecca Andrew—was written in childlike print, the letters uneven, large and blockish.

Before another question could form in his mind, Rebecca came out of the bathroom, damp hair neatly combed and pony-tailed; fresh clothes replaced her torn, striped pajamas, yet her expression remained the same.

She tentatively gripped the notebook, tugged it from his hands, closed the cover and stuffed it into a bag he hadn't noticed her carrying.

Trailing her into the kitchen, he watched as she placed the two letters, the leather book and the remaining cans of soup into the bag. She pulled the zipper closed, turned toward him—eyes acknowledging the wall as if waving him to follow—then she exited through the back door in the kitchen.

Sirens trilled in the distance—the phone call.

"Wait! Why did you draw those pictures, Rebecca? Who are those people?"

For a moment, he thought to grab her elbow, bring her back into the house to wait for the police, if for no other reason than self-preservation, but the images, the answers locked in her unspoken thoughts, intrigued him.

Without waiting for a reply, he followed her toward the door, grasped the can opener from the counter, and allowed the screen door to slam behind him, no thoughts given to the flowery sheet or the trail of unseen evidence left behind.

Thirty minutes after silently tailing Rebecca's uncontrolled running, through wild brush, thistles and thorny trees, he understood how her pajamas had been practically shredded.

The sirens quieted in the distance as the girl pushed on quickly through the thicket, her heavy bag slung over her shoulder. Several times, he managed to determine her zig or zag, beat her to a branch or thicket, and clear her path to keep her from being slapped by thorns or thistles that could easily mar her face. Each time he gained ground on her, he searched her blank expression for the key to her destination or next move, but there was no hint, no gesture, just robotic like motion. He hoped in her crazy changes of direction that she knew where she was leading him.

Within an hour, she arrived at a heavy brush wall, the length of which spanned either direction for what seemed an eternity.

Rebecca stopped, moved to her right several feet, then bent forward and disappeared through a tiny opening in the brush, pulling her bag through behind her, now invisible to the world in which he stood.

He listened for rustling but heard none.

He searched the thicket, his hand parting limbs and leaves, but more brush protruded toward him.

He lifted his eyes skyward, searching for the top, but the evergreen tangle seemed to go on forever. He found it amazing that he could no longer see Rebecca, hear motion beyond, yet he was certain she waited on the other side of the thick brush.

How? Where did this come from?

He walked a few feet to the right, bent forward, and feeling somewhat like Alice trying to follow the rabbit, found only frustration until a delicate hand poked through and waved him another foot over.

Following the retreating fingers, he knelt and disappeared through the small opening where Rebecca stood waiting for him.

She moved to the center near a fallen tree, sat on the ground, and leaned her back into the rough, dry bark, letting her bag fall nearby. Her rapid breaths began to slow; she turned her head away from him and closed her eyes.

He wasn't sure about this decision to stop here when he knew the police would be searching the area for her. He could only hope the security the tangled brush wall offered enough cover as he seated himself next to her in the small clearing.

Turning his head as far as it would go to the right, then back around to the left, he noticed the thicket appeared wherever he looked, one large circle of brush that only allowed the sun from above.

Although he understood Rebecca was unlikely to speak, he decided it couldn't hurt to speak to her, if only to collect his thoughts and allow her to gain trust in him through his voice. He spoke low and nonchalantly, as if to a frightened animal—remembering the many strays he brought home to his grandfather only to find them a new home. The only two dogs they had at the farm had followed Nathan home from the school bus stop. If he'd had his way, he would have kept every one of them.

He glanced at Rebecca. She wasn't a stray and she wasn't an animal. He changed his tone, talked to her like a friend. "I know that you can't talk to me. It's okay. My name is Nathan. Nathan Bartholomew. I live in Paradise, Texas. Well, I used to.

"Are you Rebecca? Is that your name in the notebook? Did you draw that picture of me?" He desperately sought answers to the questions that spilled from his eager mind, but his voice remained calm. He peeked around her head trying to find answers in her face, knowing otherwise, "It's a perfect likeness," he added. "I thought I was looking in a mirror." He glanced down at his hands as the silence continued. He crossed his legs, the forgotten can opener laying nearby.

"This way! I got the trail here!" A muffled shout on the outside brought Nathan to his feet.

"They can't see you. Sit down!"

Nathan spun in a circle, eyes frantically searching the empty circle for the speaker of the command.

"Yes, I'm Rebecca." The voice continued, *"Rebecca Andrew."*

His seeking eyes ended their journey on her unchanged expression, now facing him, her still lips, and her stationary eyes focused at the distance to his left.

"Who said that? Was that you? Did you... speak to me?" Disbelief emphasized the last whispered words of the question, as he moved nearer to her.

"I'm Rebecca."

While the words fell on his ears, she hadn't moved. Her expression hadn't changed.

This must be some trick; someone else hid here with them, probably the real Rebecca, owner of that backpack.

His feet stepped backward, away from her, his eyes again restlessly searching around the tree, over both shoulders.

"Over here!" A yell outside the brush grew fainter, their pursuers moving away.

"Come sit, Nathan. Sit down. They're moving away.

"See, you didn't think I knew what I was doing, zigzagging about like a crazy person." A chuckle followed.

Cautiously he moved toward her again, each step lightly, noiselessly placed, eyes squinted curiously.

"Why are you so unsettled, Nathan? This is my special place, a place I love best. This place will keep us safe, for now."

Nothing.

No moving lips, no flashing eyes, no sniffling nose.

Nothing!

"Seriously, Nathan? Why are you so shocked? Didn't anyone ever teach you it's not nice to stare?

"Really! You of all people should understand gifts.

"Look, you can hear me, because your mind is open. I'm guessing because of your gift.

"And by the way, I have seen you. I do know you. I think I can trust you, especially after your actions this morning. Thank you for the respect you showed my Grandmother. It was kind of you to cover her like that, though she hated that sheet. She wasn't a fan of floral prints. I picked that one out for my bed years ago, and it was very difficult for her to buy it for me.

"My mother understood me, could sense my words, too. I talked to her like this all the time, before she was murdered. That was the night I learned to be careful."

"So, you're not... I mean... man, I'm so stupid! You totally understood everything I said and I..."

"It's okay, really. You're not the first to assume on first impression that I don't understand what people say about me. It used to happen in school all the time. I used to think, if only they knew, but I couldn't let them know me because then they would think I was a freak...

"Or like in the fairytale my mom used to tell me,

my gift would put me in danger. I couldn't have spoken to them anyway; their minds were closed and narrowed by their own eyes and ears."

"Fairytale?" So she's... Nathan's excitement grew. "So, why are you like that? I mean, what's wrong with you?"

"Nothing's wrong with me! I'm just different from you or most others. I have my way of doing things, and it takes me longer to learn to do them your way, like cooking.

"It's not because I can't. It's just, stress kind of shuts me down. I have to take little steps to learn. Grandmother didn't have the patience to teach me her ways. When I get scared, or frustrated, my body gets different messages from my brain than what your brain sends to you, and it takes me a while to learn how to do things, sometimes days and days. My body wants to give up, though my brain doesn't.

"Mother had patience to teach me, until she d..."

"So you're like... What's that called?"

"Autistic. One hundred percent, special talent and all, stereotypically autistic, and as you've figured out, my talent is drawing. I love to draw. But there's more than that."

Nathan noted the slightest curl of her lip, or perhaps he imagined the movement when his own lips turned up with the memory of her pictures. The smile disappeared suddenly with the thought of the pictures near the end of the notebook.

He would get his answers!

"The picture... you said you know me? How? I

don't remember you."

"Not that you would. Many people forget me after meeting me. To most, I'm just a poor retarded girl who doesn't deserve recognition or remembrance from them, only pity. Once people walk away, that's it. They don't have to think about me anymore. They don't know, though.

"We didn't actually meet. If we had, I can promise, you wouldn't have forgotten, because I would have spoken to you.

"I saw you in a dream two nights ago. And when I saw you this morning, though I knew you from my dream, I felt I could trust you. I just had to know first, and now I know. Thank you, Nathan, for coming here, for helping me."

"Oh, hey, I had doubts, believe me!" A fearful chuckle escaped his lips. "Okay, so, in the notebook —what about the guy with no face?"

"I'm sure you did have doubts. I can only imagine what you were thinking when you saw those images.

"The guy with no face? He was in the dream, too.

"At first, when the dream came to me, he was the only one in the dream. Then another face appeared... yours.

"I knew then that he had something to do with you—with me—with the world.

"I don't know him, though he seems so familiar to me. I never see his face, but I feel the fear he creates, leaves behind."

"Humpf? Well... I'm pretty sure now that I can trust you. I mean, your gift, the fairytale, the dream...

"I have a dream, too—almost every night—about that guy, the guy with no face... it scares me.

"He scares me. I mean, I don't scare easily, but..." Nathan paused.

"I always try to see him, before the dream wakes me up, but I never do. It's the fear—the fear in the dream wakes me up. He does terrible things to people, to the world. I don't see it happening; I feel it. And they don't even know, the world, they have no idea.

"Normally, fear works for me. But that dream? It's the only time I feel a fear that completely paralyzes me.

"When I saw that image in your notebook—the picture of that man—it scared me so bad I dropped the notebook, but it was different, because suddenly I knew I wasn't alone... Wasn't the only one who saw him, wasn't the only one who feared him. This time the fear made me want to react by facing it, facing him, instead of running from him. When I saw the face in your notebook, I was finally able to gain control of it, I think. Now more than ever, I want to know who he is."

"Yes. Sometimes, I think dreams seem more real, locked in our head, than images on paper. Before you faced the man alone in your head, but now there's two of us, and that makes the fear more manageable.

"We have to get past that fear in our dream, and see his face. When you first appeared in my dream,

my fear changed. It was suddenly for you—for another girl—for the world.

"We have to see his face, find out who he is."

"I know. The girl, was she the one in the picture?" He held the can opener to her, and she accepted it, placing it in her bag.

"Yes, she is the girl in my dream. The boy, too, he was there and something terrible was about to happen, and darkness, but I woke up to that darkness and that was all.

"There's more than just them, us. You know that, right? You know the fairytale, well, isn't just a story."

"Yeah, I gathered." Nathan changed the subject, slowing his thoughts about the future events that threatened now to take over his actions. "How did you know to pack a bag?" He indicated the bulging bag next to her.

"Honestly, Grandmother had them packed in case we needed to leave in a hurry. Now that she's gone...

"I wanted the book, the letters; I had a feeling I might need them when this is over, at another time, when we no longer have to hide or run.

"You know Grandmother didn't fall off that chair?"

"Yeah, I figured that out, too. Are you sure nobody can see us in here, or hear us? I mean, maybe we shouldn't be just sitting here." An edgy anxiety filled his nerves, but Rebecca stared quietly forward, no thoughts passing from her to Nathan. He was beginning to notice small changes in her face, changes no other person talking to her would see, changes that indicated a thought, speech, emotion... a slight bounce of her brow, indicating that she was thinking. He would never have noticed the gestures before, but since she'd been communicating, he caught the subtle nuances as they conversed.

"No, we shouldn't leave. This place is secure. Nobody knows how to get in except me. If you go look where we came in, it appears closed. We can't be seen from the outer world. Let's be rational and calm. We should wait here, a few hours at least, until they've finished searching."

"Yeah, I guess you're right. If we leave, we might get caught, and I ain't goin back to juvie. They'd never let me out. They'd probably blame me for your Grandmother's death. I always get blamed for things I don't do."

"No, you wouldn't get blamed, and I don't think either of us would go to juvie. I think it would be much worse. Much, much worse. Especially if he got involved." A slight movement of her downturned eyes, bright blue and blank, warned him of a memory. However slight the motion, he understood because he had baggage, too, memories that hurt and frightened. Yes, he understood.

"What is it? What happened? It has something to do with your mother, doesn't it?"

"It has everything to do with her.

"That's for another time, another place. At some point, you and I will learn the truth about our parents,

and we will discover the ending to the story, the dream.

"So, do you have any thoughts on where we'll go after we leave here? It should be somewhere safe, protected, somewhere he can't find me... us. If he does he'll do what he threatened. Especially now that Grandmother isn't around to keep me safe from him."

"Who'll do what?"

"My father, the sheriff. The one who wrote the letters. He'll kill us both, just like he did Grandmother.

"Enough about him. Those other two in my notebook, I think they need help. I think we should find them and see how we can help them. Something bad is about to happen, something really bad. And I can't think clearly because of Grandmother and everything. Where were you going when you found me?"

Her eyes blurred with the slightest shine.

"Look, I know how you feel," Nathan reached over, covering her warm hand with his own, receiving the slightest squeeze on his fingertips in return.

A veiled muffle.

A rustle of grass.

They turned to the wildly sealed wall and then listened beyond their safe, brush-entwined circle. Searching steps sought an opening through the thick bushes and vines.

5

"T*hey're out there, searching for us.*

"Be still.

"Don't make a sound.

"They must have doubled back. He must think we've tricked them, somehow.

"I can't imagine he would believe me that smart, though. After all, he thinks I'm stupid and I'm sure he hopes my wandering off will result in me getting eaten by a pack of wild dogs or something."

"He must have discovered you were in the house. He wouldn't care so much about me. I'm sure he knows about you." Her brow flicked with concern.

Nathan shook his head, anger flaring at her words as he glanced first toward her, then back toward the opening. His hearing tuned to noises beyond the leafy wall. Obscured crunches, whispered words, and faintly rustling foliage did not bring fear to him, though. His fear came from beyond the ones producing those noises.

"Where is it?" a girl's muffled voice.

"I don't know. Let me think," a younger voice crackled with desperation.

A shout, "Hey, you two kids! What are you doing? Come 'ere!"

"Run! We'll find it later!" The girl's sharp order

left Nathan and Rebecca in silence, again.

The flight of faltering steps brought Nathan's vision around with the noise while Rebecca's arm muscles twitched and tensed and jerked.

"Stop! I need to ask you something! Come back! I'm a sheriff! Stop!"

Adult voices surrounded the thicket as harried footsteps pursued the two young people outside.

Nathan noted Rebecca's motions from the corner of his eye and turned to her; her arms rose, fanned, fell, hands waving as if swarming mosquitoes attacked her.

Swallowing the knot of fear in his throat, he returned his attention to the voices and footsteps as they grew distant; his hand reached out, grasped Rebecca's flailing hand assuredly, cautiously, and brought it down to her knee.

"It's okay," he whispered. "They're gone."

"That was close," she replied, a tremble in her words.

"That was him, wasn't it?" Nathan let go of her hand before his fingers flexed into a fist at his side.

"Yes. I guess I'm not the only one who knows about this place after all. Those two kids seemed to know about it. I've never come across them here before."

"Yeah, sounded like they knew what they were looking for." Nathan kept his voice low as the silence grew beyond the wall. "Whoever those kids were, they may have just saved us—running away like that."

"Yes, you're probably right. But why would they

run from the cops? Unless they did something wrong..."

"I think they'll be back. We should stay and find out. The way they ran away, the authorities must be searching for them, too."

"Nathan, what if they don't, or can't, return for days?"

"I don't think that will be the case," his head shook slightly. "They'll be back soon. The fact that they were trying to get in, that they know about this hiding spot, means they're in hiding, too. Besides, I just have a feeling they'll be back."

He glanced at Rebecca, adrenaline still roiling his blood.

"Rebecca? Did you ever hear the end of the story? The fairytale your mother told you?"

For a moment Rebecca sat silent, *"No. I always fell asleep before Mother finished. In fact, I don't know if she ever finished the story. I was going to ask you the same."*

A mocking bird warbled in the distance and Nathan resisted the urge to whistle back, to taunt him with new patterns, like he did when he was young.

"Would you hand me my notebook and pencils, please? Since there's no telling how long we'll be here, I want to draw, to calm my nerves, before the light is gone from this place."

Nathan unzipped the bag between them and pulled out the notebook. He dug around for the pencil case, too. Hesitantly, he held them out to her and waited. "What are you going to draw? Can I watch, or will it bother you?"

"I don't know—whatever I feel. Sometimes I just get the urge to draw; I don't think about anything in particular or what the image will be. And, I'm not used to people watching me draw, but you can if you want."

Rebecca flipped the cover open, allowing delicate fingers to find an empty page near the back. She opened the pencil box, selected a sharpened pencil, and fluently swept gentle curves on the paper. The lead appeared to levitate above the paper, yet lines shaped and formed the object of her mind. The consistent motion calmed Nathan, too, lulling him until his eyes drooped.

"You're tired. Take a nap. We'll probably be here long enough," Rebecca commented without pausing her actions.

"I did walk most of the night. I am pretty tired. Will you wake me up if you hear something?"

"Certainly!" Her thin hand flew over the paper, the pencil tip lightening and darkening the image with altering pressure.

Nathan lay on his stomach, positioning his face so he could still watch the image form, allowing the flow of her movement, the light, scratchy rhythm of pencil on paper, to lull him to sleep.

6

When Nathan woke, dusk had settled in their brush-thick haven, and Rebecca was gone, pencil left dangling precariously at the edge of the notebook page where it had rolled to rest.

Leaning upon his elbows, he turned his head both ways, searching for her.

No Rebecca, just her notebook and pencils placed carefully on the ground.

Palms to the earth, he pushed up and stood, moving cautiously around the large tree, "Rebecca!" His dry throat croaked. "Rebecca!" He started around the tree.

"I'm okay! Don't come any closer, please!"

Nathan released the breath he was holding through pursed lips. He returned to the notebook, peering through the dim light at the images she had drawn.

Two teenagers stared back at him. They weren't the two from his dream, the girl who saved him the night his grandparents were killed, nor the boy who shared the page with her. These were faces he'd never seen before—a girl with delicately slanted eyes, and a boy who looked of Middle Eastern ethnicity.

Who were they?

They looked familiar to Nathan. Had he seen

them recently?

Think!

Where?

"Yes, they look familiar to me, too. Perhaps we dreamed of them and don't remember; they must be part of the recurring dream." Rebecca returned to her seat next to the tree. *"Have you seen them? You look as if you have."*

"Well, I don't know exactly. I may have seen them before. Actually, I think I've seen them more than once." He squinted at the images.

"Yeah... yeah, I did! I passed them on the sidewalk when I came through town yesterday morning. Then again yesterday afternoon, I thought they were following me, but they ducked into that pizza place in town, Lone Star or something like that.

"Before that, after I ditched my Grandma's car..." Nathan's brows drew down in concentration.

His stomach rumbled. He realized he hadn't eaten all day, save the saltine cracker that sent his stomach whirling.

He couldn't think anymore. Where was it that he had seen them after he walked away from his grandmother's car, leaving it on the side of the road?

He stared at the images on the sheet as darkness settled and the moonlight filtered through the limbs above them, bright rays dancing upon the dark page.

"You'll remember. We should eat something. I'm hungry. Aren't you? It's been quiet. I think it would be okay for us to leave afterward.

"Where are we going to go? Do you think it would be safe for us to start a fire to warm the soup? Can you make a fire?"

Nathan stretched his right leg out as he returned to his place next to her, stuck his hand in his pocket, and produced a lighter. "Grandpa loved cigars. Kept a lighter in every car they owned, even Grandma's." A reminiscent smile curled his lips. He put the lighter back in his pocket. "But we would be better off to not have a fire. The smoke might draw attention. Even at night. Look, the sky's clear." He nodded upward.

Nathan pulled the backpack open and produced two cans of soup. "Well, we have chicken noodle and chicken noodle, which would you prefer?" Laughter filled Nathan's mind.

"I suppose I'll have chicken noodle. It's my favorite."

"That's stating the obvious.

"We didn't get any spoons, but I got this!" Nathan held up the hand operated can opener like a trophy. As he set it down, he noted the can tops' pull-tabs. These were different from the can he'd opened for her earlier. A chuckle again reached through the silence to his ears.

"Yeah, well, always be prepared, right?"

He pulled the tab and handed a can to Rebecca, who stared into the open top.

"What's wrong?"

"I can't eat it that way. I need a spoon, a bowl, a table, my chair. I can't eat it like this. I don't know

how to do this." Nathan jerked the can away from her hand just as her arms began waving about her.

"Calm down, Rebecca. It'll be okay. You drink out of a glass, right? It's the same thing. Just hold it like a cup and tilt it upward, like this." Nathan touched one can to his lips, tilted it up until fat, noodles, and broth spilled onto his tongue, then he brought it down slowly while he chewed. "See, it's easy. You can use your fingers, too, to pull out the noodles, like this." Again he demonstrated.

When Rebecca's frantic motions soothed, he placed the can in her hand, and she stared into it again. Nathan had almost finished his soup before he saw her arm move. She followed his motion, bringing the can to her lips, tilting it up, and dropping cold soup onto her tongue.

"I don't like cold soup, but I'm so hungry." She stopped, noodles dangling between her lips, broth dripping down her chin. With dread, she slurped.

"Well, we're kind of on our own; we'll have to accept what we have, do the best we can. You gotta eat something. You'll get used to it."

"I know I will. It's just going to take me a while." She sucked in more noodles, chewed, and swallowed. Nathan emptied his can, digging with his index finger to pull free the remaining noodles stuck in the bottom, and then he set the can aside, pulling the lighter from his pocket again. He wanted another look at those pictures.

Holding the lighter away from the book, he turned first to the man with no face, shook his head and flipped to the picture of the first two kids Rebecca had drawn.

He turned to the newest picture bringing the page closer to the light. Crickets and frogs replaced the mockingbird's call, filling the silence beyond. He held his breath.

Nathan thought about these two kids, about where he had seen them when he arrived in this town.

Are they following me? He wondered again.

"Hey, where'd you get that picture? Did you draw that?"

A flashlight beam jolted past Nathan's left ear and down onto the page just before the words reached him, overpowering the soft, sputtering glow of the lighter flame.

The notebook tumbled to the dry leaves when Nathan started to his feet, whirled and raised his fists.

7

As if they had come to life from the pages of charcoal and white, the girl he had just viewed stood illuminated by the downward glare of the flashlight, and behind her, the younger boy from the page.

"Nobody's going to fight you. Put your fists down," the girl ordered with a voice both firm and nurturing. "That's a very good likeness of us, don't you think?" She squatted, picked up the book, and shined the light on the page.

"Yes, it is. Who drew that?" The other boy peered over her shoulder, a quiver in his immature voice.

"Have you been following me?" Nathan's anger flared. "Why? Why would you follow me?"

"Calm down. We're not following you, but we do seem to be crossing your path a lot." The girl answered.

"How'd you get in here? I didn't even hear you." Nathan peered over the other boy's shoulder expecting to see a gaping hole in the brush.

"Well, if you hadn't been slurping so loudly, you might have. Besides, you learn stealth when you're on the run all the time."

Nathan released the tension in his fingers. They were on the run, too. "How did you find this place?" He glanced impatiently from one face to the other.

"I lived in Godley for a while. After my parents —well, I stayed in foster care here. This was my favorite place to hide before..." The girl gulped air and swallowed the rest of the sentence, grief lining her face.

"If you don't live here anymore, then why are you here, in Godley?" Nathan asked.

The two glanced uneasily at each other, and then back at Nathan.

"Just passing through on our way to the land of dreams..." She glanced sideways at her younger friend before stating. "...Paradise."

"Paradise?" Nathan repeated the word, too forcefully, too loudly.

"You know Paradise?" Her arched brows rose in question.

"I lived there," Nathan's suspicion grew.

"Great! Are you running from or to?" The girl's dark brown eyes shined with her question, and she tilted her head slightly, as if speaking to a small child.

"Funny!" Nathan scoffed. He didn't much like this girl, or her friend.

"We are going to." Rebecca intervened between the willful contesters.

Again, the two newcomers glanced at each other, and then at Nathan.

"Nathan, it's okay. Sit down, please. It looks like the four of us should get to know each other better."

"Who said that?" The girl's eyes had been focused on Nathan's motionless face. "How'd you do that? Are you a ventriloquist?"

"No, I'm not. You can hear her, too?" Nathan frowned at them.

"Her?" They turned a disbelieving gaze on Rebecca.

"Yes, Nathan, they are like us. They're going to the same place, in search of the same things as we are, I'm sure. The drawings make sense now. Sit down and let's work with each other instead of against."

"What's she talking about, Cai? Does she mean..." The boy leaned in closer to Cai's ear.

"Yeah, Thad, I think that's what she means." Cai nodded curiously at Rebecca.

"It seems you're more of the twelve... from the fairytale. My name is Rebecca. That's Nathan. Go on, sit down. We're not going anywhere soon. We should get to know each other, figure out how to help the other two, the ones in darkness. I don't know how or why they're stuck there, or what we can do to help them, but..."

Cai sat guardedly, her almond-shaped eyes crinkled as she squinted at Rebecca.

Thad crossed his legs beside her, distrust dawning his deeply tanned features. Moonlight glistened off their near black hair.

"Okay, well, my name is Cai Philip and this is Alex Thaddeus. He goes by Thad. Who are you, again?" Cai, the obvious leader of the two, demanded.

"Nathan Bartholomew," Nathan squinted across the dimly lit ground between them.

"Rebecca Andrew. Cai's a pretty name."

"It's Chinese. So, you know about the fairytale, too? The twelve—how?" Cai grilled before Rebecca could continue.

Nathan glanced down at his hands folded in his lap, memories of his mother, the fairytale, flooding his thoughts, her soft voice filling the dark void in his heart. "My mother used to tell me this story every night. It was scary, but really good, too. It was about twelve kids, she called them princes and princesses, and this horrible, flaming monster and..." He stopped when recognition left Cai's and Thad's mouths gaping in his direction. "Is... is that what you meant by the twelve?"

"Exactly what I meant. My mother told me the same story; Thad's told him the story. And you, what about you, Rebecca?"

"Of course—until the day she died."

"And your parents? Where are they?" Cai turned again to Nathan.

"Dead. They died in a plane crash on their second honeymoon. After that, I went to live with my grandparents, but now they're gone, too... murdered. I managed to escape, because of a dream, a girl..." Nathan turned from their probing gaze.

"And your father?" Cai asked Rebecca.

"My father lives, but he would sooner kill me than claim me."

A sympathetic growl slipped from Thad's lips

before he angrily confessed, “Like mine. He did not want me... Didn’t want me raised in America, but my mother would not leave her home. He has friends everywhere in law enforcement. They are searching for me.” A tear formed, fell from the corner of Thad’s eye as gritted teeth puckered his lips, “He’s trying to take me away from my friends, he says, but I think he never loved me. He always looked at me with hatred, like he knew something I didn’t know.”

“Where would you be if you hadn’t run away?” Rebecca’s compassionate voice calmed Thad.

“Israel. That’s where both my father’s parents are. I’ve never met them. I don’t know anyone there. I didn’t want to go. They wouldn’t protect me over there.”

“It’s alright, Thad. He won’t find you. I’ll make sure he doesn’t find you.” Cai lay a protective arm over the younger boy’s quivering shoulders, pulling him to her.

“Both of my parents are gone, too. They died in an car accident. My grandmother, in China, was ill. Father wanted me to return with them, but I had school. I stayed with a friend, until they put me in State care. Grandmother died shortly afterward, before they could send me to her.

“I had no one. I ran away from my foster parents. They weren’t the ni...” Cai’s features became stern, angry, defensive. “I’ve been on my own ever since. That was two years ago, when I was fifteen.”

“Was it you two fumbling around outside the brush this morning?” Nathan asked.

"Yes. When that cop showed up, we ran. I won't risk us getting caught." Cai replied.

"I have another question for you two. Your birthday, when is it?" Nathan inquired cautiously.

"December twenty-fourth." The two answered as one.

"Twelve twenty-four in the morning?" Rebecca's voice was barely audible.

"Yeah, Mom always made a big deal out of that on my birthday," Thad squinted.

"As did both of yours." Rebecca would have nodded at them had she been able to control it.

"Yes, exactly the same time, day. We've discovered another coincidence—Thad and I—our Mothers' birthdays."

"I guess now I know why Mom stressed that information, too." Nathan's face wrinkled with disbelief. "My mother's birthday was..."

"It's okay. I already know it's the same, all of our mothers had the same birthday... just like the fairytale." Cai's gaze returned to the notebook. "Who drew these pictures?"

"I did."

"Have you seen us before?" Thad's wariness returned. If she had seen them, who else might have noticed them.

"Only in a dream."

Thad reached for the book, flipped the page, "Agh! It's him! That faceless man!" The notebook shook in his hand. Pages rustled as his shaking hand fought to turn them from the page staring back. "It's them! Look, Cai!"

"Who?"

"The ones in my nightmare with him! They must be bad people!"

Nathan pulled the notebook from Thad's trembling fingers and returned it to Rebecca. "I don't know, Thad. I think they're the ones in trouble. They need help.

"You said you had a dream. Tell us about it. I will tell you about mine, too. Maybe it will help us piece together what's happening. Maybe it will help us find them, and the other six." Nathan offered.

"Yeah, I agree," Cai nodded. "That's a good place to start. I'm starved, though. You guys got anything to eat?"

"Uh," Nathan glanced at Rebecca, "some cold soup, Chicken Noodle ..."

"...or Chicken Noodle," Rebecca added, laughter punctuating her statement, bringing a chuckle from Nathan.

"I don't get it," Thad cocked his head.

"Sorry. Here," Nathan handed them each a can, grinning as they pulled the tab and alternately slurped noodles.

8

"Go on Thad, tell them about your dream, about the two in the drawing." Cai bumped Thad's shoulder with her own before lifting the can of soup to her lips again.

Thad peered into his empty can, tension filling his dark features, his jaws clenching with fear. He swallowed hard, focusing on Nathan, drawing from the energy of the angry boy's strength, courage. "My dream always starts with my mother," he pressed his lids closed to ward off stinging tears. "First it starts with her telling me the story, a prince named Thaddeus, but I'm always puzzled by her words. How could I be a prince? I never felt like one.

"Her voice trails off as I begin to doze and the dream overpowers the end of the fairytale. But, whenever the dream gets to the part about the other eleven royals, I don't see them clearly, like the one with no face, but they're like shadows behind the flames.

"Except Cai. I see her now, since we met.

"I see Rebecca, too, I think. At least, there's blonde hair flying and twirling like the flames surrounding it, the hot wind forcing the hair upward, circling and twisting above her head, like she's sinking in a pool of water—" Thad stared at the top of

Rebecca's head, paused and licked his dry lips—"at least, I'm pretty sure it's you.

"And the man in the drawing... without a face... he is there, too... standing in front of me. He speaks, but his words aren't clear, like he's mumbling, and the roar is so loud. I can't hear him." Thad's voice crackled like the fire in his mind. "He spins around, shows his featureless face, releases mocking laughter. As he turns, I see the outline of another kid, and another. When his back is to me, darkness and flames fill my eyes.

"As the flames die down, she appears—the one with long, brown hair. I see her face. She is angry... so much anger. I have never seen that much anger in someone's face, not even my father. Then her face kind of fades out, and I see him, the tall boy. He is angry, too. I feel like they're angry with me, but I don't know why.

"The man faces me again, a gaping, fiery oval with a center of darkness, hair and flames pushing upward, standing on end. The oval moves closer to me, and just when I think I will see his face, he releases this terrible scream, and I wake up."

Cai slipped her arm around Thad again as a tear escaped the corner of his eye, a protective sister-like squeeze, and Thad buried his face in the security of Cai's shoulder.

Nathan's jaw clenched; his fingers flexed. The images produced by Thad's dream stirred a rage within him.

Rebecca drowning in a pool of water? Nathan

rose to his feet, pacing. He wanted to kill the man with no face. Rebecca, like him and the others, had lost everything, and Nathan laid the fault of their losses on this man with a face surrounded by fire. He ducked his head away from their view, left the circle and disappeared around the large tree, muscles tensing more with each step. On the other side, out of sight, his fists clenched tightly before him, he drew back and swung at the large oak trunk, stopping short before the connection broke the knuckles of his right hand.

"Nathan?"

The young man took three deep breaths, releasing his ire, and rounded the tree from behind the two newcomers.

"I'm fine!" His sharp words contradicted.

"Sure," Cai nodded, "there's been a few times I've wanted to punch a tree, too. We'll have our chance. Sit down." She smiled knowingly at him, and at that moment his trust in her grew. They were a lot alike, had a lot in common. Together they would handle the beast.

Nathan returned to his previous position, reaching for Rebecca's hand and giving it a reassuring squeeze. He drew a strange comfort from Cai's smiling eyes. They were the same. *Two peas in a pod,* his grandpa would say.

"What about you? What about your dream?" Cai questioned, leading the conversation.

"Me?" Nathan tapped his own chest. "Mine is nothing compared to that. I haven't seen any of you. I just see him. But it starts out the same, with my mom telling me the story, a prince named Bartholomew. All through the dream, I think of my parents, and more recently my grandparents. I see that black oval and I want to..."

"Me, too," Cai reached across the space between them, patted his arm. "In time—a little time —a little patience. We will get our chance to use the pain in our favor. There are others involved, and we need to be there for them. We can't risk their lives for our own revenge."

Nathan glanced down again. "I'm not selfish. I would give my life for... for any of you."

"Me, too.

"There's more to this whole crazy world we've been living in than we know," Cai added.

"Well, here I go, then," Rebecca's soft voice cut through the wall of indignation forming around Nathan and Cai.

"Is yours similar to Thad's?

"Exactly the same, except of course, I cannot see myself. I apparently saw you, Thad, the fear in your face as the man turns to you is evident in the sketch." Thad's face ducked into Cai's shoulder again.

"You have to stop being so afraid, Thad! Sit up... listen... take note. You're not the only one who's scared. One day we will have to stand together. Don't let fear control you," Cai urged.

Thad pulled back, his chin on his chest, and then slowly let his chin rise to face Rebecca's motionless features.

"Yes, Thad, Cai is right. We all must be brave. We need you. We will all need you.

"When the faceless man reaches out, the girl appears before me. She is angry, as Thad says. So is the other. Just before the fire flickers and dies, they appear, no longer angry, but their faces swim in darkness, eyes closed, hands clasped. They lie next to each other in the darkness. I hear her soft voice repeating the fairytale, softly at first, then louder and louder, and his voice joins hers as they weave their words to the missing end that we all know, the end that begs of hope, then their voices fall silent. And next, three words fill my sleep, "'Unite, Gifted Ones!'"

"Gifted Ones?" Thad prodded as Rebecca fell quiet. "Is that us?"

"I'm guessing so."

"That's the same thing she said to me the night my grandparents were killed!" Nathan glanced around the group.

"Huh! The Gifted Ones… I like it. Still, that dream doesn't tell us much more, except that she's calling to us, which doesn't really make it clear that she's on our side." Cai flopped onto her back and stared at the few stars peeking in from far beyond the earth, hands pillowing her head.

"No, it doesn't. But she did warn me. And she knows about the fairytale. In my book, that makes her one of us. If we're going to Paradise, do you suppose those two might have been going there, too? Maybe they're there already and they got caught?" Thad poked at Cai's leg excitedly.

"Possibly," she replied more quietly. "If they know the fairytale, then they know of Paradise."

"Well, we are all together in the dream, right? And the story climaxes in a place called Paradise. I bet they are there already!" Nathan added.

"What do you think, Rebecca?" Cai asked for the sake of unity.

"Well, they do join hands in my dream, which might mean they have found each other. They could be the first to have arrived there, but I don't know that for sure."

The other three gazed from one to the other, and then turned away, eyes searching the shadows for invisible clues.

"Well, since we're headed to Paradise, we'll find out, I guess," Cai spoke toward the sky above her. "But right now, I'm exhausted. We've been on the move since daybreak."

"For now, maybe we *should* stay put, catch a few hours of sleep and then take off, definitely get out of that sheriff's area," Thad added.

"Well, I don't think that will help much. There will be others like Rebecca's father, and yours, searching for us if we are living the fairytale. Like that man that showed up at my grandparents' house, the one that ki..." Nathan stopped.

"Yes, like him, too. I'm not tired. I'm ready to go. We've been here all day, and it's much easier to move in the night. The darkness will mask us." Thad stood.

"Uhm, you know there's no need to worry

about that," Cai sighed annoyed by Thad's sudden bravado.

"That's right; Cai can mask herself!" Thad sat.

"What?" Nathan leaned toward Thad.

"Later, you two. I could use some sleep before we take off, too." Rebecca curled on her side, her back pack under her head.

Cai's breathing slowed. Thad lay next to her, deep breaths filling the air around them. Nathan grew sleepy listening to the gentle inhale, exhale surrounding him. He'd been up for two days trying to get back to Paradise. "I'm not tired. I napped earlier. You all sleep," he offered to stand guard, but within the hour, the four teens lay on their backs sleeping beneath the oak, their feet forming a four-point star to one side of the large fallen tree, shoes leaning against each other as if connection brought protection.

9

The circle of flames danced in the darkness surrounding Thad. Fear bubbled in his chest, rumbling upward through his throat, an unloosed scream squeezing his esophagus closed. His dry tongue touched the roof of his mouth attempting to form sound.

Rebecca's blonde strands floated into his vision through the seeking flames in the circle of fire, if only he could reach her.

His hand moved into view, arm tensing, fingers flexing at the twisting, spiraling tendrils floating upward in a fire forced whirlwind. If he could just get a grip on her hair, he could pull her to him—save her.

The fear in his chest moved into his arm; the hand before him trembled.

"Go on, reach!" A horrid voice filled his ears, and then the face, the laugh, the flaming circle shrunk into an oval shape—the faceless man.

The lone word erupted weakly in a dry croak before the empty oval, "No!"

Thad's hand pulled free from the fierce flames and found the hand of another. His eyes followed his hand seeking the owner's face; it was Cai, rage lining every muscle in her jaw, filling her delicate features, and reflecting in her dark eyes.

Gripping her hand for strength, Thad felt another squeeze of his right palm.

Hoping it was Rebecca's hand closing about his, he turned, and the fire shifted, providing a vision of floating blonde hair across the flames.

Nathan then, it must be Nathan, the two angry ones on either side of him, giving him strength, but when he looked, it was not Nathan.

It was the other girl, the one from his dream the night before, the angry one with the flowing brown hair, the one surrounded by darkness, and at her other side, the other boy from Rebecca's picture.

"Unite, Gifted Ones! He's gaining strength! We must find each other through the flames! Reach!"

Rebecca screamed, her body rising into a torrent of wind while flames licked at her without contact, grew taller, and forced her upward.

Almost out of reach, Nathan jumped, grabbed for her hand as it spun before him, and pulled her back into the circle. Rebecca's hair still whirled with the fiery wind, as did Cai's and the other girl's.

"You will not win! You were destined to die!" The heat-filled, hoarse voice rumbled into Thad's heart. His grip on Cai's hand loosened, but she tightened her own not giving him freedom.

Thad turned a grateful look toward Cai and saw Nathan on her other side gripping her left hand, Rebecca beyond him, and another hand, an arm, leading to one hidden by flames.

Another Gifted One? A prince?

"Stop looking at them! Look at me! I own you! I

am your leader! You were never one of them! Look at me!" The voice roared, shaking free the hands that provided support and kept Thad focused.

"Noooooo!" Thad's body twirled upward in the hot whirlwind his grip slipping.

10

A choked scream woke them all. Thad swallowed hard, trying to find his voice.

Darkness swam where flames once stretched.

Stars sparkled in the dark oval formed by leafless branches.

Soon six eyes peered through the lightless night at Thad.

"I'm sorry. It was the dream. I didn't mean to wake you." Stunned silence followed his quiet words. "I said I'm sorry!" Thad repeated; feeling their stares, he jerked his body into a sitting position.

"It's not that," Rebecca's eyes met Nathan's for the first time; Nathan turned to Cai; Cai squinted at Thad, then back to Nathan.

"I've never seen myself in a dream before," Nathan spoke flatly.

"Me, either."

"Nor I," Rebecca added. "I'm not sure I like it. Thank you for saving me, Nathan."

Nathan's head turned, from one to the other, settling on Cai, "You saw it, too?"

"Yes," she glanced between the three, and then down at her shoes. "Look," she nodded.

"What?" Thad followed her gaze.

"When we all finally slept, our feet were

touching."

The four looked now at the triangles their legs formed in the four-point star. They hadn't moved since waking, sitting straight up with the abrupt noise.

"That must be how he did it," Nathan looked at Thad.

"Did what? I didn't do anything!" Thad's voice trembled with tears.

"Your dream," Cai answered, "we dreamed it, too."

"Yes, and I'm not thrilled with my prospects," Rebecca's voice filled their heads. She pulled her feet from the star, crossed her legs and began rocking nervously. *"I seem to be the weak link. A burden to everyone."*

"No, Rebecca! We're in this together. What happens to one, will happen to all," Cai comforted.

"Yes, that's what I'm afraid of."

"You... you saw my dream? All of you? Then Rebecca, you know you didn't seem to be the only weak link." Thad angrily plucked brown grass from the ground before him and tossed it over his shoulder.

"No, Thad, we saw *our* dream, you just channeled it to us through touch." Cai calmed him with a pat on his shoulder.

"We'd better get out of here. I have this feeling that we're running out of time." Nathan jumped to his feet, reaching for Rebecca's hand. Reluctantly, she allowed him to help her to her feet, then he bent forward for the backpack.

"Where are we going to go?" Thad dusted the dirt off the seat of his pants while Cai dusted off his back.

"Home... I mean, Paradise, where my Grandpa lived. I know my way around there. And there's food if we can get to the farm, and maybe another vehicle. The sooner we get there the better."

"Well, how far is it?" Cai fell in behind Nathan and Rebecca.

"I don't know. By car, it was only an hour or so from here, but walking? I don't know. It's like sixty or seventy miles."

"Well, even at three miles per hour, that will take us twenty hours, or two days, given that we'll need to rest." Cai did the math.

"I don't suppose any of us have any money for bus tickets?" Thad asked.

"Well, actually..." Rebecca stopped.

"You have money in this bag, Rebecca?" Nathan lifted the bag from his shoulder.

"Not the bag. At my grandmother's house. She hid it in a tin under a loose floorboard. It was for me, but I didn't have time to get it."

"We can't go back there," Nathan shook his head. "They'll be waiting for her."

"Besides, it'll be all roped off, right? Like a crime scene?" Thad asked.

"Oh, I doubt that," Nathan replied.

"We'll just have to be careful. He is probably lurking, waiting for us to return," Rebecca agreed to

the plan.

"You're not seriously thinking about going back to get it?" Nathan asked.

"It is my money!"

"But if we get caught..." Cai argued.

"We won't, Cai! Not with you there!" Thad smiled at her.

"Well, we would save a lot of time taking a bus. But is it worth the risk?" Nathan questioned.

"I don't know. The four of us showing up at a bus station for tickets might set off some alarms. On the other hand, we don't know what the other two are going through right now, how long they can hold out." Cai shrugged indecisively.

"Where's the loose floorboard, Rebecca?" Nathan asked.

"In the bathroom, right inside the cabinet under the sink."

"Whew! That's all the way in the middle of the house! I don't know." Nathan paced away.

"We can do it, the four of us! The house is small." Rebecca urged.

The other three peered at Rebecca's motionless features.

"I think we should do it, too! I'm in!" Thad agreed.

Nathan and Cai searched each other's eyes.

"We could end up without the money, and it would delay us, especially if we get caught." Nathan checked each for acknowledgement.

"That's true, but if she goes, I go," Thad

nodded.

"I'm going back for it! We need it." With that, Rebecca disappeared through the brush.

Thad followed her. Cai and Nathan shrugged apprehensively at each other. They had no choice but to follow Rebecca, "I guess we're in, too," Cai punched Nathan's shoulder.

11

Moonlight stretched through the trees, sprinkling beams upon the darkened house, shadows playing upon them in the breeze.

No voices broke the silence.

"It's dark. See, there's no tape. I'll go in alone. I know where to go. I can do it without turning on the light. If someone is in there waiting, then you three will be safe here."

"Safe? If one of us gets caught, what happens to the fairytale? We're coming in with you so we're there if something goes wrong! There's four of us, and they may not know that, yet. We won't leave here without you! Unite! Remember?" Cai's harsh whisper filled Rebecca's tilted ear.

"Of course."

"No, wait," a light touch froze Rebecca's housebound step. "I've been in your house, too. I know where the bathroom is. I'll go. I have a little experience with getting in and out of places quickly." Nathan peered through the trees at the dimmed doorway, stepping out ahead of Rebecca and the others.

"Maybe that would be better," Cai nodded.

"Nathan, I'm perfectly capable of going in there and getting the box," Rebecca defended.

"Oh, I know. I just... well," he stammered.

"We'll both go." Nathan paused, allowing Rebecca to move up beside him.

Nathan tensed as they approached the door they had exited from that morning. Something wasn't right; he could feel it in the quivering of every nerve.

The hair on his neck rippled, but he couldn't risk speaking. Somewhere... something... someone was watching them, waiting for just the right moment to grab them.

Rebecca reached for the cool, brass doorknob just as Nathan rested his hand on her wrist.

"It will be alright, Nathan." Her voice resonated in his mind, but he couldn't respond in the darkness enveloping them. She turned the knob and slowly pushed the door inward.

She slid her left hand in his and tugged him through the dark kitchen, living room, and hallway without a bump.

She felt for the bathroom doorknob, twist, push... squeak... pause.

Nathan cringed.

Rebecca let go of his hand.

Blindly his unadjusted eyes searched for Rebecca.

The cabinet hinges made no sound, and for a brief second, the deafening quiet in the blackness left Nathan trembling. Never in his life had he wondered what it would be like to be without sight and sound, but he experienced it now.

As if it would help, he squeezed his eyes closed,

concentrating on sound.

Then he heard a light thump, low and in front of him, a metal on wood sound. He imagined Rebecca removing the box from the hole in the floor.

A scratch of wood to wood.

Rebecca's hand touched his chest causing his body to jerk with fear.

Her fingers crawled upward to his shoulder and down his arm to the back of his hand.

She turned his palm upward and placed the box in it.

Next, she turned him around in the doorway, found his free hand and led him down the dark hall.

The sigh Nathan had been holding since they took those three steps into the house filled his chest; choking it down made him dizzy. He realized he wasn't breathing at all.

A memory, buried deep, pushed its way forward, his dad spinning him around by his hands in the backyard, his dark eyes turned downward, smiling at Nathan as he slowed and released the young boy's hands.

Dizziness filled the boy, and he stumbled around the yard, laughing until he fell onto his back in the cool grass, stars above him spinning and spiraling into a black sky.

Rebecca's right hand touched Nathan's shoulder, breaking through the melancholy dizziness he felt. He slowly released the breath he held.

He knew they were in the kitchen and moved farther right to avoid the table he remembered from that morning, stepping around the missing body as if it still lay there.

As they neared the backdoor, Nathan wished he hadn't responded to his grandfather's rough, echoing voice when they had entered the dark house, *"Close that door, boy! I know you weren't born in a barn!"* How many times had his grandfather said that to him in the course of the two short years he lived there? Thirty? Forty? Finally, closing doors behind him became the habit that he now wished he hadn't developed. Right now, they were trapped in the darkness, closed in with no exit, almost against a wall. If only he had left the door open.

The feeling Nathan had before they entered the house grew stronger.

The hair on his neck danced as if a mountain lion stalked him from the outside.

Somewhere... something... someone...

Releasing Rebecca's hand, he felt for the doorknob, but grasped only air.

The countertop cooled his fingers as they glided over it, and he shifted left, Rebecca pulling his elbow, *"Left, Nathan, hurry!"*

She felt it, too.

He was there!

Nathan had been wondering if she had the same sudden urgency, too; now he knew.

Left—wall, doorjamb, too high—Nathan's hand slipped down the wood frame until the metal plate felt cool against his fingers.

The doorknob grazed the back of his hand and

he grabbed for it.

Grip... twist... pull...

A blinding light filled his eyes as he stepped from the darkness.

"I'll take that!" A large, strong hand reached toward him from beneath the blinding circle. "It belongs to me, anyway."

"Move, Nathan! Don't let him have it!" Rebecca pushed Nathan down the steps, out of the light.

A glowing halo filled Nathan's eyes while his feet skipped, slid, and stumbled down the porch steps forcing him into the shadows.

Rebecca's mute scream filled his ears as the cool, metal box flew from his hand into the night.

12

Dried, brown grass poked between Nathan's bared teeth, though his elbows broke his fall. Blinded by the flashlight's momentary glow, he pushed up on his knees and felt the ground in front of him for the box.

Nothing but grass.

Hands grabbed roughly at his shoulders, pulling him upward and he turned, swinging his fists.

"It's me!" The whisper ducked beneath his swing and moved near the back of his head.

Cai spun Nathan toward the house, kicked her right leg out, and turned it hard into the back of the attacker's legs.

Thad swiftly ran out of the trees as the man howled in pain; the man's knees buckled and thumped hard into the concrete below, leaving him to topple to his side in the grass, grasping his aching knees.

Rebecca fled from the large, rough hand that had been squeezing her arm, and while she quickly moved away, Thad scooped up the box with one hand and grabbed Rebecca's hand with his other.

Cai led the light blinded Nathan behind them.

"Back to the brush! Hurry!" Rebecca's voice quietly led them to their secluded spot by the old oak

tree.

"Stop! I'll shoot!"

A beam of light bounced to the right of Cai, and she dodged into the darkness on her left, pulling Nathan with her.

A loud pop brought a flinch from Thad, and Rebecca squeezed his hand reassuringly.

"We're not going to make it there in time! Give me your other hand, Rebecca!" Cai whispered, reaching forward.

An army of trees advanced to the right, and Cai tugged Nathan and Rebecca along with her, forcing Thad to follow. Into the bouncing light and out again the four moved. A bullet grazed Thad's jeans near the back of his calf as he turned, jolting him ahead of the others.

"Where are we going?" Nathan's vision slowly returned as a tree appeared before him.

"Just a little farther! Whatever happens, don't let go of my hands!" Cai answered.

Nathan wasn't about to let go. A sheriff tailed them, and he looked to shoot somebody. Nathan followed her order and gripped Cai's hand tighter, tree or no tree, until Cai ran their hands dead center a hackberry tree.

"Stop! We'll find you! You can't hide from us!"

The hackberry drew closer and Nathan tried to free his hand from Cai's, expecting a broken wrist if he didn't.

"No! Don't let go!"

"You're going to break my wrist!" Nathan's

voice squeaked.

"No, I won't. Just hold on!"

Nathan's eyes squeezed shut as they approached; he opened them when he knew his wrist should have snapped from the impact, but all he saw were trees.

"Okay, just relax. Everyone breathe and don't move." A barely audible whisper reached the three pair of ears in the night.

Nathan glanced at Cai, but she wasn't there.

Thad was gone too.

The light shone upon and through them. Rebecca could see the light move around her. Nathan watched as it bounced toward him, shining light on his back. No! Not on his back!

The shadow cast before him was that of a tree.

His shadow?

He still felt Cai's hand in his, yet there were no connected arms in the shadows.

There were no heads, no legs, no bodies.

There were only shadow trees.

"Damn kids! I'll find you! We'll find you! You watch and see!" The crazed officer yelled into the night. "And if I find you first, you're all dead! I don't care what he says!"

13

Nathan's hand cramped from holding onto Cai's so tightly. An exhausted sigh burst from his lungs as she let go, breaking the long held silence.

"We have to get out of here... tonight! They will be looking for us first thing tomorrow. I'm sure assaulting an officer of the law is a good reason for them to pursue us, not that they didn't apparently already have a reason." Cai took the lead moving deeper into the trees until she found a thicket of brush. Who has the box?"

Thad's eyes jumped from Cai's face to the box in his hands, and he immediately stiff-armed the box to her. "Here," she offered, "put it in Rebecca's bag. We'll count it in the morning, somewhere safe." She passed the box to Nathan who obediently unzipped the backpack and placed the box snuggly inside.

"Alright, come on! That cop might come back with others. They might even bring dogs." The angst in Cai's voice seeped into her words, bringing the rest of them into harried flight. "Thad and I know a fast way out of town. We've found it a couple of days. It will provide us cover for a while! They will be looking for us since he's seen us all now. It's going to be difficult to hide Rebecca." Cai glanced at Rebecca before leading them out.

"I think they already knew who we were from the sound of it. We need to find another place to hide, to make a safe plan." Rebecca added.

"We'll have to be careful in open spaces. The four of us together will draw suspicion. For now, in the cover of darkness and woods, we're safe, but once we're out of cover, or in the daylight, we'll have to split up." Cai added.

"We can't. Rebecca's... well..." Nathan moved up next to Cai.

"Too obvious, you're right, Nathan, I am." Rebecca agreed, *"Especially since he knows me."*

Moments of silence, broken by the light crunch of fall leaves under their steps and the quick breaths of brisk movement, surrounded the fugitives.

"We'll have to find a way to disguise you somehow, Rebecca. And one of us should stay with you, maybe disguised, too."

"A disguise? That will be fun!" Rebecca's positive mood brightened them. Cai glanced over her shoulder at the expressionless face of the taller girl. Nathan and Thad followed her gaze. *"Well... I never had many chances to play dress up, or wear a costume at Halloween. Not as far I can remember, anyway. Mother died when I was very young. Grandmother didn't have the money for luxuries like that."* Rebecca's words drew them to her.

"Well, I'm glad you're so positive about it, at least," Cai added. "It's a scary situation, but we can't let fear rule our actions or we will get caught."

"Yeah, but where will we get a disguise?" Thad

asked.

Cai grinned, remembering younger days when she twisted herself among the line dried sheets in their backyard on laundry day, “Clotheslines?”

“Hey, yeah! That might work. We could find a ball cap somewhere, too. Maybe pull Rebecca’s hair up under it.”

“Good idea, Nathan. Maybe we could find Cai one, too.” Thad offered.

“True, we need to hide all of our distinguishing features so it will be harder to identify us. And we’ll split the pairs. After all, they’re looking for four of us, or the pairs of us they’ve seen, but not two girls and two boys separately!” Nathan pointed out.

“Yes, that should keep us hidden in plain sight.” Cai agreed.

“You know, there’s only one problem with that idea... It’s dark. Who’s gonna leave their laundry out after dark?” Rebecca asked.

“Also true.”

A roadway emerged beyond the tree line, but Cai kept them as far from it as possible, paralleling the pavement. “Thad? Do you remember seeing any Goodwill drop boxes? Or Caritas stores?”

“Well, I wasn’t really looking.”

“Grandmother always took my old clothes to the church. They have a collection shed,” Rebecca suggested.

“That might be an option. We’ll have to keep our eyes open. Clotheslines, donation boxes, whatever we can find.” With the threat of discovery past them for the moment, Cai slowed their pace.

"I've seen caps and shoes and shirts on the highway before. Maybe we'll get lucky and find a couple," Nathan added.

"Me, too. I always wondered how they get there. One time, before Thad and I connected, I saw a pair of shoes hanging over a telephone wire up high. I wonder why people do that." Cai frowned at the worn sneakers on her feet.

"Well, one reason is school buses. I heard kids take other kids' shoes and throw them up over power lines at bus stops.

"Some people say that gangs do it in big cities as a sign of ownership... territory. Around here, I would think it's bullies.

"Once I threw a pair of my tennis shoes up over a line when I got off the school bus... because I wanted some cool Nikes I saw. My grandpa made me run barefoot in gym for a month because he saw my shoes dangling way up high when he came back from town. The line was still bouncing, which is what made him look up. That was when I first moved in, and the line was right in front of the property. Smart me!" Nathan chuckled.

"Ouch!" Cai grimaced.

"Oh yeah, it hurts to run barefoot in gym. I guess it taught me to appreciate what I have. It was a real challenge getting those shoestrings to catch on that line, too.

"I sure miss my grandparents, and my parents." Nathan fell silent.

"I miss my mom, too," Thad turned his eyes toward the empty highway.

"Look, we all miss somebody, but we can't let that get us down right now! We are being hunted by crazy people..." Cai picked up the pace again, jogging through the brush in front of them.

"For sure!" Rebecca chimed in, following Cai's lead. *"... and we need to focus on finding the other two 'Gifted Ones.' So, let's not get stuck dwelling on the past. We need to figure out what dark place those other two are stuck in.*

"In the fairytale Mother told me, there were many followers of the monster. And if there were only mine and Thad's fathers, then how did the other two get caught?" Rebecca stated.

"That's right. That's the way my mother told the story, too. Everywhere the princesses and princes went they fought off some version of a monster, an ogre, a troll or a dragon. Of course, those creatures don't live in our world. They have to be real people in our case. And probably numbers of them!" Cai added.

"I hope they're people because there's a dragon in my dream," Thad huffed.

"Huh! In mine, I just see fire and that guy with no face. Do you suppose the dragon in the story represents him? He's at the center of the fire in the dream." Nathan asked.

"Perhaps. I wish one of us knew the ending to the story. Have any of you seen his face... ever?" Thad asked. Three unanimous NOs filled the air around him.

"How are we supposed to identify him? How are we supposed to find the others? According to the story, there are twelve of us. And where are the two in my picture and the dream... the darkness? Though dreams are never real or right, are they?" Rebecca feared this one was.

"There's too many questions with no answers. I just don't know." Nathan shook his head.

"Stories aren't always real, either. Maybe we're wrong about the whole thing. Maybe Thad's suspicions are right and those other two are a danger to us." Cai tossed loosely into the pool of ideas.

"But, then, why these unusual... powers? None of it makes sense to me." Rebecca gave up.

"One thing is sure; my instincts tell me that girl is reaching out to us for help. She guided me out of the house that night. I believe the two have been caught—and they're still alive—which means that whoever is behind this, man or beast, wants us alive. But why?" Nathan asked.

"That's true. If they are still alive, then the threat of cops and dogs won't stand true. There hasn't been anything following us since he threatened us." Cai stopped jogging.

"I wish I hadn't fallen asleep before the end of that story!" Nathan pounded his right fist into his left palm.

"Me, too," Cai added. "And I wish I wouldn't wake up before the dream ends. We all seem to have the same problem. We don't know the ending. Why would that be kept from us?"

"A story with no end, a dream with no end... maybe the ending is up to us, The Gifted Ones. Maybe we don't know it because it can go either way. Maybe it's all about our powers? Maybe they want my telepathic speech, and Thad's dream communication. And Cai's, well..."

"Yeah, what exactly was that back there? Did you make us disappear?" Nathan recalled the shadows of trees. "I could still see myself when I looked at my arm, but the shadows..."

"Not disappear, no," Thad smiled at Nathan, eyes lighting with excitement.

"Well, I kind of... I don't know, go camo? And like King Midas, whoever I'm connected to changes with me," Cai shrugged.

"Camo?" Nathan almost yelled. "Wow! I was a tree!"

"Nice! So what do you think the other two are like? I mean, we know what they look like, but I wonder what they can do." Rebecca stared into the darkness before her.

"It appears she communicates like you, Thad. She did call out to us in the dream." Nathan pointed out.

"But that's a dream. I don't know that I've ever used my power in the dream." No further comments followed Cai's. Silence moved with them through the cover of brush.

The sun inched its way into the night sky over the eastern horizon reaching out to the four travelers, an early morning chill sent them shivering into the daylight. True to Texas weather, the first days of December warmed, but the nights brought cold. Cai briefly rubbed her bare arms as the darkness made way for light, the sun attempting to warm them as it rose higher, bringing silent memories.

"Cai, darling, it's the first day of school! You can't be late! Come on now!" her father's voice filled the house.

Cai sat on her bed, hands folded in her lap. She didn't want to go. She was an outcast all through middle school. The first day of high school didn't look promising, either.

"Cai, come on!"

She wanted to hide, run away. She'd begged her parents without success the night before to let her home school. They both worked; they couldn't leave her home alone all day, every day. No points she argued convinced them. Not even the fear she felt of the person who had bullied her all through school. "It builds character. Learn to deal with her."

Her father's footsteps tore her from self-pity, and she gripped the comforter of her bed, searching the room for a hiding place.

The door creaked open as she bit her bottom lip, flopped backward on her bed and prepared for one last desperate attempt to disrespect her father's wishes by screaming that she wasn't going to school.

The doorway filled with his silhouette and her mouth opened, "Cai? Huh, she must have left already." The door closed. Cai searched the vanity mirror opposite her bed and discovered nothing on the bed but the multi-colored, geometric patterned comforter.

On the third morning of school, the phone rang during breakfast, and her father returned to the table, anger darkening his handsome face. "Where have you been going? You have not been attending school the last two days. That was the secretary calling to see if we had changed schools. I want answers!"

How could she tell them? She didn't even understand it herself. She did tell them, though, and when her father's temper rose in answer to her ridiculous story, her mother turned defensive, reminding him of the fairytale, of her past, and during the high level of emotional tension filling the room, Cai's fear showed them both what she could do.

A year later, her parents were dead.

A tiny smile touched Cai's lips as she recalled the first time she blended with her surroundings, the fear she felt upon first discovery, the fun she'd had after acceptance, but the smile faltered quickly, replaced by sorrow.

The first peek of the sun battled the last chill in the air as the four walked on. Though they remained in the shadows of forest, their path pulled them toward a residential area.

Like casing burglars, they crept along the outer edges of houses along the highway, hoping to avoid discovery from slumbering dogs.

Their cautious steps brought them to the bank of a dry riverbed as the first highway noises rose with the golden orb of daylight.

"Do any of you even know what direction we're going? I mean, suddenly I'm feeling a little lost. Are we going the right way?" Cai directed her questions at Nathan not really expecting an answer, looking to break the silence that had brought the painful memories of death.

"Well, I don't think we're going the right way to find disguises," Thad added.

"No, but there's less chance of getting caught out here. That highway turns into 171, which goes to Paradise. I drove my grandma's car this way to 35... until it ran out of gas."

"Where exactly were you going, Nathan?"

"I don't know... anywhere away from there. Mexico, maybe. Grandma once told me I still had family there."

"Too bad we don't have your grandma's car now," Thad moped. "I'm getting tired of walking. These shoes are too small. Can we take a break? My stomach is growling again."

"Thad! We're all tired and hungry, but our

safety is more important than your feet and stomach at the moment!" Cai argued.

"Well, I'm not trying to be weak, but I'm hungry, too. It couldn't hurt to stop somewhere soon and take a break. We've been walking most of the night. Nathan, is there any soup left?" Rebecca sided with Thad.

"No," Nathan tossed the backpack up and caught it to show them how light it was. "We do have money, though."

"We might need to use that money," Cai reminded. "But, we don't even know how much is in the tin. Maybe we should stop for a break. How much farther do you think it is to Paradise, Nathan? Do you remember?"

"Right in here somewhere there was a sign coming from Paradise to Godley was about 60 miles? We've been keeping good pace, so maybe we have about 40 miles left?"

"That's too long and too far," Cai pouted. "At that rate, it's still a two day walk. Plus, we don't even know where to go when we get there."

"No, but we're pretty sure it's Paradise, because of the story," Nathan added.

"But is Nathan's Paradise the right one?" Rebecca wondered.

"Good point." Cai stopped. "I wonder how many cities in the world are named Paradise?

"Let's rest here," Cai ordered. "We've been careful to stay hidden, and they don't seem to have followed us. I guess we could all use a break, if for nothing else than to think." A tree struck down by high winds long ago had fallen crossways of the creek bed, leaving the top half lying on the ground in the opposite direction. Cai took a few steps beyond the dry roots poking out from the uprooted trunk and sat, resting her back against the rough bark. Rebecca sat next to her, while Thad climbed upward, planting himself onto the fallen log.

"Get the box out, Nathan. We might as well check how much we have," Cai held her hand out. "Maybe we could swing enough for food."

Nathan handed the Christmas tin to Cai and waited for the tally.

Cai counted the bills, counted them again and set them back in the box. "One hundred and twenty-six dollars... and one necklace," she concluded thoughtfully. "Definitely not enough for bus fare, which we should probably avoid anyway, given that the law may already have posters up in every station."

"Right, but there has to be a quicker way to get there than walking," Thad suggested.

"Maybe we could pay someone to give us a ride. It's not that far. People drive that way every day!" Nathan added hopefully, bringing a shrug from Thad.

"I like that idea," Thad snapped a piece of bark from the dead tree as he and Nathan continued their discussion.

"A necklace?" Rebecca peeked over Cai's arm.

"Yeah," Cai pulled the delicate chain up between finger and thumb.

"Oh, that was my mom's!" Rebecca held the delicate chain in her hand, a slight smile of reminiscence playing on her lips.

"Do you want to wear it?" Cai offered.

"No, just put in the small pocket of my bag. I don't want to lose it."

Cai placed the necklace in the pocket and zipped it closed. A minus later, she patted the top of her head for flying bugs. Pulling a piece of bark from her hair, she glanced up Thad's grinning face. "Knock it off, squirt," she threatened a fist at him. "The problem with catching a ride is we don't even know who we can trust, Nathan. If there're posters in the stations, wouldn't they be in the post offices, too? How many people go to the post office every day? Since we don't even know the faces we're up against, it's hard to trust anyone. We don't want to wind up like the other two."

Silence surrounded them until Thad's stomach growled again, forcing a round of laughter into the morning air.

"We better find some food before Thad decides we would make a good meal." Cai snapped the lid back onto the tin and replaced it.

"Leave the food to me. It's one of my specialties!" Nathan stood, turning from the others.

"Where are you going, Nathan? You shouldn't go alone. I'll go with you." Thad jumped down.

"He's right. None of us should go anywhere alone," Cai ordered.

"But one won't be as noticeable as four, or even

two. I got this!" Nathan waved Thad off before moving away from the creek bottom.

"True. Stay here, Thad!" Cai replied.

14

"Come on, Son. We better get back to camp before it gets too dark!"

"Hang on, Dad. I found something," Nathan called from the brush beside the hiking trail.

"We still have a mile or so to go, and if that sun sets, it'll be difficult to find our way back. Come on!"

"Okay, okay," Nathan ran to catch up to his father, the wild onions flopping in his hand.

"What in the world?" His dad studied the fistful of onions. "Where did you find those?"

"Back there, off the trail where I stopped. Didn't you smell them?"

"I sure didn't. Well, those will go quite nicely with that fresh fish waiting for us at camp."

"That's what I thought, too," Nathan's broad smile caused his dad to draw him close in a one-arm hug. Nathan felt he was getting too big for hugs, though. He ducked away from his father's embrace with a grin. "Wanna race?" He jogged backward, taunting his dad.

"You're on!" His dad nodded and sprinted past him.

The winner's bragging rights were put on hold when they reached camp. Someone, or something, and tossed their tent, destroyed their food, and dumped the fresh fish, water and all. Their camp had been trashed.

"Dad?"

"Bear, Son. It was a bear. We forgot to raise that cooler full of fish and the rest of our food before we left. Rookie mistake." His dad eased into camp, turned a chair up and sat down. "I don't know what we'll do for dinner, now. The bad thing is, it'll be dark in a half hour, and we're spend ing the night. We're really gonna have to rough it." He shook his head at the mess, the overturned tent, and the scattered wood.

"We have onions!" Nathan held the handful of onions up. His dad's weak smile made him frown, though. "You fix the camp, Dad, build a fire, and I'll be back. I'll find something for dinner."

"Wait, Nathan! That bear may still be out there. I really don't want you running off on your own..." His father's last words trailed him down the incline to the creek.

"So what if I see a bear. I'll wrestle it for our fish!" He yelled back.

"Nathan!"

The boy returned just before the last light disappeared behind the trees, bringing the cool air. A chilly fog followed him up the slope tagging him before he glimpsed the crackling orange and yellow reflections lighting his father's features. He held two large fish shoulder high, an ear splitting grin announcing his success.

"So, I see you found the bear," the pride on his dad's face trumped the disrespect his son had shown

earlier.

"Yeah, he was just sitting down to dinner, turned his back to cough—I sneaked around him and slipped the fish from his plate. What can I say?" Laughter over Nathan's ridiculous story filled the reordered campsite as his dad stuffed the two fish with the cleaned onions before skewering them hickory branches.

The memory turned up the corners of Nathan's lips for a moment before his knees struck the hard dirt, palms collecting grit and grass.

Nathan pushed to his toes and up, glancing back at the immobile prankster, half buried in vines and dry leaves. He brushed the leaves and dirt from his knees and hands, pulled the prankster from its hiding place, and smiled as he continued on, eyes searching the ground before his feet.

He hadn't been away long before returning to his companions, the front of his shirt bulging. "Here," he handed a tomato to each of them. "Late blooming tomatoes. Good thing we haven't had a frost, yet. And here's a cantaloupe that missed the frost. All we have to do is break it open and eat around the rind."

"Where did you find these? Did you steal them?" Cai narrowed her eyes at him.

"No, well, not technically. I found an

abandoned, overgrown garden. The house was empty," he shrugged. "I imagine they're volunteer plants grown up from rotted plants left behind."

"Wow, that was lucky!" Thad hungrily bit a chunk out of his tomato.

"I can't eat this. I need soup..." Rebecca palmed the tomato.

"No, you don't. You can do anything you want to do, Rebecca!" Cai firmly reprimanded.

"No... I mean... all I've ever learned to..." Rebecca's hands fluttered.

"I know. I know what you mean. You just have to learn. Look, I'll show you." Cai rubbed the tomato on her shirtfront like an apple and bit into it, juice and seeds spewed from the corners of her mouth. She emphasized her chewing in Rebecca's direction. "Mmm... sweet."

Rebecca pushed the tomato toward her shirtfront, cautiously moving it up and down until the skin started to rub off.

"That's enough. Now just take a bite. Actually, they're very good tomatoes. Were there anymore, Nathan?"

"No, I only found these. At least it will take the edge off our hunger until we find something else."

"Can you break that cantaloupe? I'm still starving!" Thad begged wiping his hands on his gritty jeans.

Rebecca pressed her front teeth into the tomato, causing juice and seeds to drip down the front of her shirt. *"Oh, no! I don't have clean clothes."*

"Don't worry; when we find some disguises, we'll wash it out. Just eat," Cai's patient words calmed Rebecca. Nathan found it interesting that Cai handled Rebecca with such ease. His eyes remained on them as he smacked the cantaloupe against the tree.

Using his fingers, he dug out the stringy, slimy, seedy guts. Next, he smacked each half to break it into smaller chunks. Thad grabbed the largest piece and began gnawing out the sweet insides.

"Dang! You are hungry!" Nathan chuckled. The tomato seemed to fill his stomach enough, so he took a smaller piece.

"The only thing we had to eat yesterday was that can of soup you gave us." Cai bit into the yellow-gold meat of the fruit, its juice trailing from a corner of her mouth. As she wiped at it with the back of her hand, a gunshot sounded nearby.

The teens started, stood, and faced the alarming sound, hands reaching for each other, cantaloupe pieces falling from their fingertips.

Seconds later, a medium sized, gold spotted, white dog barreled through the scruffy underbrush, paused at the fallen tree, and ducked behind it, quivering with fear.

Cai followed Rebecca with her eyes as Rebecca moved behind the tree and huddled with the dog.

Nathan moved closer to Cai, the two guards, standing tall with fists clenched.

Thad disappeared behind the tree, back sliding down its rough edge as he crouched near Rebecca, fear turning his legs to jello. Rebecca calmed the shaking hound with gentle strokes. The dog's torso hardly moved with breath as he buried his nose beneath his forelegs.

"Damn dog! Where'd you go? I told you to stay off my property!" An angry, loud voice preceded the burly man, long barreled shotgun slung over his shoulder. "Hey, you kids see a dog?"

Cai and Nathan glanced toward each other, then back at the large man, "No, sir," Nathan shook his head in unison with Cai's answer.

"He must have cut left. I hope he cut right onto the damn highway. Maybe a car will get him!" The man's face pinched into a hate raged image.

"Is... is something wrong with the dog?" Nathan worried about Rebecca, remembering the time a rabid dog wandered onto his grandpa's place.

"Nothin' that some buckshot won't cure. Dog keeps chasing my stinkin' chickens."

"Did you tell his owner?" Nathan hoped there wasn't one.

"What? Are you one of them there animal rights people? I am the dog's owner! Stupid dog! Argh! Maybe shootin' at 'im run 'im off this time!" The man turned, stomping back through the woods.

When the man's back disappeared beyond the trees and he couldn't hear them, Thad peaked around the tree, the piece of melon near his lips, "I guess we're five now, huh?"

"Absolutely!" Cai's eyes widened in agreement. "That dog will not go back to that man!"

Nathan climbed over the log, bouncing down to the other side. He ran his hand over the dog, checked his teeth and nodded his approval. "I don't know how we're going to feed him, but he's in pretty good shape. We should've asked his name."

Rebecca's hand swept from the dog's head down his back to his stubbed tail.

"Let's call him Splash! He looks like he was splashed with a bucket of soft golden-red paint."

"Hey, that's a good name, Rebecca," Nathan picked up the dog's chin. "Splash, how 'bout that, Splash? You like that name?" He stood, backed away, and called the dog, patting his thighs. "Come on, Splash, come here." The dog rose to his haunches, panted at Rebecca, and remained seated, reluctant to leave her.

"Go, Splash. It's okay," The dog's head tilted at Rebecca, then glanced over his back to Nathan before lifting his hind end and trotting into an affectionate rub down.

15

Splash trotted near Rebecca's side, tail tucked, head dropped low, steps silent, as the four continued on their journey. When they stopped to rest several hours later, the dog laid his head protectively on Rebecca's lap, relaxing his guard; she massaged his noggin, ears raising and flopping with her motion, his stubbed tail wagging in response.

"Look at her, just sitting in the floor playing with that doll. She's such a good child."

"She's so quiet, Barb. Isn't there a way you can get her to open up? Did the doctor give you any ideas?"

"No. Her teacher suggested a dog."

"Oh, that would be wonderful. I bet she would love that," the neighbor agreed.

Rebecca's doll lay still in her tiny hand for a moment.

One of her classmates had brought a puppy for show and tell once.

She would like a puppy, a soft, warm, licky puppy.

"I'm afraid I couldn't afford another mouth to feed. Now, if her father would step up and help out, I could pull it off, but..."

"Ask him. Surely he wouldn't deny that sweet girl a puppy."

"Humpf. I have asked. Many times. He denies that sweet girl as his daughter, and he won't do anything to help her." The angry bitterness in her grandmother's voice drew Rebecca back into her quiet place where she couldn't hear, see, or feel anything in the outer world, the rag doll slipping from her hand to the floor.

In her quiet place, a soft, brown puppy bounced around her, licking her face, tugging at her shirtsleeve, chewing on her rag doll, but that was just her happy, otherworld place where nobody could reach her, hurt her, yell at her.

The memory lifted a corner of Rebecca's lip as she stroked Splash's warm head. He wasn't a brown puppy, but he was soft and warm—Splash lifted his nose to her chin, his wet tongue venturing a swipe below her bottom lip—and licky.

"Somebody is in love," Cai nodded toward the dog.

"Yeah, I think it's mutual, too. Thad and I are

going to slip out near the highway... take a look around."

"Okay. Be careful." Cai joined Rebecca and Splash.

Nathan and Thad took turns walking the right of way near the highway, searching for articles of clothing to use for disguises.

They lucked out on the last jaunt and found a cap for Rebecca. Though it took her a little time to accept wearing it when they returned, she now wore the well-used Longhorn ball cap, her straight blonde hair tucked beneath it.

This venture to the right of way produced a pink Cowboys cap for Cai—it appeared to have been collecting dirt while tossing in a past wind. At first, her thick, dark hair escaped capture at the sides, and she continually readjusted it.

"Splash really likes you," Cai plopped down next to Rebecca on their next break, still adjusting her hair under the cap.

"I always wanted a dog. He's so sweet. Why would that man want to shoot him?"

"Why would your own father want to shoot you?

"It's a horrible world we live in today. Not at all the way people were when our parents were alive." Cai picked up a twig and stirred some dry leaves. Then she picked up a handful, palmed them, and then crumbled them to pieces to blow from her hand. "There's so little happiness, anymore. It seems like nobody cares about anyone else... so different from when I was little. This time of year, Mom and I would make almond cookies and spiced nuts to take to the homeless shelter. She always volunteered to cook for them, too. I helped her cook, and I liked them, the homeless, the poor. They told interesting stories. They didn't judge me, like the kids at school did.

"I've seen so many homeless people since I've been on my own, and less and less people who care about them," Cai frowned. "You know how many soup kitchens I've seen boarded up? I can't count them," she shook her head.

"Where are you from?" Rebecca felt nosy, but she often wondered about the lives of others and never had the chance to speak to them.

"Actually, not far from here. Burleson. I can still see our home on Eden. It was huge! I miss my bed, my mom's cooking, my dad's concern, even his yelling!" Cai allowed herself a rare moment to reminisce, tears welling. Rebecca shocked her by placing her delicate, pale hand over Cai's and patting in a stiff but gente way.

"We have all lost someone we love, our most precious possessions, but I know there is a greater reason for our suffering. If you could help those people you've seen, those people we ourselves have become, would you?"

"Of course!" Cai wiped away a stray tear, a response to the calmness in Rebecca's thoughts and words, outer world silence surrounding them.

"As would I, and Nathan, and Thad. We are the Gifted Ones, apparently—whatever that means for our

future. We must find the other two in our dream, the ones in my picture. Where they are is where we should be.

"We have all suffered, and yet, our mission, as in the story, is to stop the dragon—the faceless man—from his plan. Yes, we have suffered, are suffering still, but maybe it is so others will no longer suffer, so the world will be a better place, become one again. As hard as it is, we have to stay focused on that."

"I know, Rebecca," Cai's chin lifted. This was close to the speech she had given to Thad when they met, and Rebecca had reminded her how even she, Cai Philip, needed reassurance at times. "It is very hard to be alone, without family. I get so mad about my parents, my grandmother, the foster home I stayed in after their deaths, the way nobody has offered to help Thad and me. Yet, if I had a sandwich and a hungry person longed for it, I would give it away and suffer myself. What's happened to us, to the world we live in?" She frowned, eyes distant, head shaking.

"My theory is him, the faceless man in our dream. I think he has done this to our world, somehow. We have to stop him."

"What if we can't? What if he stops us?"

"Hmm... I wonder, would that be so bad? Per the beliefs of my grandmother, we would be reunited with our families," Rebecca's voice trailed off with the thought of seeing her mother again.

"But then, the world would be ..."

"... a very, very sad and hopeless place, worse

than now."

Nathan's return from the right of way brought him discomfort as he listened to the melancholy conversation between the girls. He moved toward Thad meeting him from the other direction; they sat, shoulders pushed into each others, backs against a tree. They closed their eyes and listened to the silence around them, until Thad's stomach startled Nathan's eyes open causing them to roll toward the younger boy.

"Again?" Nathan's brows rose.

"I can't help it," Thad's nose wrinkled. "What are the girls talking about over there?" He jerked his head toward them.

"They're just talking about the past, the future. Then Cai started to cry… I hate it when girls cry. Well, I hate it when anybody cries."

"What? Why was she crying?" Thad stiffened, but Nathan laid his hand on Thad's forearm to stop him from running to Cai.

"Rebecca's got it covered. Let's get some rest during our break, and then I'll go see if I can get tripped by some food again."

Thad laughed, "I bet that was funny."

"Probably to the cantaloupe, but that fruit ain't laughin' anymore!" Nathan rubbed his stomach.

"Where did you live before Paradise?" Thad asked Nathan as he closed his eyes to the flecks of light filtering through the trees.

"Let's just keep it at Paradise. I don't want to think about before then, with my parents. What about you?"

"Denton. We lived on Paradise Lane. Isn't that funny?"

"Yeah. What's even weirder is Cai lived on Eden Street, Rebecca's from Godley ... Paradise, Godley, Eden... if you think about it they're all kind of synonymous."

"Hey, that is weird," Thad sat up straight. "Do you suppose that the other two, the ones in Rebecca's picture, were from similarly named places. Do you think that maybe those others are looking for your Paradise, too?"

Nathan straightened, "I think we might be onto something, Thad. If we're all connected somehow through our locations, Eden, or Paradise, or Godley, then, yeah, they might be, too.

"We all are! We may not have to go looking for the others. They may already be in Paradise! Or, at least on the way!" This time, Nathan and Thad rose to share their discovery with Cai and Rebecca.

"We need to find a faster way to get to Paradise, Nathan. If what you and Thad are thinking is correct, then all of the others could be in danger, not just the two in our dream!"

"Yeah, but even if we find a faster way to get there, how are we going to find them?" Thad asked.

"The dark place, could it be a shed or garage, or a storage building?" Cai wondered.

"Sure, but do you know how many of those there are in Paradise? Especially on farms," Nathan added. "Some farms have three or four out buildings, at least."

"It would have to be sealed tight. No light shows through wherever they are. I could barely see their faces through the darkness in my dream, until that brief moment of light disappeared, like a door being closed, or lowered on them," Thad offered.

"Are we sure they're not hiding on purpose?" Cai's headed tilted.

"No, we can't be sure, but I had a sense of fear, loss, hopelessness in the dream. It felt like they were in danger. The darkness... it was so deep, what I always imagined that's what it was like for the dead, being buried beneath the earth." Rebecca volunteered.

"You imagined that?! That's a little morbid. I know for one, I don't like darkness. Maybe they don't, either?" Thad shivered.

"Hence the flashlight," Cai nodded at Rebecca.

"Deep dark? Like an underground kind of darkness?" Nathan closed his eyes. "Can any of you remember the angle of the light as the door closed?"

They paused, eyes closed trying to recall the details of the dream. Rebecca's eyes widened, *"It was like the door was above them, the light crossed their faces, their bodies in darkness until all I could see was a thin line of light drawn between them right before the door closed."*

"Sounds like they are underground?" Cai's voice rose in uncertainty.

"You think they're buried alive?" Thad shivered again.

"Or maybe in some kind of an underground storm shelter or cellar? My grandparents' place has a cellar on it. I used to hide in it when I was in trouble. There was no light, but I hid battery-operated lanterns down there so I could turn one on and read, or just sit and think. Everything Grandma canned went down into that cellar. Grandpa hung a lot of smoked meat down there, too. I used to sneak down there and eat Grandma's peaches. Mmm... they were so good!" Nathan rubbed his stomach, the tip of his tongue circling his dry lips.

"Did you have to say that?" Thad placed both of his hands over his stomach as it ached with pangs.

"Sorry, Thad. They could be in a cellar, though," Nathan nodded.

"Could it be your cellar?" Cai turned to Nathan. "You said you escaped when your grandfather was killed by a man. Do you think..."

"Maybe somehow, the other two wound up at your grandparents'? If they came to the same conclusion as we have about Paradise, perhaps your family's farm is being used to hide them?"

"I guess that could be. Now that I remember, that killer wanted my grandparents gone. I didn't hang around long, but it seemed he wanted the farm —or maybe he wanted me.

"I guess our cellar is as good a place as any to start looking. If the other two did end up in my cellar, they're lucky to have all that good food to eat. If they're okay, that is. Speaking of food, I better start looking." Nathan lifted a corner of his lip at Thad, his long hair swinging from side to side as he left the group.

"I wish there was a way we could get to Paradise sooner. I'm afraid what might be happening to the others at this moment... all that darkness. If they're on Nathan's farm, and that man killed his grandparents..." Rebecca grasped Splash around his thick neck in a desperate hug, her cheek resting against his head.

"Don't worry, Rebecca. Think of it in terms of the story. As far as we know, none of the twelve die before they are all together... right?" Cai suggested. "We'll get to them in time. They're in the dream, too, remember? So they have to be okay—for now."

16

Cheater rolled from side to side in the darkness. No warmth encompassed her in this lightless world, and she cringed remembering the fall down the cellar ladder—with the aid of a broken ladder rung—her tailbone striking hard against the floor beneath the ladder. She writhed in discomfort, slight moans slipping from her parched lips.

Aside from the pain, this dark place brought cold shivers. The refrigerator feeling it gave her brought memories of younger years and hot days when she would come in from playing outside and open the refrigerator just to cool down.

She rubbed her arms to create a warm friction.

In the little time she had dozed off, a new dream plagued her. Slightly different from her usual frightening dream about the faceless man, it left an odd sense behind. "Jaz, are you there?"

"Yeah, I'm here. Where else am I gonna be? Are you okay?" His low voice drifted through the quiet darkness.

"Yeah, I think so. My tailbone hurts from falling, I'm hungry, and really thirsty. I keep smelling barbecue or something.

"I had a strange dream. It was different than the other one." Cheater moaned, trying to sit up.

"Yeah, I dreamt about something weird, too. Circle of fire, some blonde chick's hair spiraling upward..."

"Yes! And I saw the faces of other Gifted Ones, I think. I called to them. I told them to unite. I don't know if they heard me over the roar of that fire and that gaud-awful laughter."

"I heard you, in the dream I mean." His voice rippled through the darkness. "I saw the faceless guy, and then some kid got picked up in, like, a whirlwind or something."

"Yes, I was holding his hand. I didn't feel like he was one of us. He was afraid and that man talked to him. Did you hear what the faceless man said to him? I wonder why that kid was there.

"I want to think that it really is all just a dream, but after all that has happened in my life, I know it's not," Cheater sighed.

"I know, that's some crazy story that brought us together, isn't it? At least we got each other down here in this hole."

Cheater didn't think her eyes would ever adjust to the blinding darkness; she reached out to her left, her strong, thin fingers seeking the one whose voice had become her greatest comfort.

"Would you mind taking your hand off my forehead?"

She laughed. "Sorry, I can't see a thing. Can you?"

"What? Do I look like an owl? Or maybe a bat? No, I can't see anything, but both of my hands are touching wood."

Cheater resisted the chuckle that inspired the Pinocchio reference hovering on her tongue and instead ran her hands over the hard coolness below her. "Mine, too. My back hurts so bad when I move, but I don't think anything's broken. Do you think we've been buried alive or something?"

"Nice! Yeah, way to scare me. Don't say that! That's always been my worst fear. Besides, there was a wooden door they opened before throwing us into the hole, remember?" Jaz's voice came from above her, indicating he'd stood up.

"Sorry," Cheater giggled. She cautiously rolled to her hands and knees, and inched her way around. "Do you think oxygen filters through here somehow? What if we run out of air? I remember a fence, and then a shed with a tunnel-like area going downward to the ladder. How long did we walk to get out here?"

"Man, I don't know." His hopeless words fell silent. "Wherever we are, there's something else here with us."

"What do you mean?" Cheater stood still.

"I mean, you know how empty rooms echo. When we talk, there's no echo. There must be something else in this space, maybe something we can use to get out." Jaz felt around some more.

"I found a wall, I think. It's wood, too." Cheater's hands crept upward.

"Where are you?"

"How would I know? In a room with you!" Cheater replied smartly.

"Yeah, well, I found another wall!" Jaz called from behind her.

"It's probably the same one. Ow!" Cheater rubbed her head.

"What happened? Are you okay?"

"Yeah, there's something hanging above me. I bumped my head on it."

"In this darkness, it's probably a bat!"

"Yewww! No, it was too heavy."

Jaz yelped.

"What?"

"A shelf, I think."

"I wish they hadn't taken our backpacks. I'm starved. It feels like we've spent days down here?"

"I don't know, but ..."

Cheater's face basked suddenly in a warm glow of light, and with her, shelves and shelves of canned fruits, vegetables and dried meats, "Yum!" She cried.

"I found a lantern. Now I know where we are. A cellar! I don't think the owners will mind if we help ourselves seeing as they threw us down here!" Setting the lantern in a corner, Jaz scanned the labels. Heavenly smoked meats hung from ropes above them.

"I don't care if they do!" Cheater pulled a jar of peaches from the shelf and started to twist the top off.

"Wait, do you think this stuff is still good?" Jaz's concern didn't even phase Cheater.

"Can't be any worse than food out of a dumpster!" The aroma of peaches filled the dimly lit space. Cheater wiped a hand on her jeans and pulled a firm, sticky slice from the jar, offering one to Jaz.

"You first," he waited.

"You're such a jerk!" She giggled, shaking her head, and bit into the peach slice, syrup slipping down her chin. "Oh my, these are so good. As good as Sadie's pies!" She pulled another from the jar.

"Hey! Let me try one!"

"Get your own! There's a ton of them!" Jaz searched the faded labels on the jars. "Cherries! Oh, man, my favorite!"

Cheater lifted her chin to allow the drips from the peach slices to fall into her mouth—and her eyes found the wooden door. She chewed the peach, scanning the broken rungs on the wooden ladder. "So that's why I fell. Hey, think you can reach that door?"

"Maybe." Jaz ate a cherry, and then another. "But you don't really think they would leave it unlocked, do you? I mean, seems like they're pretty much using us as bait to draw the others. Otherwise, we wouldn't be alive. The door has to be sealed." He set his jar on the shelf and stretched upward to the first unbroken rung. Pulling on it a few times to make sure it wouldn't pop loose, he flexed his arms, pulling himself upward, and walked his hands up the ladder while pressing his feet into the wall for leverage. He climbed farther up, until his feet stood on the closest unbroken rung and he advanced to the door, pushing up on it with his right hand.

It didn't budge.

"Hey! Let us out of here!" Jaz pounded his fist

against the solid oak door.

"So that's it; we're stuck in here." Cheater ate another peach slice.

"At least until they come back and open the door. We need a plan." Jaz gingerly climbed back down the ladder the way he had climbed up, so as not to break any more rungs. "At least we have good food!" He lifted the jar from the shelf and plopped another cherry into his mouth.

"And water." Cheater nodded toward the corner where ten or so plastic gallons of water sat in the shadows cast by the lantern.

Finishing the last peach slice, Cheater recapped the jar, licked her sticky fingers clean, and picked up the lantern to have a look around. Where Jaz set it on the floor, light filtered to the lowest shelf and the floor beneath it, but the other side of the cellar remained dim.

"Batteries, a couple of bulbs... Hey, peanut butter, crackers in a tin... Wine?" Her eyebrows raised and a smile dawned her lips.

"Ha, we can have us a party!" Jaz joked.

"Riiight! The labels are handwritten. It must be homemade."

"You ever drink any of that stuff?"

Cheater stopped searching the shelf, the bottle suspended by her left hand, the lantern in her right; she turned her head slightly toward Jaz and frowned. "Once, on Christmas Eve a long time ago. My parents' friends came for the holidays. They brought a bottle of homemade wine to share with us."

"Never tried the stuff. What's it like?" Jaz stuffed two cherries in his mouth.

"Like fruit juice; I don't know. Not long after I sipped it, Mom carried me to bed." Cheater shrugged.

"You little wino, you!" Jaz peered over her shoulder at the bottle, a grin lightening his features. Cheater's head remained turned; her brow furrowed in thought. She glanced up at him. "No, but it does give me an idea how we might get out of here."

"Oh, yeah—that's a good idea!"

Cheater pursed her lips at him defiantly, then carefully vocalized the plan even though he already knew it. Talking about the plan gave them a chance to clear up details. Jaz filled in where she stumbled, closed gaps, posed questions.

"It might work," he nodded.

"Then we can find the others. They're coming for us, you know? The blonde girl..."

"... spoke to you in the dream, yeah, I know. I was there."

Cheater huffed, "Oh, yeah!"

"Yeah, yeah, okay. I won't read your mind anymore. Let's see what else is up there?" Jaz lifted the lantern from Cheater's hand and held it higher. "Mmm, how much ham can you eat? Smoked ham sure sounds good. I mean, we don't have anything else to do but wait, right?"

"That's why I smelled barbecue, and what bumped my head. Yes, I could eat some more food... absolutely!" The thought rumbled her stomach. "You know, adding up the kids in the dream, I count..."

"Six. You, me, that kid on the other side of you, that hot Chinese chick..."

"Oh, sheez! Really? I'm sure she would love to hear that!" Cheater shook her head. "Another guy on the other side of her..."

"I bet he's the one that lives here... the grandson."

"Yeah, maybe, and then that blonde girl. Where do you think the other six were?"

"They must have been in the dream, too. We just couldn't see them through the fire," Jaz managed to chew a hole in the netting around the ham, peel away the cloth covering it, and tear off a large chunk with his fingers. He passed the piece to Cheater.

"Mmm... this tastes as good as it smells." She bit into the tender meat. "I bet Danny could make a good breakfast out of this ham."

"Danny? Oh, yeah, that diner guy. Yep, it would be good with some eggs, biscuits. Mmm." Following Cheater, who bent to pick up a gallon of water, Jaz moved to sit against the hardwood wall opposite the ladder. Cheater gritted her teeth through the pain of crossing her legs and sat next to him.

17

"Hey!" Nathan called quietly as he stepped around the tree, a fast food bag in hand.

"Where'd you get that?" Cai's suspicious gaze set Nathan on the defensive.

"What difference does it make? It's food!"

"Did you buy that? With our travel cash?" Cai screeched.

"Whoa, *our* cash? I thought it was Rebecca's cash!" Nathan's eyes rounded.

"It's okay, Nathan. It's our cash... for the cause," Rebecca's voice calmed them both.

"It doesn't matter. I didn't take any of the money. I found a cafe. I went it to see if they had any scraps. I told them it was for my dog, but it just so happens that this lady ordered lunch for her office, and they accidentally made it twice. The waitress gave it to me."

"Huh, that's weird. That doesn't happen very often," Cai squinted, her eyes nearly closed. She eyed Nathan's apparel. "She must have figured out you were homeless. She didn't act like she recognized you or anything, right?"

"Hey, sometimes it works to look grungy! No, she had more important things on her mind than figuring out some kid like me!" Nathan scanned his filthy clothing and shrugged.

"Wow, wonder what that lady ordered? It sure smells good!" Thad reached for the bag.

Nathan lifted it out of his reach. "Hang on, human vacuum!"

Splash's nose crinkled twice in his sleep, his eyes popped open, he raised his head and sat, nose twitching to the scent.

"Looks like we got some fries, some kind of sandwiches... one, two, three... hey, there's five!"

"Well, gimme one!" Thad held out his hand. "I hope it doesn't have onions on it."

"Really, Thad? You're going to get picky, now?" Cai reprimanded. "Brush them off."

Cai handed a sandwich to Rebecca, and Splash rose, stub wagging in wait.

"Is there a little one for Splash?"

"Yeah, actually, this one isn't very thick." Cai opened it, "No veggies, no mustard or ketchup. Perfect—hamburger and cheese, just the way dogs like it!" She handed that to Rebecca, too.

Thad had his sub sandwich half eaten before Nathan and Cai opened theirs.

"Man, this is so good!" Thad chewed and swallowed.

"Splash agrees!" Rebecca tore another piece away from the cheeseburger and fed it to the dog. He took it gently from her fingers.

"Anyone want my tomatoes? I don't like them on sandwiches." Cai held two slices between her thumb and forefinger.

"I'll take 'em!" Thad grabbed them up and stuffed them in his mouth. "If anybody doesn't want their fries, I'll take them, too!" His words muffled around the food filling his cheeks.

"Dang, Thad! The way you eat, you should be 600 pounds!" Nathan laughed. "You know, once, I had a friend in school that had tapeworm. She ate like a horse and kept losing weight. Maybe you have tapeworm, Thad."

The fries in Thad's hand stopped in front of his mouth. "Huh? Worms? How do you get those?"

"Ask Splash! He's probably had them," Nathan smiled.

"Uhm, no, he says he never has but that they come from eating fleas," Rebecca answered.

"Good one, Rebecca! Oh, yeah, I remember. That is how you get tapeworm. Did you get so hungry you ate some fleas, Thad?" The girls giggled at Nathan's teasing.

"Man, leave me alone!" Thad shoved the fries in his mouth.

"Was that pepper on that French fry, or a..." Cai squinted.

Thad stopped chewing, choked down his swallow, and peered into the nearly empty French fry carton.

Cai, Nathan and Rebecca burst into laughter.

"Sheez, why does everybody always pick on the youngest kid?" Thad shook his head.

"We're not picking on you because you're young. It's because you eat so much!" Cai's closed mouth grin angled around a cheek puffed with food.

They chuckled again.

"Too bad they didn't give you any drinks!" Thad licked the salt from his fingers. "I'm gonna see if I can find some water somewhere. I'll be back."

Nathan and Cai glanced at each other, shook their heads and grinned, but a second after he left, Thad returned.

"Hey! We gotta go, now! There's a sheriff walking through the woods over there. I think that somebody called the law about Nathan or something!"

"Maybe the waitress did recognize you and called the law about..." Cai went silent, she and Rebecca rose, picking up their trash. "Don't leave anything behind for them to find. They may be able to use it to identify us."

Once their trash was back in the bag, Nathan stashed it in the backpack, and the teens left the area, crouching and ducking behind any trees or brush to stay out of sight.

18

"Hey, kid! Aren't you supposed to be in school?" The deep voice caught Thad by surprise. Ducked behind a shrub, he slowly straightened, swallowed hard, and glanced at the others. "Should I say kids? Come on out."

"We're... working on a project... uhm, bugs... collecting bugs for science," Nathan lied.

"Zat so? You know, you look a little familiar. What school you go to? You have class with my son?" The sheriff squinted his eyes at Nathan. "You're not too far from the high school. You drive out here boys?"

"Uh, no sir." Thad shook his head and looked down at his ragged shoes.

"Huh." The officer glanced at Thad, then stared harder at Nathan, a curious glint catching his eyes. "Wait a minute! You don't go to school with my son. I've seen your picture... yeah, at the station. You from Paradise? You better come with me, son."

Nathan glanced around at the others and then back at the sheriff.

"Wait, don't run. This may be our way to Paradise. Play along, Nathan." Rebecca cast the thought quickly.

"All right, yeah, I'm from Paradise. So, you

found me... and my friends. What are you going to do with us?"

"Well, I'll get a hold of your family up there. Of course, I have to contact the law in that district, let 'em know we have you in custody. Stealing a car isn't something you can walk away from, son."

"Stealing a car? It was my grandma's car! And my family is all dead! There's nobody there to call!"

"Oh, now, just because you had a spat with your grandpa don't mean you can disown him. He still loves you, son. Now come on, turn around so I can put these cuffs on. Standard procedure."

Approaching Nathan, the young officer took a closer look at Rebecca's tilted head. "You..." he nodded toward her, "...take off that ball cap!" When she didn't respond, he stepped nearer her. "I said, take off that cap!" Within three feet, he leaned his head to the side, taking a closer look at Rebecca. "Just a minute! You're that girl they're looking for in Godley!" His hand slowly reached for the cap, "I'll have to take you back there young lady. You understand me, right? You're not fit to be running around out here in the wild!"

"Run!" At Rebecca's silent command, the four ran in different directions.

"Wait! Come back!" The officer drew his phone from his belt requesting help, although he knew by the time backup arrived, the kids would be too far away. Turning in a circle, glancing in the four directions they ran, each one already out of sight, he tucked his phone back in his pouch and moved in the direction of his car. Knowing the kids were in this area would be helpful finding them. Chances were the one kid was on his way back to his hometown, anyway. He started back to his car but turned when a crash of brush sounded not far from him.

Rebecca huddled among green shrubbery at the back of somebody's yard. Splash sat by her side, listening. When his mouth dropped open, his tongue slipped out, and he began to pant, Rebecca took it as a sign of safety.

"Is he gone?" She patted the dog's head gently.

The dog smiled up at her, pulling his tongue in and baring his front teeth on one side.

"You're so cute!" Rebecca rubbed his head again and pushed through the leafy growth into a patch of sunlight. Strands of blonde crept from beneath the cap and she fruitlessly pushed them upward.

"What are you doing in my backyard, kid? Why ain't you in school?"

Cai waited long enough to know the officer hadn't followed her before returning to her normal appearance.

"Now, where to find the others?" She closed her eyes, listened to the quiet surrounding her, and looked up at the sun. She was thankful for her years of experience in the scouts. Given the location of the sun, she could tell which way to walk.

She took a few steps northeast before she heard it—the cry for help.

It was Rebecca.

Nathan waited and listened. He'd found a fallen tree, gathered loose leaves, and lay as close to the motionless protector as he could, covering himself with the leaves.

He peeked through the crispy colors of fall, allowing the tiny openings between to aid his hearing. No sounds moved on the light breeze except the rustling of branches.

Then he heard it—a cry for help.

It was Rebecca!

The crispy colors crashed and swirled as he rose into a full run.

Thad huddled at the base of a shrub-covered tree. His body quivered as each crunching footstep drew closer. Fear bubbled in his chest, threatening a loud eruption of breath he held.

Knee bones pressed into his deeply tanned forehead, his arms cramped from the tight hold on his calves.

He'd heard Rebecca's cry for help, but the approaching crinkle of dried foliage held him in place, too scared to move.

The running steps slowed. Silently he begged whomever it was to keep going. Visions of his wrists in cuffs, riding in the back of the tan car, his father's angry face sneering at him when he arrived at the county sheriff's office to pick him up, froze every exterior quiver in his body.

Someone stood next to him.

Dizziness filled his head.

A firm hand tightened around his right arm, bringing a cramp to the tense bicep.

"What's wrong with you, girl? Can't you speak? I asked why you ain't in school."

Rebecca remained silent as the old woman approached her. Splash wagged his tail, stepping toward the woman.

Rebecca reached out again, hoping her friends could hear her cry.

"Ain't no reason for you to cry for help! I ain't gonna hurt ya'. I just want you to answer my question."

Splash moved tentatively toward the elderly woman, sniffing her hand. The woman scratched his head. Rebecca turned toward her.

"You can hear me?"

"Of course I can hear you, girl. I ain't deaf, just old and mostly blind. Now, why aren't you in school?"

Rebecca chanced a closer look at the woman. Wrinkles filled her graying features. She was much older than Rebecca's grandmother had been. Thin patches of silver hair poked out from under the large straw hat mounted atop her head. Dark gaps shone where once many teeth resided. Her rheumy eyes couldn't see well enough to know Rebecca wasn't moving her mouth.

"I... I don't go to school," Rebecca replied.

"Ah, finished it then. You got a job?" The old woman scratched Splash behind his ear.

"No, ma'am."

"Want one?"

"Uhm... well..."

"Oh—Rebecca—there you are!" Nathan huffed between breaths.

"Who 'zat? 'Zat your boyfriend?"

"No, ma'am. My name's Nathan. Sorry to bother you," Nathan gulped air.

"T'ain't no bother. You need a job? I got a job

needs doin' and nobody to do it."

"A job? Well... no, but I'll be happy to help you out if it won't take too long."

"Well, we'll see just how long. Come with me." The old woman turned toward her house.

Nathan searched the area behind him for Cai and Thad but they couldn't be seen.

"Why don't you and Splash stay in the backyard and wait for Cai and Thad? I'll see if I can help her," Nathan leaned in to whisper near Rebecca's ear.

"No! I won't go with you! Let go of me!" Thad jerked his arm free.

"You idiot! It's me. Get up! We have to find Rebecca; she's in trouble." Cai slapped the back of his head.

Thad's chest lightened when he looked into Cai's stern, sisterly stare. "Oh, Cai, it's you."

Cai jerked him up by his shirtsleeve, and they sprinted in the direction of Rebecca's scream.

19

"That's it? That's all you need?" Nathan looked at the wooden bed.

"May be easy for you, kid, but for a ninety-eight year old woman, it ain't so easy. I need this room cleaned out, and I can't lift a thing."

"If you let me get my friends, we can get it done twice as fast."

"What's your hurry? 'Fraid to be around an old person? You youngsters! Bah!" She flipped a frail, flimsy hand his way.

"No, ma'am. My grandpa was old, and I was around him all the time," Nathan assured, immediately biting his lip at the possible offense.

A crackly, old chuckle followed.

"It's just, we're kind of in a hurry. We're on foot, and we need to get to... somewhere really soon. We have some friends that need our help." Nathan didn't mean to tell her that much, but for reasons he couldn't understand, he trusted her.

"Help, huh? They in some kind of trouble with the law? I don't need kids like that around. If that's the case, you just go on now!" Bent arthritic fingers waved him toward the backdoor.

"No, ma'am, not the law... Just let me get my friends, and we'll break this bed down and move this stuff out to your shed for you in no time. Honestly, I would like to have more time to visit with you; I really would. I used to love listening to my grandpa talk about the old days."

"Old days! Ha! Bet I got years on him if you wanna hear about some real old days."

"Yes, ma'am. I'll just go see if my friends are here, and I'll be right back." Nathan moved toward the door as the old hand caught his forearm, "Where you trying to go, son?"

He glanced at the semi-crippled, arthritic fingers lightly gripping his arm, then up to the dull, sightless eyes, "Paradise, ma'am, where my grandparents live... lived."

"All right, then! You go get your friends, and let's get this done."

Nathan hoped he was doing right, trusting the elderly woman. She seemed honest and kind enough, though somewhat bossy. Stepping out the back screen door, he caught sight of Thad and Cai running toward Rebecca. After explaining, the four quickly went to work in the room without argument.

"We need to hurry. We don't have time to waste!" Cai hefted one end of the headboard, while Thad carried the other. Most of the bed was already in the shed.

Once finished, Cai swept the vinyl floor for the woman, wiped her hands on her worn jeans and declared, "Done!"

"And a fine job, too! Now, I wanna pay ya'. How much?" The elderly woman opened a worn wallet.

"No, ma'am, that's fine. We don't want to take your money. We'll be on our way, now, though, if that's all you need," Nathan argued.

"Oh, I ain't got much money to give. I got this, though!" She pulled a key ring from the old wallet gripping it between thumb and forefinger. The keys clanked and swung from her fingertips, tapping a silver cross key chain. "Which one of you Gifted Ones can drive?"

Nathan and Cai traded glances warily. "You—you know about the Gifted Ones?" Cai swallowed hard.

"I do. Now get on your way! Who's driving?" The woman asked again.

"But how?" Nathan exclaimed.

"Who cares? I got this!" Cai wrapped her right hand around the key.

"Wait! How do you know about us? Can you tell us anything about him... the faceless man?" Thad asked her.

"There's an old story went around years ago, a fairytale of sorts, about twelve children... Yap, heard it a long time ago when I was a wee thing. Most people have forgotten it, 'cept those involved, I s'pose. Can't tell ya' who that horrible monster is, but today, he could be anybody, any higher up in this country if ya' ask me. You'll find him. Or... he'll find you. Whichever happens, the prophecy will be fulfilled." The old head nodded solemnly.

"Prophecy? What are you talking about? What prophecy?" Nathan asked.

"The end of the story..." The bluish lips stopped moving as she slipped into solemn consideration. "Now, go. And if you need to come back here, you do it. Old Maive has nothing to live for anymore. A little danger's good for the heart... keeps it pumpin'. I'll help you any way I can. Go, help your friends!" She shoed them out the garage door.

"Thank you, Miss Maive," Nathan wrapped his arms around her frail shoulders.

"Bah!" She accepted the hug, but quickly pushed him away. "Git on outta here! Ain't got time for mushy stuff! Go! And don't forget to unplug that thing before takin' off! Likely pull the whole dern garage down, you will!" She rapped her knuckles on the door frame. "Almost done that very thing first time I drove it out." She chuckled at the memory.

Maive held open the kitchen door leading to the garage for each teen as they exited. A car tarp hid their prize ride; Thad and Nathan carefully pulled it free. The dusty, silver cover revealed a like new, all electric car.

"Right back there, there's a plug. See it?"

"Yes, ma'am!" Nathan gripped the plug and pulled it free tucking it away.

"Don't forget to plug it in somewhere in Paradise, you know, so you can get back here if you need me. I ain't worried about that car. Haven't driven it in years. Can't see. Gotta girl comes by and drives me when I need to go to the store or whatnot. We use her car instead. Use it as you need it."

"Will it get us to Paradise on a charge?" Thad

ran his hand over the glimmering hood.

"Shoot, that thing'll git you halfway across the state of Texas. Just make sure you turn everything off when you stop. Now, git in and git gone!" She flipped her old hand toward the gaping garage door behind the car, then she pushed the kitchen door closed on the four.

Nathan opened the backdoor for Rebecca and she climbed in. Splash whined and Rebecca called to him, but he wouldn't follow her.

"Come on, Splash, get in!" Nathan picked him up and put him in the car, receiving a wet lick on the chin from the nervous dog. Splash slipped onto the seat between Rebecca and Thad. "I don't think he's been in a car before. He might get car sick," Nathan crinkled his nose.

"Great! Don't get sick, Splash, okay? You won't be in here long." Rebecca held his snout in the palms of her hands, and then rubbed behind his ears.

Nathan lifted the large garage door, waited until Cai backed out, then closed it again, climbing into the front passenger seat and pulling the door closed behind him. "Crank it up! Let's go!"

"It's on, silly. I just backed it out. Why would I turn it off again?" Cai laughed.

"Wow! I've never ridden in an electric car. It's quiet. Cool!" Nathan checked out the dashboard.

Cai proved a better driver than Nathan. Under his direction, and with the help of the navigation system, they were on their way to Paradise and would arrive within an hour, instead of two days.

"Does this seem too easy to anyone else?" Thad's voice quivered cautiously.

"What do you mean?" Cai glanced in the review mirror at Thad.

"An old lady needs help, knows about us, and offers us her car... What if it's a setup?"

"Nah, she was very supportive. She wants to help us." Cai shook her head.

"Yes, I think so, too." Rebecca agreed.

"Yeah, but, maybe the other two, the ones in a cellar somewhere, maybe someone helped them, too," Thad frowned. "And look what it got them."

Cai caught his eyes in the mirror and took it seriously. "What makes you say that?"

"'Or, he'll find us.' That's what she said. She got all quiet after that. I just don't know whether we can trust her!" Thad looked down at his hands on his lap.

"I know I can. I've had dealings with one of the followers. I saw him kill my grandparents. She's nothing like them, not like that." Nathan's jaw tightened and flexed.

"Well, we can't worry about that now. Let's try to stay focused on finding the others. I think we'll have a better chance of dealing with everyone involved if we stick together. We'll worry about trust issues when we need to. Right now, enjoy the ride, and the fact that we don't have to walk sixty miles!"

"Agreed!"

A foul odor filled the car, wafting to the front seat and under Nathan's nose. He waved his hand below his nose and pressed the window button.

"Oh, Splash! Windows, quick!"

The dog's tongue dripped on Rebecca and Thad as he smiled, moved between their laps and chomped at the fresh breeze entering from both sides. "Whew! Car sick dogs do not smell good!" Thad fanned his nose.

"Could've been the hamburger!" Nathan suggested.

"Very true! Some dogs don't digest people food well. Once we had this little schnauzer, and he ate some of our Christmas candy. Let's just say it wasn't pretty," Cai added.

"Yeeuw!" Rebecca squeezed her eyes closed.

"Yah," Cai nodded.

"Oh, right here, Cai. There's the sign for FM 151 N!" Nathan directed just before the navigation voice told her to make a right, then left, then right again. "Won't be long now," Nathan's anxious voice added.

"Yeah, then what? I mean, once we get there, we need a plan. We can't just rush into town and start asking questions, you know?" Thad pointed out.

"True," Cai agreed.

"If we're sure they're being held in a cellar, then we should start with places with cellars," Rebecca offered.

"You don't think it will look suspicious, checking out every cellar we find?" Nathan asked. "We don't have to go looking; we'll start with the one I've seen, the one on my grandparents' property."

"Right, but how will we get on the property unnoticed?" Thad wondered.

"At dark. I know that place better than any other place in the world. I know every hiding place on that farm. We'll come in from the back. You'll see."

Silence filled the car as the four considered the dangerous quest they were about to embark on to help two people they had never met, but the deep quiet proved too much for the dog and he started yipping impatiently.

"What is it, boy? What's the matter?" The dog calmed while Rebecca stroked his head. The solemn threat of impending peril seemed to momentarily set him on edge.

"It'll work, don't worry, you guys," Nathan's voice quivered with uncertainty.

"Yeah, sure it will," Cai agreed, swallowing her sarcasm.

"Well, I'm just..." Thad began.

"Be quiet, Thad," the two in the front seat warned in unison. "Stop overthinking things. You doubt everything, all the time!" Cai stared Thad down in the rearview mirror for a second, taking her eyes off the road just long enough for an old model Dodge pickup to jerk right out from between some storage sheds directly in front of her.

"Look out!" Thad pointed between the two front seats.

20

Scratch… scratch… scrape.

"Turn off the light, quick!" Jaz wiped greasy hands on his dirty jeans and turned the lantern dial to the off position.

"What is it?" He whispered.

"I don't know," Cheater listened intently.

Scratch… scratch… scrape. Scratch… scratch… scrape. Yip! Yip!

"It's just the dogs!" She released the breath she held.

"Whew, I thought it was a shovel." Jaz rubbed his hands together.

"No, I think they're scratching at the door, trying to figure out how to get us out." Cheater drew her brows together in concern.

A long, loud, muffled howl filled the air beyond the door.

"Uh, do dogs do that?" Jaz asked.

"Sure, but usually when they hear train whistles, sirens, or… coyotes!" Fear filled Cheater.

"Oh, crap! Why are they scratching at the door?" Jaz jumped up.

"Food. I wonder if they smell the food?"

"They're gonna eat us!" Jaz had never seen a coyote and knew little about them.

"No, not us. They tend to run from people. They smell the food in here, the hams and stuff. If you were to climb up the ladder and bang on the door, I bet they would run away." Cheater hesitated.

"Seriously?"

"Sure... well... maybe."

"That's good to know. Wonder if they can get through that door?" He asked.

"They already would have before tonight. It would take them longer than we'll be in here. Besides, they'll give up first."

"Are you sure?"

"Yeah, sort of. Or the dogs will run them off. It's okay to turn the light back on now." Jaz rotated the dial and Cheater pulled free another hunk of ham.

"They're creeping me out... all that howling!"

Cheater ducked and cringed at the two cannon-like noises above them, muffled, yet loud enough to shake the ground around them.

"Gun shots!" Jaz whispered. "They're coming to kill us!"

21

"Look out!" Nathan and Thad shouted just before closing their eyes.

Cai slammed her foot down on the brake pedal and turned the wheel right. The old truck,—driven by an even older man—slid inches past the left bumper, leaving the small car on a precarious path to a power pole.

"Whew! That was close!" Nathan's hands pressed into the dash, his head bent forward to avoid the broken glass he imagined. Minus the crunch of metal, Thad pulled his index fingers free of his ears.

"I think I need to get out for a minute." Thad pushed the door open, disregarding the lot of empty outdoor sheds to his right. His knees trembled fiercely as he tried to stand. Gaining control of his balance, he moved behind the car and off the right of way where he casually bent forward and relieved the flux of stomach acid that rose from his bout of fear.

Cai eased the car backwards and straightened it out on the shoulder. She turned on the flashers while waiting for Thad. "He always does that when he gets extremely scared," she shook her head.

"How long have you been watching out for him?" Rebecca asked.

"Seems like forever, but I only just found him

huddled between two buildings a few months ago, scared to death, shivering, starving, untrusting." Cai's eyes crinkled with the memory.

"Does he have a gift, like you? Me? Nathan?"

"Oh, yes. He's very insecure about it, though. Well, he's very insecure, period. I mean look at him." She glanced out the passenger window.

"What is it? His gift?" Rebecca asked while stroking the window sniffing dog that now straddled her lap in search of Thad.

"You know, I don't think you'll believe it. I've only seen it once, and I still don't believe it. When I think about it... well, you'll just have to wait until he needs it."

"Hard to believe he has that awesome of a gift, looking at him right now," Nathan commented sarcastically. "The question is: will he be able to use it when we really need it? He's awfully timid."

"Yeah, that is the question," Cai frowned.

Thad returned to the car, "Sorry." His pale face turned away from them.

"I bet you've never been on a roller coaster," Nathan glanced around the back of the seat.

"Actually, no, I haven't," Thad answered quietly.

"It's okay, neither have I," Rebecca awkwardly patted Thad's arm.

Splash licked his right ear.

The now reddened face of the young man turned a grateful eye to Rebecca and Splash.

"Hey, it's all right! I'm just razzin' ya'!" Nathan

grinned at him.

Cai checked her left mirror and eased out on the road again.

"Hey, what's going on over there?" Thad indicated. He'd been watching the buildings through the windshield as they approached them. Just beyond a flapping yellow banner in front of a place called Chad's Pizza, a group of people circled in the parking lot, chanting. A body lay on the ground inside the circle.

One glance forced Cai to jerk the steering wheel left into the parking area of the pizza building. Thad flung his car door open simultaneously with Nathan, Cai not far behind. Rebecca debated whether to leave the dog and the vehicle, especially since Cai left the keys in the ignition and the quiet car running. She remained in place, let the window down, and listened.

"What's going on?" Nathan strolled into the gathering as if he belonged. Teenage faces turned toward him. The man on the ground, however, was rather old. He covered his face with the arms of the old, tattered leather jacket covering his shoulders. Patches on the jacket indicated that he might be a military veteran, or the jacket had belonged to one. Nathan recalled his grandfather's war stories and grew defensive. His jaw tensed, fists clenched.

"Who the hell are you? You're not one of us!" An older guy with a spiked, green Mohawk stepped toward him.

"No, he's not, Spike! And neither am I. Why are

you beating on this old guy?" Cai moved to the center of the circle and bent forward to help the older man up.

"Touch him and you'll get beat, too!" A girl moved in front of Cai.

Cai stiffened as she straightened. She'd been in more than a few scrapes in her lifetime, especially after her parents died. Jaw set in anger, she rose slowly to meet the girl's gaze. "For what? Being different?" She eyed the girl without flinching. "Is that why you're beating *him*?"

"That's none of your damn business. This is our territory. Get out of here!" The girl took a step closer. Cai felt a hand grip her ankle in warning and turned just in time to see Thad moving into the circle. She was glad to see him take control of himself, get out and help, but the look on his face surprised her more. She glanced at Nathan and nodded toward Thad.

Thad's face had changed to a blank, yet focused stare.

His gift took over his body. Cai knew that when he was finished here, he wouldn't recall what had happened. He hadn't mastered his gift, yet. It didn't matter though, because he would quickly clear out this crowd.

As Nathan looked on, he saw Thad bend forward, take the old man's hands in each of his, and then Thad closed his eyes.

Out of nowhere, a strong, warm wind burst from the center of the crowd of criminals and pushed outward, circling before the intimidators, their feet stumbling backwards, arms covering their faces.

Thad's free arm wrapped around the old man's waist just before the two twisted into the wind, distorted and skewed, until neither were seen in the center by the onlookers who fought to keep their feet balanced, hair out of their eyes, and shades on their faces. The wind moved through and away from the crowd, east to west, and back again. When the wind calmed, Thad stood alone in the center of the crowd.

"Hey, where'd that guy go? He has our money! Our check! Where'd you take him?" Green hair advanced on Thad, who opened his lips as if to blow out a candle, releasing the wind again, blowing Green Hair backward onto his butt, hushing him to silence. The crowd dispersed warily, running this way or that way, glancing now and then behind them at the three left standing with arms crossed, backs forming a triangle.

Cai turned to Thad's side, motioning Nathan to join her. Just as Nathan stepped up, Cai circled an arm around Thad's waist, holding his hand at her shoulder to support him as his eyes closed and his knees buckled beneath him. Nathan supported him from the opposite side and helped her guide Thad to the car, the toes of his shoes dragging slightly behind him.

"So, that's what he does!" Nathan nodded in disbelief as he closed the passenger door securing Thad inside.

"Yeah, now you see why he doesn't remember.

He passes out. He won't even remember stopping, even though he was the one who saw the incident."

"What triggers it, though? He didn't do that with the sheriff?"

"The only other time I've seen it was when some guys were slapping around this kid. It's like it only works for him when he sees others being hurt or abused. I don't know."

"I have to say, I was impressed. I had to put the window up at one point, the wind came back so strong. Those kids sure weren't too eager to hang around, either." Rebecca added as they returned to the car.

Cai glanced over her shoulder, first one way and then the other. She checked the rearview mirror, noted a couple leaving the pizza building and eased backward. She slipped out the driveway, turned left, and set the car back on course.

"Where'd you learn to drive so well?" Nathan asked. "I mean, that accident could've screwed up our plans."

"A friend taught me, a long time ago. That and video games!" She smiled at Nathan.

"Me, too!" He laughed. "The only thing video games didn't teach me was to have the money for gas and how to put it in the car!" The three chuckled.

"What's so funny? Where are we?" Twenty minutes later, Thad rubbed his eyes and looked around.

"Should we tell him?" Nathan whispered.

"Nah, it won't matter." Cai shook her head. "We

just left a place called Weatherford. We're almost there." She glanced back at Thad in the mirror.

The navigation system indicated a left ahead, and Cai turned on her blinker.

Nathan inhaled deeply, exhaled slowly.

"We're getting very close, I take it," Cai commented on Nathan's sigh.

"There's a church up here on the left. Past the church, there's an intersection. Turn left. It's Olde Towne Road... if there's a sign."

"Is that the road where your grandparents' house is?"

"Yeah."

Cai turned her signal on, waited for a few cars to pass, then made the sharp left. Following Nathan's directions, she let her foot off the accelerator around the S curve and eased toward the house. The four stared out the right side windows as the car slowed more while passing Nathan's house. Cars filled the driveway, as if a major holiday gathering were in session.

"Looks like more than two people," Thad observed through the back window.

"Definitely. Where's the cellar?" Cai asked.

"At the back of the first section of the property," Nathan turned toward her.

"Is there road access at the back?" Cai's eyes remained on the house until she could no longer see the road and the house.

"No, not for a long way. We'll have to walk in." Nathan frowned, swallowing hard.

"What is it?" Rebecca felt his tension.

"Dogs... my grandparents had two dogs. They bark at suspicious activity on the place."

"But, they know you, right?" Thad assured him.

"Yes, but I don't know if they'll bark at us before they figure out it's me."

"Hmm..." Cai's limited memories of dogs included the bark of announcement.

"We could send Splash in first. He carries our scent. Maybe then they won't bark at us." Rebecca scratched the dog's ears. *"Right, Splash?"*

"But what if they bark at Splash and he gets shot?" Nathan advocated.

"If they would shoot Splash, then maybe they already shot your grandfather's dogs," Thad pointed out. Nathan swallowed, again. He loved those dogs. They had been his best friends since his parents' deaths.

Cai stopped at a crossroad. "Just stay on this for a bit. It will take us into town, past the school. I guess we'll find someplace to wait," Nathan instructed.

"Okay." The depression in Nathan's voice thickened the silence in the car. Cai followed the road, leaving Nathan to his thoughts.

22

The sun began its dip to dusk as three of the four sat in the car outside a little convenience store. Thad helped Splash out of the backseat and released him on the pavement, walking near while Splash relieved himself.

Nathan ducked his head when anyone neared the car, afraid they might recognize him.

Cai drummed her fingers on the steering wheel, her impatience rearing.

"There sure were a lot of cars back there." Rebecca's voiced Cai's thoughts.

"Yeah. It makes me so angry, them moving in, taking over my grandparents' house." Nathan's voice cracked with ire.

"Let's take it back!" Thad demanded as he climbed in next to the dog, who willfully jumped into the backseat.

"How exactly? They have guns," Nathan emphasized.

"We don't have guns, but we have gifts!" Cai pulled her bottom lip between her teeth and turned to Nathan.

"Okay, fine, but if our gifts would stop them, how come the other two got caught? Surely, they have gifts, too."

"Yes, but like the dream we had yesterday, perhaps if we work together, combine our gifts... Maybe they discovered that too late, or not at all. Maybe their gifts are like mine, passive." Rebecca added.

"Deceptive, you mean. I would have never guessed you could speak telepathically," Cai grinned. "But you're right. Maybe they didn't catch on beforehand. So if that's the case, then we need to get to them, combine our *gifts* and devise a plan to run those murderers out of Nathan's house."

"Well, I only use it when I'm afraid, or uncertain, or when I just don't want to speak," Rebecca voiced.

"That's good to know! Nice to hear your voice!" Thad's shocked expression brought a chuckle from Cai. "Apparently, the house is important enough for them to want to gather there," Thad nodded.

"Yes, which makes it more important for us to take it back," Nathan agreed.

"Now, I'm almost certain the other two are in your cellar, Nathan. They have to be! It just makes sense!" Cai shrugged. "I guess we'll find out for sure when we rescue them later tonight."

"I'm hungry!" Thad commented, breaking the solemnity and receiving an outburst of laughter in response.

"I guess since we didn't have to use your money for transportation, we could buy something to eat?" Cai asked Rebecca.

"Yes, but I have a feeling we'll need money for

something later," Rebecca suggested.

"I'll go into this store, see what they have cheap," Thad held out his hand for some money, which Nathan handed over after returning the tin to the backpack.

"Thad, be sure to think of the rest of us," Cai cautioned.

"I will!" He shook his head and exited the car again. They watched until he disappeared around the front of the store.

Having not been gone longer than a few seconds, he returned with two pieces of paper in hand, pushing them through Cai's downed window. "Look what I pulled off the outside of the front window!" He shoved the pictures toward her.

The exact likenesses of Nathan and Rebecca stared back at her. Cai passed the pages to Nathan, revealing the second sheet of paper, which contained the images of her and Thad. "Hand me your ball cap," Thad leaned into the backseat toward Rebecca for her cap and pulled it on.

"Wait, Thad, you can't go in there, now. They've seen your picture! We'll look elsewhere. Get in!" Cai ordered.

"No, look, there's just a kid working in there. I'll just go in, buy some chips and drinks and get out. I'll keep my head down," Thad argued.

"Maybe I should go with you. With this cap on, I look different. Besides, all Asians look alike to some people," Cai giggled.

"That's just wrong," Nathan shook his head.

"Still, you have to consider how few Asians live in this area," he added.

"Well, come on then, Cai, but keep your face down. Don't draw attention to yourself." Thad hurried.

"Okay, windbag." Cai tucked her hair up in her cap to follow Thad inside.

"What's gotten into him?" Nathan asked touching Cai's arm. "Suddenly he's the brave bossy one?"

"Yeah, it happened before when he stood up for that kid. I guess it gives him confidence, subconsciously, or something."

"His subconscious knows he did something good," Rebecca added.

"Yeah, something like that, I guess." Cai pushed the door open and hurried to catch up with Thad.

23

The store clerk wiped the counter where a drink had overflowed. She didn't even look up when Thad entered the store.

He moved quickly to the drink cooler, stopped, selected colas, and slipped down the chip aisle, grabbing a giant bag of flavored chips.

Whisking everything to the counter, he kept his head bent forward—eyes on the money in his hand—out of line with the camera behind the clerk.

"Z'at all for ya'?" She snapped the gum she chewed.

"Uhm, hm. Yes, thank you," Thad attempted to deepen his voice.

"Hey, you look familiar. You don't go to school here, though. I know everyone who goes to school here. That's $9.45." She held out her hand and Thad placed a ten in her palm.

"Nope." He kept his answer brief.

"Huh, I bet you played football against us or something. Dj'a hear about that kid from our school, that Nathan kid? He disappeared. Stole a car or something. He doesn't go to school anymore. My sister liked him. His picture's on the window. She comes up here and drools over it sometimes. She's so weird!" She handed his change to him, and he offered a quick thank you before stepping away from the counter.

"You're weird, too..." He heard her whisper as the doorbell tinkled and silenced. Cai shot a look of warning at the girl behind the counter before turning down the aisle behind Thad.

Rounding the corner toward the door, his head down, Thad bumped into the brown-shirted chest of a very tall man. He nearly dropped one of the four bottles of Coke cradled in his arm when Cai's downturned head struck him between the shoulder blades adding a comical air to the sticky situation.

The store clerk laughed.

Without lifting his head, Thad peeked at the shirt. On the left side was a security patch. "Watch it kid!"

"Sorry, sir." Thad skirted around the man and briskly hurried past.

"Hey, kid! Come back here. You plannin' to steal that stuff? Hey! I'm talking to you!"

The clerk chuckled again, "He paid for it!"

Cai beat Thad out the door and ran around the corner. She started the car at the same time Thad closed his door; then she backed out of the parking lot. "Okay, Nathan. We need someplace to hide for a while before that security guy catches on to us." She drove away quickly making a right into town, then a left down a side street, glancing in her mirror frequently to see if the security officer followed them.

"It doesn't look like he followed us," Cai said after a few turns.

"We can go sit at the football field. Kids hang out there sometimes. Football season is over pretty much at this time of year. That or we can get out close to my house, park out in a driveway to a field or something," Nathan suggested.

"I like that idea. I don't think we need to get too far from the car."

"How much battery do we have? Maive told us to plug it in," Thad reminded.

"It says half," Cai glanced at the dashboard.

"Where're we gonna charge it?"

"That's a good question. We might need it to get back to Maive's house, I mean, if we can't take over yours," Cai raised her brow at Nathan.

"We may have to chance the field house. There's outside plugs there. At least until the battery's back up," he suggested. "It'll be dark then."

"True, but will that make us more suspicious?"

"Two girls, two guys, the bleachers? I don't think so."

"Hah! That's funny! Well, then, direct me, *Oh Leader of this Paradise.*" Cai made her voice robotic and alien like.

"Whatever. Can we hurry, though?" Thad asked.

"Certainly, *Oh Hungry One*!" Cai continued speaking in her halting manner until she parked the car as close to the field house as she could get. Nathan found the plug, put on the adapter, and plugged it in. They entered the chain link fence in the darkest corner of the field. Fortunately, the deep blue car hid well behind the building.

"Here, take your soda," Thad passed each of them a bottle he still cradled.

"This way. We can get through the fence down here. My friends and I always used to do that when I lived here." Nathan led the way.

"Did you have a lot of friends?" Cai asked.

"Nah, not really. One or two, but we weren't real close or anything." Nathan pulled the gates apart, slipped between the pipes and held it for the rest of them. Splash squeezed in behind them and trotted next to Rebecca.

"Apparently he had a girlfriend he didn't know about!" Thad joked.

"What are you talkin' about?" Nathan made a face.

"The clerk at the store. Apparently her sister liked you. Drools all over your picture." Thad puckered his lips, made kissy noises, and nodded.

"Shut up, you idiot! I don't even know who you're talking about!" Nathan rolled his eyes and shook his head.

Finding a dark spot beneath the bleachers, Nathan sat down on the firm ground. It felt good to get out of the car and stretch his legs. The Coke popped and fizzed as he twisted off the top. He took a long swallow, not realizing how thirsty he had gotten.

Thad passed the chips around, the only sound in the night the crunching of chips and gulping of drinks. Each ate one chip and gave Splash one, too, not paying attention to the actions of the others in the darkness.

"How much longer should we wait, do you think?"

"I don't know. How long to charge the car?" Nathan asked.

"I've never had an electric car. I'm not sure," Cai shrugged.

"It'll probably take a long time in that outlet," Thad guessed.

"Can we leave the car here and walk to your place? It didn't seem that far. Did you ever walk to town?" Rebecca asked.

"Sure, plenty of times."

"Maybe we should do that," Cai added.

"But what if we need a quick getaway? I don't think it's going to be so easy to take over the farm, but we should have the others out by morning," Thad said.

"Let's just focus on getting the other two tonight then. We can go back to the farm later. Maybe it would be best that way." Cai's one shouldered shrug brought nods.

"Okay, what if they're hurt? How will we get them back here?" Nathan questioned.

The four sat in silence for a while.

"We'll leave the car here, charging. If one of them is hurt, we'll hide them out in the field and come back for the car. It's our only option. We may need that car fully charged to get back to Maive's," Cai decided.

Chip bag and soda bottles emptied, Nathan's

white teeth reflected in the distant streetlight as he spurred them on, "Okay. Everybody ready to start walkin'... again?"

Thad licked seasonings from his fingertips and wiped his hands on his pant legs leaving orange streaks behind, "Yep!" He pushed up from the ground.

"I guess so," Rebecca succumbed to giving up the short break.

"Let's do it, then," Cai and Rebecca held their hands upward, allowing Nathan and Thad to pull them to their feet. Splash's head remained inches from Rebecca's dangling fingers, sneaking licks of orange seasoning from them now and again.

24

"What was that?" Cheater huddled close to Jaz, burying her face in his shoulder.

"Sounded like a shotgun, a big shotgun."

Whimpering drifted in from above, the scratching silenced. "Oh, no! They shot one! They are gonna shoot us!" Cheater whispered desperately near Jaz.

"I don't think so. I think they're just keeping the coyotes from scratching at the door. Maybe they think the scratching will weaken it or something. Maybe they're afraid we'll get out."

The door above them rattled, opened, and the light cast behind the man above blinded Cheater and Jaz, leaving only a big silhouette facing the two in the cool dark. "You kids just be patient. There's plenty of food and water down there. See ya' found the lantern, oh and that good ol' ham. Good. You might need this, not that I really care, but he wants you alive and well. You won't have to worry about them coyotes scratchin' up the door, either. They won't be back before the others arrive. Eat and keep up your strength. Someone will be back in an hour or so to check on ya'."

"Why are you doing this?" Cheater demanded.

"You'll know soon enough." The door creaked

as it lowered again.

"Wait! What do you mean others?" The question hung in the dark, unanswered; the rattling of the lock echoed in the silence.

A large box had hit the ground close to the ladder.

"What is it?" Cheater wondered.

Jaz waited until he could no longer hear any sounds above, then he turned the lantern on. Cheater rubbed at her chilly arms. Jaz turned the box over, revealing black cardboard. He searched Cheater's face warily as he grabbed the open flap and pulled.

"Blankets. A couple of pillows, and this," he pulled out a portable camper's toilet.

"Oh, I am so not using that, but I will take one of those blankets." Cheater grabbed at the blanket, unfolding its corners and wrapping it around her.

"I guess we'll use it if it gets urgent enough," Jaz frowned. "There's a lock and chain on that door up there." Jaz gave the door a calculating stare.

"I know. I heard." Cheater shivered.

"How are we going to get out of here?" He tossed her a pillow.

"Just like we planned. When they come back in an hour, we'll use the plan. Grab a couple of those jars of homemade wine. Now we know what to listen for when they come back. We'll have a few seconds to prepare."

25

"How much longer is it before we get there?" Thad trudged through the clotted black dirt field, tripping over clumps every few yards.

"Whining already? Man!" Nathan shook his head. "It's not too much farther. I gotta admit; it's hard walking through a freshly plowed field." Nathan stepped out in the lead, directing them out of sight of any onlookers or backyard sitters. The five of them moved into a planted field of winter oats, slipping between the high shoots and trying not to stumble. The walk to the house took about thirty minutes, and they were twenty minutes into it when they heard the cry of the coyotes followed by the blast of a shotgun.

Splash whimpered and hid behind Rebecca.

"Okay, what was that?" Cai froze.

"Somebody's shooting coyotes, I think. Sounded really close to my house, too. It might have been them. Grandpa used to shoot at the coyotes when they would try to get into the cellar or the chicken coop."

Nathan felt the group stop behind him. He turned, noting the concern in Cai's city-girl face. "Where are the coyotes he missed?"

"You don't have to worry about coyotes. They stay away from people for the most part. They're afraid of people."

"It's no wonder with people shooting at them. Look at poor Splash," Rebecca leaned to her right and reached down to pat the crouched dog, offering reassurance.

"I'm not worried about the coyotes; I'm worried about the guns," Thad glanced at the shadows in the fields and trees.

"Me, too. But, we do have Splash. Even though he's afraid of loud noises, which most dogs are, I'm sure he wouldn't let anything or anyone come near us without warning. He certainly won't let anything happen to Rebecca." Nathan nodded toward the dog.

"You're right," Cai's courage returned, and she waved Nathan forward. "Lead on!"

Within moments, the four exited the tall oat field, the back border of Nathan's farm in the near distance. He stopped, led the group into some trees and used the half moon's light to scout out the barn, the cellar, and the back of the house. A man's silhouette moved between the cellar and the house.

"We'll have to wait. Somebody just left the cellar, and it looks like he's headed toward the house. There might be more of them, though. He's carrying a shotgun, too."

"Where's the cellar?" Cai peered over Nathan's shoulder while he pointed it out to Cai and Thad.

They watched and waited; time passed too slowly for Thad. He began to pace, anxiety filling him. After a sufficient amount of time, when he knew nobody else waited near the cellar, Nathan signaled for them to follow him. He moved closer, leaning his body into a large tree and peering around it, his back open and unprotected. His hands hung at his sides as he watched.

A familiar wet feeling touched Nathan's fingertips and he turned excitedly. His grandfather's two dogs stood behind him. Apparently, they had been hiding just beyond the trees. Nathan dropped to the ground, ruffling their matted fur, kissing their heads and hugging their underfed frames.

Splash cowered and moved tentatively toward them, ready to bare while the newcomers sniffed him. Cai, Thad and Rebecca gathered around the three dogs.

"Look how thin they are, the poor dogs. I don't think they're feeding them, Nathan." Rebecca's words added to Nathan's heartbreak.

Nathan glanced through the darkness at Rebecca's downturned features and nodded, remaining silent in the event that one of the men was on guard and in earshot. He motioned to the dogs to be quiet and returned to the tree, anger tightening his lips. Peering around the tree, again, he noted nothing. After all the cars they saw there earlier, he imagined the grounds teaming with armed men.

The three dogs accepted their positions in the mission and stood near Nathan's side. As if reading his thoughts, they bravely pushed past him out of the trees and toward the cellar, drawing away possible attention from Nathan and the others.

When the dogs safely veered to the left of the

shack leading to the cellar, Nathan stepped out from behind the trees.

26

"Did you hear that?" Cheater's brows drew down in rapt attention.

"Yeah, I did. A girl's voice?" Jaz whispered.

"Yes. Do you think...?"

"Maybe. Wait, there's somebody else, too. I'm picking up their thoughts, faintly. The boy, Nathan, it's him. He's back!" Jaz's eyes widened and he looked up at the cellar door. "They're coming to get us! Man is he angry! Wait there's another girl, too. She keeps repeating to herself, 'We can take it back. Be careful. Don't get caught.' And she's thinking about a kid named Thad hoping his courage will last. Who's Thad?" Jaz frowned into the darkness.

"How would I know? The kid that lives here is back, though. He'll know how to open the cellar door. He knows we're here. We're almost free, Jaz, and there are more of us!" Cheater sighed, relief rolling through her into the cool, dark air.

"Yeah!" Jaz threw an arm over her shoulder and shook her excitedly.

"Ouch!" Cheater rubbed her tailbone.

"Oh, sorry." Jaz removed his arm and patted her hand. "We'll be out soon... I hope."

27

Nathan motioned for Cai to wait at the door of the shack in case the man with the gun returned, then he slipped between the door and frame, motioning Thad and Rebecca to follow him. They crinkled their noses, cringing as they passed a dead coyote hanging from the eve at the back of the shed.

Darkness overtook them as the door fell closed behind them, but just enough light shone through a crack in the slanted cellar door for Nathan to find his way around. He signaled Rebecca to speak to them and find out who was down there.

"Hello? Is anyone down there in the cellar? Hello?"

"Did you hear that? It's the girl's voice we heard!" Cheater excitedly rose. "Yes! Yes, we're here!" She kept her voice low through her excitement.

Jaz, rising to his feet, stood next to her, eyes turned upward.

Nathan searched the wall of the shack for the hidden key.

"It could be a trap for us. Wait. Who are you?

How did you get stuck in there?" Rebecca asked.

Cheater turned her face up toward Jaz, waiting for his read. Disheartened by the questioning.

"They think it's a trap. At least they're careful. More careful than us," Jaz whispered.

"But how can we prove to them that we're part of the twelve?" Cheater eased down to the ground again, a sense of defeat filling her.

"The fairytale?" He suggested. "Our names are Cheater and Jaz. We're two of the Gifted Ones. They locked us in here to wait for you and the others." He called out.

Thad nodded at Rebecca, but she shook her head.

"How do we know you're Gifted Ones? We've met a lady that knows about the Gifted Ones. For all we know, many people know about them." Rebecca waited.

"There's a fairytale our mothers used to tell us —we don't know the end."

Rebecca grew sad with thoughts of her mother and the story, but others, elders, seemed to know of the tale, too.

"I'm sorry. Others beside the Gifted Ones know of the story, too. Tell us... tell us about the dream."

Cheater and Jaz searched each other's faces, now. He knew the teens on the other side of that door were real Gifted Ones because of their thoughts, their caution.

"Well, there's this circle of fire..." Cheater began calmly. "And there are twelve of us, trying to hold hands outside the fire..." She glanced up at Jaz. How much did they want to know? How much would secure their freedom?

"There's a faceless man in the dream..." Cheater continued.

"A girl with blonde hair is whirling upward..." Jaz added.

"Yes, that's me! We're going to get you out of there! Hang on!" Rebecca told them. She watched Nathan as he tugged a piece of wood loose to retrieve the spare key. *"Hurry!"* she prodded. He turned a frustrated look her way, and returned to feel the black space beneath the board. His fingers traveled lightly along the inside board, found the hook, and lifted the key.

Nathan fumbled with fitting the key in the lock. If the crack of light were only on the same side as the lock...

A light tap on the shed door stopped his fumbling.

"Someone's coming this way. We'll be back!" Rebecca told them.

"So far only one man has returned. We have a plan! Wait!" Jas whispered as loudly as possible.

"We have to go! We'll be back when he leaves."

"No, stay close. You could help!"

No reply.

Rebecca slipped out first, then Thad, and last Nathan, who turned an angry gaze toward the man coming his way, head bent forward, a whistled tune announcing his progress.

28

The door to the shed stood open as the imposter dug the key from his pocket and unlocked the cellar. Shining the flashlight into the gaping darkness, he peered in at the two teens. Two empty jars lay beside Cheater. The sweet smell of homemade wine drifted out the cellar door. Cheater lay on her back in slumber.

"He wants to see you two. Get her up! Which one of you's been into that wine?"

"She has." Jaz motioned toward Cheater. "Her back hurts really bad. She thought it would help."

"Well, wake her up. She prob'ly won't be much use to him drunk, though."

Jaz pushed at Cheater, lightly at first, then more aggressively. He called her name, fear filling the small space.

"What's wrong?" The old man yelled.

"She won't wake up! Cheater! Cheater! Come on, wake up!" Jaz became desperate.

"Ah, crap! Is she breathin'?" The old man asked.

Jaz feigned searching for breath. He put his ear to her lips. Using every lesson he ever learned in drama class to make the old man believe him, he shook his head in panic.

"Damn! How many of those bottles did she drink?" The man leaned into the opening moving the flashlight around the floor.

Jaz searched around her, "Three... four," he counted. He pushed at Cheater, again, lightly slapped her face.

The bearded man filled the opening as he leaned into the cellar. Jaz watched as the man's concerned look changed to fear and his face grew closer. His own features turned to panic as his feet lifted from the ground and he tumbled through the cellar door.

Cheater rose to her feet.

Jaz stood ready with a large jar of wine, but there was no need. The unprepared man landed on his head, a loud snap suggesting he might not wake up again.

Cheater and Jaz didn't wait to see if he was alive or not. Jaz easily lifted Cheater upward so she could reach the bottom rung of the ladder, Nathan waited at the opening to pull her through. Jaz tossed up the partially eaten ham and strong armed the cardboard box he filled with canned food. Cradling the box under one arm, he started up the wooden ladder. Nathan reached for the box and passed it to Thad. Then he reached behind Jaz, grabbing the waistband of his pants to secure him as he neared the top.

"Hurry! We have to get out of here before they realize he's gone!" Thad peeked around the shed door where Rebecca and Cai stood watch. At Cai's signal,

Thad exited the shed, followed by Cheater and Jaz. Nathan hung back, closing the cellar door and replacing the lock. He placed the spare key in his pants pocket for future use, and removed the key from the lock to replace in the spare's hiding place.

Cai and Nathan simultaneously reached to close the shed door—cringing once more at the hanging mammal on the outer wall—and then they ran to catch up to the others.

Cheater's sore back brought a slow limp, but Thad eagerly relieved Jaz of the box of food so Jaz could support Cheater's effort to keep up.

Only the crunching of the dry December ground followed them into the shadows as they moved quickly back through the woods, the oat fields, and the silent streets to the little blue car awaiting them at the field house.

"Ow, ow," The pain in Cheater's back grew more intense as they neared the street leading to the field house.

"Just let me carry you, girl!" Jaz offered.

"We're almost there. Just hold on," Rebecca assured her with a pat on the shoulder.

"Okay, who said that? You?" Jaz tapped Cai on the arm. The group moved silently until now, and Jaz scanned the others for an answer.

"I said it... without saying it. We'll talk about it later. We need to get out of here before they come looking for us." Rebecca continued on without a hint that she had spoken.

This time Jaz pinpointed the voice, and he

turned an open mouth to Rebecca's closed one.

"Yeah," Cai nodded before racing ahead. She pulled the car key from her front pocket, popped the trunk button and opened the doors.

"We're not all gonna fit in that car!" Jaz viewed the inside of the small vehicle with doubt. Thad placed the box in the trunk and closed it, keeping the ham with him.

Nathan unplugged the car and climbed in beside Cai. "Sure we will. Two in the front, four in the back."

"Three will barely fit in the back!" Jaz exclaimed.

"We'll have to make it work if we all want to get out of here!" Cai started the quiet car, buckled her seat belt and waited impatiently tapping her fingers against the steering wheel again.

"We need to go someplace to plan," Nathan whispered.

"Yes, I know. Maybe we should return to Maive's. She said she would help us in any way. And I think she needs help." Cai glanced in the rearview mirror at Cheater.

"Who's Maive?" Cheater groaned as she squeezed in next to Rebecca.

"The old woman who owns this car," Thad answered.

"Whoa! Wait a minute! We trusted an old person already. That's what got us where we were!" Jaz protested.

"I don't think Maive will turn against us. She

knows the story. She knows about us. And she's not the only one, apparently," Cai explained.

Jaz pulled his knees up, slid as close to Cheater as he could, and grunted as Thad squeezed himself in, barely forcing the door closed.

"I hope we don't get stopped for having this many people in the backseat," Jaz commented.

"Somebody will just have to duck if we see a cop. Speaking of ducking, I can't see out the mirror. Can you lower your head a second?" Cai asked.

"Wait! Splash! He didn't come with us!" Thad realized.

"He's with the other two dogs. He'll be fine until we get back. They know the area," Rebecca's positive tone eased their minds.

"Yeah, they may have been skinny, but they're getting food somewhere. He'll be all right," Nathan added.

"Speaking of food, anybody want a piece of ham?" Thad asked.

Three of the six burst into laughter as the car eased out onto the highway per the navigation system's directions.

"What? It's really good ham!" Jaz pulled a chunk free and began chewing.

"Heck, I'll take a piece! I know how good it is!" Nathan wiped his hands on his shirt and reached over the backseat.

"As many hungry people as there are in this car, it won't last long," Cheater noted. "We should have taken more."

"We got a box of goodies in the trunk," Jaz mumbled between chews.

29

Maive's house lay in darkness when they returned, except for a lone light in the garage. Cai eased the car into its place while Nathan returned the plug to the wall.

Hesitantly, Cai turned out the light and rapped on the garage door that opened to the kitchen.

No answer.

"She might be in bed," Nathan offered.

Cai knocked again.

"Who's that?" A rough sleep-riddled voice called from the other side.

Cai glanced around her in the darkness, sending a thin, unseen smile to the five behind her, then she turned to the door. "The Gifted Ones," she answered.

The door opened quickly, and Maive rushed them into the kitchen, "Hurry, now!" Her tired, wrinkled, old face followed each one through the door as she counted. "Oh, my! You did it! You got the others!" She excitedly closed the door behind them.

"Well, two of the others. Now we're six," Nathan told her.

"Yes, but you saved them! Oh, let me look at you, as best I can see. What a wonderful group you are! Come on, I got some soup in a pot on the stove.

Something told me you would be back. I just knew it! How'd the car do for ya'? Good? It's a fine little machine! Wish I could drive it." She rambled as she took bowls down from the cabinet. "I fell asleep in my chair waitin' on you all to return! You there, what's your name?" she called to Cheater.

"Che... Sarah, ma'am," Cheater responded.

"Well, now, Sarah, if you'll turn a bit, you can get seven spoons out of that drawer behind you. I don't like eating alone! I'm so glad y'all made it back!" Maive cast a toothless grin their way.

Cheater counted out seven spoons.

"You come over here one at a time and get you a bowl. I smell ham. Now, I didn't put no ham in this here pot! Why am I smelling ham?" The woman cackled as Thad moved to get a bowl first. "Growing boys! Yessir, I bet you're the one smellin' like ham! Where'd you find a ham, boy?"

The woman noticed Cheater rubbing her lower back as she walked away with a ladle full of soup in her bowl. Cheater didn't have the heart to tell her she wasn't hungry. She'd eaten so much these past weeks that her jeans were snug.

"Girl, you need to be looked at! What happened to you? We'll take care of that soon's we finish the soup. Eat as much as you like now!"

"Yum!" Thad exclaimed. "This is the best soup I've ever eaten."

"Not bad for an old lady, huh?" The woman's gaping smile filled her face again. "I fixed up that room for you. The one you took the bed out of?

Figured you'd need time to rest up and make plans. Stay as long as you need to stay. Use the car when you need it."

Cheater's spoon paused before her lips, and she peered uneasily at Jaz. He shook his head in her direction. Her intuition having been tested, she now relied on Jaz for his skill at reading minds, though that failed them recently, too. They still hadn't figured out why.

She couldn't help distrusting the elderly lady. Cheater let her spoon clatter into the empty bowl. "We can't stay here. We need to find someplace else to stay... someplace far away from innocent people."

"What are you talking about? We need a place to plan!" Cai fired back.

"Maive doesn't mind, do you Maive?" Nathan, sitting closest to the old woman, already viewed her as a replacement grandma.

"Oh, of course not! I love company, and you all are the best kind of company! Now, what's got you all stirred up young lady?"

"If... if we stay here... You'll die." Cheater's blunt reply blurred her vision as she remembered the others. "Everyone who has ever cared for me has died..." The tears punctuated her resistance as they rolled down her cheeks. The months of traveling alone—finalized by the sympathy of those around her —released the pent up grief she'd carried on her own for so long.

Maive rose as quickly as her ninety-seven-year-old frame would allow. She wrapped Cheater in a hug that brought more tears from the young girl. "Now, now, you let it out, you poor baby. Probably got a little shock. You just let it all out." Maive stroked Cheater's head and squeezed her gently.

The other five cast eyes downward, thinking of their own families, but self-pity did not belong to them. Cai cast a look of concern to the newcomer, Jaz, whose own tears glistened over his tensely angered jaw line. "We've all lost everyone we love, except those whose fathers are trying to remove them from this mission. I think you've seen a lot more death than us, and I'm so very sorry, but Sarah, we have to stay strong. There is a reason for all of this, and we will get our revenge on the one at fault." Cai assured her.

"I don't care about revenge!" Cheater pushed away from the comfort of Maive's arms. "I don't want any more innocent people to die! I don't want any more homeless people in the world! I want things to go back to the way they were when I was younger! I want Christmas! I want my mother and my father and my brother!" She covered her face with her hands, wiped away her tears, and turned back to the group, "Every place I stay burns down. Everyone who cares for me risks death. The longer we stay here, the more likely it will be your fate, too!" She turned a tear stained face toward the rheumy eyed hostess before her, one of the few compassionate people left in their world.

"Baby, you don't have to worry about old Maive. I'm ninety-seven years old, done outlived my family, my husband, everyone I know. I'm just like you, in a way. I'm ready to go, and I can't think of any better way to do it than to help the ones who can make a difference in this world! I've seen so much change for the worst. It's time to bring the world back to its senses!"

"She's right, Sarah!" Cai set her bowl on the table, rose and put an encouraging arm around the younger girl, recharging her with the strength she'd lost from distrust. "It's time. And you won't lose us. We're the Gifted Ones. If one goes, we all go, right?" She looked at each of the others. Jaz was first to agree and move behind Maive to Cheater's other side. Nathan and Rebecca joined them at the same time, standing together. Thad rose last, after finishing his bowl of soup, and tentatively stood next to Rebecca. Unknowingly, the six formed a circle around Maive.

Jaz took Cheater's right hand in his left, then grasped Cai's left hand in his right. Thad stepped up to take Cheater's free hand, and Rebecca took his free hand. Nathan quickly reached out for Rebecca's free hand. When the protective circle around Maive closed with Nathan and Cai, Cai raised both of her hands, pulling the others with her. "We are The Gifted Ones!"

Cheater felt the wave coming.

Her vision tunneled until Maive's face filled the circle of light in her vision, shrinking to only Maive's eyes, to one eye, to the one pupil, and then the warm, welcoming darkness.

family, my husband, everyone I know. I'm just like you in a way. I'm ready to go, and I can't think of any better way to do it than to help the ones who can make a difference in this world. I've seen so much change for the worse. It's time to bring the world back to its senses!"

"She's right, Sarah!" Cat set her bowl on the table, rose and put an encouraging arm around the younger girl, reinforcing her with the strength she'd lost from this attack. "It's time. And you won't lose us. We're the Gifted Ones. If one goes, we all go, right?" She looked at each of the others. Jaz was first to agree and moved behind Maive to Chester's other side. Nathan and Rebecca joined them at the same time and did it together. Thad rose last, after finishing his bowl of soup and tentatively stood next to Rebecca. Unknowingly, the six formed a circle around Maive.

Jaz took Chester's right hand in his left, then grasped Cat's left hand in his right. Thad stepped up to take Chester's free hand, and Rebecca took his free hand. Nathan quickly reached out for Rebecca's free hand. When the protective circle around Maive closed with Nathan and Cat, Cat raised both of her hands, pulling the others with her. "We are The Gifted Ones!"

Chester felt the wave coming.

Her vision funneled until Maive's face filled the circle of light in her vision, shrinking to only Maive's eyes, to one eye, to the dark pupil, and then the warm, welcoming darkness.

30

Cheater felt Maive's dry hands on her face as she refocused. Understanding left her. Why would her gift show itself now? Nobody needed help; Maive certainly didn't. She was as strong as the six of them combined.

"Oh, my precious baby girl!" Maive exclaimed, tears following the wrinkles down her hollowed cheeks to her mouth. "M-hm-hm..." Her tight lips turned down in a bittersweet smile. "That was the most wonderful gift anyone has ever given me!"

"What happened?" Cai blinked to focus her eyes.

"I don't know. I feel like... like I blacked out," Nathan said.

"Me, too!" Rebecca shook her head.

Thad filled the small room with paranoia, "It was the soup! Something must have been in the soup!"

"Oh, oh, oh! You poor darlin' children!" Maive turned, shaking her head at each of them.

"It wasn't the soup. It was Cheater's gift," Jaz announced with a grin.

Thoughts of the dream returned to the other four. "Wow!" They exhaled in unison as their eyes followed a trail from their clasped hands to each confused face.

"Well, tell us what happened, Maive!" Rebecca was the first to shake loose of the hands clasping hers and reach out to Maive. A complete openness transformed Rebecca into one who no longer hid behind her panic.

"Each of you, oh, each of you became my lost family. You," she rested a dry palm on Nathan's cheek and searched his eyes, "my darling husband. And you," to Rebecca who now stood in front of her, "my sweet, sweet oldest girl. You and you," she placed a hand on a shoulder of Jaz and Thad, "my own precious boys. You," she put her hands on Cai's face, "my lifelong friend, my sister. And you, you precious, precious girl, my own baby girl, the first one to leave me." She hugged Cheater again, her tears drying and smiles lifting her tired face. "It is a miracle!" She nodded in silence a moment before turning her thoughts to their future. "No time to waste, though. Get back to that soup. It's gettin' cold and you'll need your strength.

"Thank you!" Maive bowed her head before she retired to her room alone, leaving them to their thoughts.

"Okay, that was weird," Thad commented as he went back for seconds.

"Definitely!" Nathan nodded.

The soup pot empty, Nathan and Cai took over clean up duty.

When the two returned to the living room, the others were discussing Cheater's gift. Jaz filled them in on what he had seen. Thad shared the idea that when they were touching in some way their gifts were shared, like the dream.

"We can't stay here. We're still putting Maive at risk!" Cheater shook her head.

"Well, if it helps any, we're not planning to stay. We have a place to stay," Nathan contributed.

"Really? Where?" Jaz's brows rose.

Nathan took a deep breath and exhaled slowly. His lips tightened to a thin white line as he looked Jaz in the eye, "We're taking back my farm."

"What?" Cheater and Jaz asked in unison.

"It's my home! And if Paradise is *the* Paradise—which it appears to be—then we should be there waiting for the others, not the bad guys. We have to get them out of my house!"

"But how?" Cheater shot an impossible look toward Nathan.

"Depends on how many are there. Do you two know?" Cai asked.

"There were only two when they took us to the cellar. And only the imposter came to check on us," Jaz answered.

"Imposter?" Nathan's brows rose, "You mean murderer. He killed my grandparents! How did he catch you two, anyway?"

"The car you left on the side of the road. We were sleeping in it. Guess he thought when it was tagged that he might find you in it. I'm glad he didn't. You knew where to find us," Cheater cast a smile of gratitude his way.

"Yeah, well, we've got some planning to do if we are taking back my house," Nathan sat down. "There were about six cars in the driveway when we passed it earlier, right?" He looked to Rebecca and Thad for reassurance.

"Yeah, about that," Thad agreed.

"One should have been your grandpa's truck and the other a sheriff's car," Jaz pointed out.

"Two were trucks. One was a sheriff's car," Rebecca added.

"So there were six to twelve people there, at least," Cai stated.

"Yep. Per each car," Thad noted.

"Six..." the others repeated.

"There's six of us here," Nathan smiled back at them.

"Still, they are armed. We're not," Cai's brows drew together in contemplation.

"Exactly! Is it necessary to take the house, though? We don't know if the others will find it, let alone find Paradise," Jaz commented.

"Well, there's something on that farm they're looking for, and I'm betting it has to do with us. How will we find the others to keep them from getting caught?" Cheater offered.

"The dream," Rebecca suggested.

"Speaking of dreaming, it's really late, and I'm wore out," Thad yawned.

"Yeah, we all are. We'll talk in the morning. How are we sleeping?" Cai asked.

"Girls take the spare room. We'll stay out here,"

Jaz offered.

"That'll work," Nathan rose from his chair to find a space on the floor, stretched back with his hands under his head, and closed his eyes.

"Before you young people head off to dreamland, *you*" Maive pointed at Cheater, "come back here. Let me take a look at that back." Maive wrapped a loving arm around Cheater as they hobbled down the hallway.

"Ah," Maive raised Cheater's shirt, "that's a nasty bruise, young lady. Here, take this to your room, plug it in and turn it on low. Cai!" Maive called out.

Cai appeared in the doorway, "Yes, ma'am?"

"There's an ice pack in the freezer. Would you dig it out and bring it to me?"

"Sure thing! Be right back," and Cai returned with the ice as quickly as she'd disappeared.

"All right young lady. You lay down on this ice pack until you hear a ding. Cai is gonna go back to the kitchen and set the timer for twenty minutes. Then, you take this heating pad, set the timer for twenty minutes, and lay down on it. If you're still awake, put that ice pack back under you again."

"Thank you," Maive told Cai to help Cheater to the spare room.

"Guys, you need to see this," Cai returned to the living room.

"Huh?" The three rose from their spots of rest, following Cai. In the spare room, Maive had fanned six sleeping bags so the open spaces formed a hexagon. If they slept this way, some part of them would be touching the ones next to them.

“How’d she know about the dream?” Thad frowned at each of them, searching their doubt-filled faces.

“I think she knows more than she’s telling us.” Nathan claimed a bag under the only window, while Jaz took the one nearest the door. Across the room, the two nodded knowingly to each other.

31

Cheater pushed the heating pad beneath the top layer of the sleeping bag closest to the outlet, turned the switch to on, set the timer, and lay back, positioning the pad so the iced small of her back was on top of the pad. No matter how hard she tried, though, she couldn't get comfortable. The ice had helped some, but not with the internal pain. As the pad heated, she relaxed, though she still lay awake, staring at the ceiling, thinking about the evening, about Maive, about her safety.

Apparently none of the others had been through all she had gone through, the various homes and families. The thought that something bad would happen to Maive if they remained with her haunted Cheater's mind while the others inhaled deeply, exhaled lightly in slumber. Jaz's hand flopped onto her sleeping bag and rested near her shoulder. She drew strength from the light touch of his slightly bent fingers leaning against her.

Thad rolled onto his stomach, pushing his left hand under his dark head, which forced his pointy elbow into Cheater's upper arm. Though slightly uncomfortable, it added to Cheater's sense of safety. She lay still.

The muscles in her back relaxed more, but she

couldn't stop thinking of Tommy and his new family, wondering if he could be Stevey, a Stevey who had forgotten his life before the fire.

The longer she thought of him, the sleepier she grew. Her eyelids drooped to slumber; her back less painful, yet her knuckles white with tension.

At least she was free again, out of the darkness of the cellar, out of the hands of death—for now. Her eyelids embraced the night without haunting images for a short time before a tiny orange and yellow flame flickered and grew deep in her mind's eye.

"Daddy! No!" The house glowed orange and yellow as the flames licked through the windows in an effort to reach the little girl on the lawn.

"No! Don't think about it! That's not your dad! Focus!" The voice of another girl—one Cheater couldn't see—roared over the flames to Cheater, refocusing her mind to the present.

Not her dad? The faceless man stood before her, his iniquitous laugh filling her ears.

Flames danced and swayed inside the circle of the Gifted Ones, forcing each to tighten the grip they had on each other's sweat drenched hands.

"It's now—the present—that we need to focus on," Jaz yelled over the billowing flames.

"Yes, if we don't stop him, the world will suffer

as we have!" Rebecca concentrated solely on the missing face, her eyes clearer than they'd ever been.

"But we don't know who he is! Look at his face!" Thad turned away, the thought of identifying the man too torturous for him.

The whirlwind pulled at them, attempting to lift them off the ground, and they fought to weigh each other down.

"Wait! I know this place," Nathan dared a glance over his shoulder, "I know where we are!"

"Remember it!" Cai ordered over the roar. "Try to see the other Gifted Ones, too! We need to know who they are. We need to find them!"

Jaz turned his head right, his eyes following the path from the hand he held, upward to the shoulder, and to the lighter hair rising and falling onto the pale shoulder of a girl. Squinting through the flames, he glimpsed her cheek before her face was overtaken by the orange, hunting fire.

"Look!"

At the center of the circle, Mr. Johnston's imposter stood with the man who tormented their dreams. Flames clawed at the imposter's body, licking his face, singeing away his beard, tiny trails of orange traveling toward his chin. His screams louder than the roar of the fire as each of the Gifted Ones turned away opting to tighten their handhold instead of cover their ears.

The gruesome screeches grew to an unbearable level, and suddenly stopped. All eyes turned to the circle, the large man a crumple of smoldering flesh at its center, unidentifiable.

"Defy me?" The evil voice roared into Cheater's face, the breath of the dragon touching the tip of her nose. "And you also will burn, just like your family!"

"Leave her alone!" Jaz kicked at the tormentor without success, his feet moving through the seeking flames.

"Keep your head! Stay focused! Don't let him anger you, or he will win!" Cai's limbs trembled with control as her words reached Jaz through the roaring flames.

Cheater's feet lifted from the ground when the whirlwind wrapped its heated tentacles about her. Her hair rose and twisted with sultry gusts. Jaz and Thad tightened the hold on her hands tugging her downward.

She had to let go of the past, of her family. She had to focus on the mission, the story, the ending. This was it. It was time to let go of yesterday.

"Sarah! Sarah!" Outside the flames, as she spun to one side, Cheater's mother called to her. "I'm here baby; I'm here and I will never leave you, again. Come with me!" She held her hand out to Cheater.

"Mom!" Cheater struggled to let go of Thad's hand, but he grasped hers tighter. "Let go! My mom's here—right there!"

"Yes, Sarah, I'm here. Come home with me. Stevey's waiting, so is Daddy. Come on!" The delicate reaching arm closed the distance between Cheater's body and her mother's gentle hand.

"Mom..." Cheater smiled at the image over her

shoulder, pulled her left hand free from Thad's grip and reached behind her.

"No!" Thad yelled as her body rose in the billowing heat that twirling her upward.

He jumped, catching a burst of hot air to ride upward, and grasped at her forearm, but his fingers barely grazed her skin.

32

Cheater felt the tips of her mother's fingers on her own before she started awake. Looking past her shoulder, she saw Thad's hand disconnected from her own. The heat on her back brought reality to the dream, until she remembered the heating pad. She sat up and pulled it free from beneath the sleeping bag. She froze when she heard footsteps and voices beyond the bedroom wall.

"You sure that was the car?" The muffled voice slipped through the walls around the window.

"Yeah, I mean, it looks just like it."

Cheater shook Jaz awake and pointed toward the voices. He rose to a sitting position, which created a domino effect for the rest.

"Then, the kids that were driving the car must be in this house. Who owns the house?"

Cheater glanced at Jaz who stood, then crouched to move into Maive's room.

Maive sat on the edge of the bed, trying to find her robe and slippers. Cheater helped her. "I heard them. These days, I don't sleep so well. Older I get, less sleep I need. Let's find a place for you kids to hide. I'll git rid of 'em."

Maive went to the closet, opened the door and pulled out a baseball bat. Cheater raised a brow.

"An old lady's got to have protection to live this long! Since they banned guns, had to get rid of those." Maive shared a gaping grin. She moved to the doorway of the spare room and motioned for the youngsters to roll up their bags and follow her. Leading them to the kitchen, she opened the pantry door, pulled back a carpet, and pointed for Jaz to pull open a door in the floor.

Cheater immediately recognized it as a cellar. Back into the darkness, she thought, but at least this time it was for protection.

The six stuffed themselves into the small area with their bags, cramped, warm and safe as Maive closed the door. Listening quietly to the footsteps that softly scooted across the floor overhead, they visualized Maive with her baseball bat opening the front door.

One thing was for sure, that woman was not afraid of anyone or anything.

Cheater sought Jaz in the dim light. He shook his head, relieving her doubt about Maive. Maive was an honest person and every thought she had was filled with good intentions toward them. To Cheater, though, it meant giving trust to another person and winding up in another cellar.

Two muffled voices, much deeper than Maive's, spoke to the old woman through the screen.

Maive complained to them about respecting an old lady's privacy, threatened if they didn't leave her to her rest she would 'conk 'em one' with the bat, and then she slammed the door.

Minutes passed, unknown time spent in the darkness for those anticipating freedom.

Were the men gone?

Who were they?

Thad knew one of the men must be the security guard from the store, but who was the other one? Why were they looking for the car? Had he figured out who they were?

Light filtered into the cellar as Maive attempted to lift the heavy door. Jaz being the tallest, pushed upward, helping her, while the other five climbed out.

"None o' their business who I loan my car to! Who does that sheriff think he is?"

"It was a sheriff?" Rebecca turned anxiously toward the nearest wall not wanting to vocalize in case they were still waiting there.

"Yep. Lookin' for you and some other kid, he was. That security guard spotted Thad at some store, called it in. Sheriff's been looking for the car. I told him I loaned it to my housekeeper and I don't know what she done with it. They won't be back for a while," Maive assured them.

"You're wrong. They won't give up. We have to leave!" Cheater pushed past everyone to the back door.

"No ma'am! Young lady, they ain't gonna find my housekeeper. She went on vacation today for a week. You got at least that long!

"Now, who could sleep after all that excitement? Cocoa anyone? That should help us get back to our rest and your plannin', right? Hot cocoa on a cold night like this, mhm!" Maive pulled a large pot out of the cabinet, milk from the fridge, and instructed Cai to get the cocoa, sugar and vanilla from the pantry. "I ain't had nobody to drink cocoa with in years. Kinda nice." She sent a wink toward Cheater and nodded at her to join the others.

Quiet sipping filled the small, lamp-lit living room as they contemplated the dream they shared just before waking. Going back to sleep was out of the question. As their caregiver suggested, it was time to start planning. They were already being hunted and had no time to waste.

But the danger they were placing on their caretaker was first and foremost in their mind. It was only one reason for wanting to take over the farm, but what would happen when they did that? The thoughts flowed slowly like each sip of hot cocoa on their tongues, warming their throats and insides. All the thinking at once sent Jaz reeling. He couldn't keep up with everyone's thoughts that they hid from the elderly lady.

"Okay, would everyone just stop thinking? I can't think myself."

All eyes turned to him before he realized they didn't understand.

Cheater smiled at his confusion, "That's what you get for being nosey!" She laughed.

"So, Mr. Mind Reader, huh?" Cai smiled.

"Yes, if they're willing and open."

"Like me and speaking," Rebecca pointed out silently.

"Then, how did you get caught and thrown in my cellar? Couldn't you tell that man was an imposter?" Nathan asked.

For the first time since waking up, the thoughts were silenced while they all remembered the dream, the imposter's ending.

"His mind was blocked or something. I didn't get anything from him. He played the part really well," Jaz frowned.

"Even down to spilling a few tears over you," Cheater added, glancing at Nathan.

"Sh—Tears? Now that's pure evil! He killed my grandparents without batting an eye, then pretended to be my grandpa and shed tears? Who could do that? I'll be glad if the dream's true and he's gone!"

"Well, now, we shouldn't wish bad on anyone, kids!" Maive interrupted without reluctance. "Don't let the evil behind their actions infect you. You are filled with good. Keep your focus on what's good and right."

Focus? Isn't that what was in the dream? Isn't that the word that kept cropping up throughout the dream? Cheater thought about her mother, the past. "Maive's right. We have to let go of the past—all of us. It was part of the dream. If we hold onto the past, it will control us, he can control us, and he will win! He's going to use the past against us, like he did me with my mother."

"How? How are we supposed to forget what happened to our families when it's first in our minds? How are we supposed to let go? We have no one! It makes me so mad thinking about my parents, my grandparents. I want revenge!" Nathan balled his fists, stood, moved toward the wall, his face turned toward it.

"Well, as I see it, that ain't true. You got somebody—me! And you got each other, plus six more somewhere," Maive reminded him quietly.

"I'm sorry, but you're not family!" Nathan spat angrily.

"I don't know. I consider Cheater my sister. We haven't known each other long, but..." Jaz smiled at Cheater.

"And I consider you family, Nathan," Rebecca contributed, now upset by the outburst. *"You saved me. You took care of me. That's what family does. And yes, we'll always think about our families, but that's not the first thing that comes to mind with us. We think about others, helping others, unlike so many today. You're all I have, Nathan. You, and the rest of the Gifted Ones."*

Nathan searched the stained, pilled carpet below as Rebecca spoke. He did think of her as a sister, someone to look out for, take care of, protect. Everything she said was true. Each of them put others before themselves, before their pasts. "You're right. I'm sorry." He returned to his place, next to Rebecca in the circle on the floor.

"Sure, you got me. You got each other. But that ain't all you got; you got gifts, your own personal gifts that will see you through any trouble," Maive pointed out. "Maybe that's a good place to start, with your gifts. Figure them into the thoughts. It's those gifts that will change this here world... take down that monster. Get those gifts figured into the equation and you got a solution! I'll leave alone now if you'd rather."

"No, you don't need to go, Maive. You already know about us, our gifts." Cai felt Maive would be safer sitting with them than in her room.

"All right. I'll just sit here and drink my cocoa."

"So, you read minds, you speak without speaking, and you turn into dead people," Cai began.
"I go camo," she shrugged.

"Camo?" Cheater questioned.

"Yeah, like camouflage? Chameleon?"

"Wow!" The younger girl nodded,

"Yeah, you should see it!" Thad turned excitedly to the group.

"More like be it..." Nathan added.

"What about you, Thad?" Jaz asked.

"Who? Tornado boy?" Nathan laughed.

"Wind, apparently," Thad humbled, though I never remember.

"Same here," Cheater acknowledged.

"He can't forget he's hungry!" Nathan joked.

A fleeting thought of the whirlwind in the dream brought glances around the circle.

"What about you, Nathan?"

Nathan thought a moment. He really didn't have a gift, not that he knew, "I don't know."

"What? You don't know or you don't have one?" Cheater couldn't hide the surprise in her voice.

"Oh, Nathan, you've managed to find food very easily. Where most people don't care about others, you seem to make them care enough to give you food. We would have starved without you. With you, we're full," Rebecca comforted.

"Well, except Thad!" Cai's jab brought shrill laughter from the group.

"Sh... I'd call that a pretty lame gift!" Nathan noted.

"Even if that's not your true gift, your gift will come when you need it to, when we need it. I didn't even know I had one—what it was until Jaz saw it," Cheater shared.

"Yeah, you're probably just a late bloomer." Jaz grinned at the younger boy.

"I hope so!" Nathan twiddled his thumbs nervously. If he didn't have some sort of gift, why was he involved? The farm? Was he selected because of his home?

"Okay, we know we can share our gifts and dreams if we're physically connected to each other." Cai changed the subject, smiling at Nathan's relief.

"Yeah, we'll have fun tripping over cantaloupes together!" Nathan's sarcasm brought a laugh from Cai and Thad.

"Maybe we should spend some time getting used to each others gifts," Rebecca suggested.

"Well, we can, but Thad's only works outside—" Cai offered.

Thad nodded, glancing around at Maive's pictures on the walls and dusty knickknacks on the shelves.

"Well, we can practice with mine indoors," Rebecca offered, raising her hand palm up to Nathan, who slapped his palm onto hers. Rebecca's other hand went to Jaz, who took Cheater's hand. Cheater took Thad's and Thad took Cai's. The circle closed when Cai took Nathan's opposite hand. *"Focus on speaking without moving your mouth."*

Each closed their eyes, concentrating on her words.

"Can you hear me?" A quiet voice broke through the long moment of silence.

"I hear ya', girl!" Maive replied aloud.

"That's Cai! I recognize her voice!" Thad asked.

"We can do it!" Cheater exclaimed.

"Soon I will hear thoughts and speak them without sound!" Rebecca filtered through each of them.

"It is pretty sweet! Think about something!" Cai suggested. *"Everyone think about something."*

"I got mine!" Maive interjected aloud. The six giggled when they heard her thought simultaneously. "Well, I been alone a long time—goin' on forty years now! I could use a man around this house."

33

Discovery complete, the teens waited until sunrise —knowing the visitors must be gone—to took their gifts to the outdoors.

"I wonder if, when we connect, would we be able to read a reluctant person's mind? Would we be more powerful?" Thad cocked his head in curiosity.

"That's a good question," Jaz answered.

"Yeah. Guess we'll know when we find one," Rebecca added.

"You kids go way back there in the woods so won't nobody see y'all!" Maive pointed toward the wooded area behind her house.

In the woods, the team of six blew up dust devils and camouflaged into trees. When the sun began its trek from east to west, they returned to the paint-chipped house where Maive struggled with making French toast for breakfast. "I'm afraid I don't have much in the line of breakfast, but I'm working up some toast." She carried a few eggs over to a round cake pan.

"Let me do that," Nathan carefully took the eggs from her hand. "You've been up with us all night, you made soup and cocoa; let me make the French toast. I love to cook!"

"Oh! Uh... okay. Ain't never had a man cook for

me, unless you count restaurants of old. There's not much in the line of food here. Probably enough for one piece each, and there's no syrup, but, you go on ahead!" Maive waived Nathan by and let him take over in the kitchen. She retreated to her chair to listen to the others strategize.

"So, we have wind, camo, thought, speech, dead people and food, how can we turn that into a plan to take over the farm, or find the others?" Cai recapped.

"That is the question of the day. How?" Jaz queried.

"Maybe we could blow them out!" Thad offered.

"And wreck up my house?" Nathan rejected.

"Wait! What if our gifts don't work on them, like Jaz. We have to have a backup plan. If we go in there and our gifts don't work, we're sitting ducks." Cheater suggested.

"Whew!" Thad sighed. "Well, maybe it was just the ruse that kept Jaz from being able to get through the thoughts of that man. Maybe combined, we could get through."

"We need to test that. And the only way to test it is to go back to the farm, get as close as we can, and still connect." Cai wrinkled her nose.

"I don't know if I'm ready to go back there. It scares me, the thought of getting caught, again," Cheater said.

"We won't get caught. There's six of us now, and more powers to use," Cai reassured her.

"Well, I guess there's no time like today." Jaz

wasn't sure it was a good idea, but why put it off?

The aroma from the kitchen drifted to the living room, and they remembered Nathan in there alone, cooking breakfast for all of them. Rebecca was the first to rise and join him, but he sent her back to the living room.

"He doesn't want any help. He said it's almost ready, though." Rebecca updated the group.

"It smells incredible!" Thad held his stomach with both hands as if to quiet the pangs.

"Yes, I don't think I could have done a better job myself from the smell of it!" Maive added. "Been a long time since somebody cooked me breakfast."

They thought about and discussed the problem of getting onto the farm without getting caught. Within minutes, Nathan announced that breakfast was ready.

"My, my! You do have a way in the kitchen young man. I'd a-swore on the Good Book that I didn't have all this in my stores!" Maive spread her hands over the breakfast setting.

"This is the best thing I've eaten in weeks, except your soup, Maive," Thad complimented as he chewed a corner of bread he'd cut off.

"Oh, you ain't got to lie to this old lady. I know this is better than any meager soup."

Silent contemplation filled their thoughts while French toast filled their mouths. By the time the toast was gone, so was any pang of hunger left among them. Even Thad was full for the first time since they met him.

"Feeding the multitude is definitely a gift, Nathan. That was fantastic!" Cai rubbed her belly.

"Thanks!" Nathan grinned. "So, where are we with plans?"

"Well, we're stuck actually. There didn't appear to be many trees around the house on the farm."

"There's a few," he nodded.

"Do you think being outside the house is close enough to see if we can break through their thoughts?" Cai asked Jaz.

"Most likely, I mean, I could pick up people's thoughts across a parking lot," he shrugged.

"Whoa, we can use both gifts at the same time!" Nathan commented.

"Yes!" Rebecca suggested. *"And if we stay quiet, they won't even know we're there!"*

"I think that young 'un is right. And whatever you need of me, I'll do. You wanna blow me over with your wind, that'd be fine," Maive cackled.

"We wouldn't do that to you, Maive," Cheater shook her head.

The teens carried their plates to the kitchen and helped with cleanup, leaving Nathan and Rebecca talking to Maive.

"So, what's that got you all locked up inside yourself, Rebecca?" Maive asked.

"Autism," Rebecca's now trusted Maive enough to speak to her, but in most cases of new or untrusting people, she spoke with her mind.

"Well, don't that beat all? Nobody would ever guess that you could speak like that. What's even more interestin' is the way the rest of you can work each other's gifts, too," Maive nodded. "That kinda gift would'a' come in mighty handy for me when I was younger, I do say."

Rebecca and Nathan laughed as Maive shared situations in which she might have used that gift of silent speech on siblings, boyfriends, girls she didn't like and teachers.

"The only thing is, the person has to be open minded—like you—to hear it," Rebecca added.

"Yeah, and those men out there at the farm may not be that way. I don't know." Nathan pointed out.

"Oh, but the things you can do to them fools! Talking trees, dead, windy people readin' their minds!" The image Maive conjured made them all laugh as the rest joined them.

"The other thing is, those men probably expect it. They apparently know enough about us and our gifts to not be affected by them. What if we can't do anything at all to run them out?" The thought of Cheater's question angered Nathan.

"Maybe you just gotta be a little sneaky about it, you know? People have to sleep. Not us, but others," Maive added. Another round of laughter filled the room.

"Well, let's see! Would you come with us, Maive, to help us?"

"I wouldn't miss this for the world! You kids are about to turn this old world around, and takin' part of that before I move on might be the feather in my cap that will put me through those Pearly Gates!"

"Somehow, I don't think you need that feather." Cheater smiled at her.

"Bless your heart!" Maive patted her cheek.

Maive stood at the center of their circle, a broad smile deepening the wrinkles on her face. The teens concentrated, eyes closed, ready to experience all that their powers could give.

Among the trees, more trees appeared, one at a time, beginning with Cai, a circle of trees, branches stretching to touch the ones nearest them.

"Can you hear me?" Rebecca began, flowing the power of speech to the others.

"Or me?" Cheater added.

"What about me?" Nathan asked.

"And me?" Cai offered.

"Maive?" Jaz focused on the old woman.

"Hello?" Thad's impatience lifted his word.

"Oh, my! I see six blurry trees and they are surely speaking to me! I ain't had a drop of liquor in years, but people wouldn't believe it!" The elder woman turned in a circle, her arms stretching out at her sides, a jerky dance of joy filling her soul.

"Cool!" Cai returned to her normal appearance, speaking aloud, followed by the other five.

A rustle of leaves brought their attention to the

near distance; fear that somebody may have seen them caused them to drop their hands and form two lines of three facing the noise, putting Maive between them. Poised in their defensive stance, their laughter relaxed them when a jackrabbit bounded into view.

Their joy quickly diminished, however, when a gunshot rang out and the rabbit bounded out of sight. The gun barrel, followed by running feet, sprang from the shrubbery hiding the group.

"Dang rabbit!" The young face was set hard with intensity; a thin frame shod in ragged clothes caused the youngster to remove one hand from the gun and pull his loose fitting jeans upward. Turning away from the rabbit, his eyes caught sight of the seven facing him.

"Hey, what're you doin' out here? I ain't never seen you before!" His eyes squinted to a wary gaze.

"Well, we've never seen you before, either," Cheater answered.

"You live here?" He took a step closer.

"Yes, you nosey youngster! They live with me!" Maive moved forward, pushing her way between Cai and Thad. "Why aren't you in school?"

"Ah, that! I ain't got no reason to be there. They ain't learnin' me nothin'!"

"Apparently not!" Maive placed hand's on hips.

"Hey, you ain't got to be mean! I home school so I can take care of my mother and little sister."

"What's that? Why are you taking care of them?" Maive's interest was peeked.

"'Cause, we ain't got no money." The boy

frowned.

"Where's your dad?" Cheater asked.

"Dead. Killed himself when he lost his job and couldn't find another. Ah, they said it was a hunting accident, but it wasn't. I know. I saw him changing—got worse every day." His eyes glazed with moisture, but his forced family position wouldn't allow him to loose the tears. That didn't stop Cheater from letting hers fall. She hadn't had to care for anyone else in so long, and the hurt emanating from this small boy brought her past back to her forethoughts.

"Oh." The seven felt an immediate kinship to the boy, having lost so much themselves.

"Times is so hard. A rabbit would give us a couple of meals."

"My, my, you poor baby!" Maive remembered how her late husband had predicted these changes in the world, and how he had started stashing away funds for their old age. She still had plenty to live on, even taking care of these six. She'd been frugal since his death.

"I ain't no baby! I'm ten years old!" The boy defended.

Rebecca remembered the money in her bag.

Cheater thought about what was left of the money Danny had passed to her without her knowledge—money that was still in her pocket.

Both girls moved away from the group and into Maive's house where Rebecca located her bag. Cheater retrieved the cash from her pocket to add to Rebecca's box. When the two girls returned, they spoke to the group about the cash. There wasn't much, just a little over two hundred dollars, but it would help with groceries.

They really had no reason for it. They had Maive; her car was electric; they had done without before, and it was them, what they do. They didn't have family to take care of and no real need for the cash.

Letting go of it wasn't even a difficult decision for them.

The teens had nothing, but what they did have, they were willing to give up.

"Cai, you go get that car started. Young man, where do you live?" Maive ordered.

"Why you wanna know?" The boy's jaw set tight, as he stood taller.

"Because, I'm gonna send some things over to your house for your momma and sister and you."

"Oh." He wasn't too sure about how his mom would feel about that. He started to say no, but his stomach panged with hunger. "I live down that way. I walked down here to these woods through the fields, chasing that rabbit. It's a long walk."

"That's alright. Nathan, you go make this boy something to eat. You'll find something, I'm sure. Son, you come with us!" He couldn't refuse the command from Maive being brought up to respect elders. He followed what was left of the group, looking up at Jaz, who walked protectively next to him.

"My dad died, too, a long time ago." Jaz rested

his comforting hand on the younger boy's shoulder.

"Oh, did he lose his job, too?"

"No, just his life. Cancer. Do you know what that is?" Jaz frowned at the memory.

"Yeah. Were you poor, too?"

"No, we were okay," Jaz shook his head. "What's your name?"

"Stevie," Cheater turned. The irony, though Steve was such a common name, drew her attention. This young boy could have been Jaz's brother, though he had the same name as her own brother.

"Why you looking at me so funny?" The boy's brows drew down in a wide V above his nose.

"My brother's name is Stevey, too." Cheater's lips formed a bittersweet smile.

"Which one's that? That short one there?" He pointed at Thad.

"No, we're not related." Cheater giggled, shaking her head.

"Well, I didn't think so, but I thought maybe you was all adopted by her." He nodded toward Maive.

"Boy, my name is Maive. You call me that. I'm not '*her*'." The elder woman corrected.

"Yes, ma'am!" He lowered his face in shame.

"Oh, now, don't you feel bad. Here, sit here in this chair. It's a nice December day. Let's enjoy it on the back porch!" Maive pointed to a tattered patio chair, foam bursting through holes in the cushions.

Nathan brought the boy a tuna fish sandwich and a glass of juice.

"Z'at tuna fish?" Maive sniffed. "Where'd you find that, Nathan? Where'd you get that bread?"

"The tuna was in your pantry, behind some other boxes and stuff. The bread was in the freezer," Nathan frowned.

"Well, I'll be. Didn't even know it was there all this time. Can't see a thing!

"Now, Cai and you other two girls, there's a little grocery store I go to when the girl drives me. I want you to go buy some things for this boy and his momma. Try not to be noticed."

"I don't know if we should split up, Maive," Cai suggested.

"Well, then all of you go. I just think it would look more..." She looked down at Stevie. "I'ma tell you what to get so they can eat for a while on that money. Who writes good? Go get a pencil and a piece of paper out of that drawer by the fridge!"

Cai went for the items. She sat in another patio chair, poised to make the list. She slowly penned each item Maive called out. "Now, you buy the cheapest brand; brand makes no difference when you're hungry."

The boy ate half his sandwich. "May I have something to wrap this in to take to my momma?"

"What? You eat that up. We'll make another one for her and your sister. Nathan?"

"Yes, ma'am!" The newly appointed house chef retreated inside to fulfill the order.

Stevie ate the second half of the sandwich greedily. His hunger satiated, he sipped his juice slowly. "That was the best san'ich I ate in a long time." He wiped juice from his lip with the back of his free hand.

Maive shook her head. The boy's shirtsleeve slid up to his elbow when he put cup to lip, showing his bony arm. Even a blind woman could see how starved he was.

"Maive's right. It won't take all of us, the less the better. How far is that store, Maive?" Cai folded the list and placed it in her pocket.

"Oh, not far at all. You just go to the light, take a left, about a mile down. We'll take this youngster home after you get back. How far a walk is it, you think, Stevie?"

"I don't know. That way, about two miles, maybe," he pointed.

"That shouldn't be any problem for you young'uns to handle. Now, get goin'. This boy can't be all day."

The girls disappeared behind the other side of the garage. A half hour passed before they returned safely with the groceries, and using the coupons Maive gave them, they almost doubled their purchase.

"We're probably gonna have to take the car to his house. There's a lot of bags in the trunk."

"Oh, I see. Well, we can't all go in the car. I'll ride with you, Cai. One of you boys walk with Stevie. That should be okay."

"I'd rather we all go, just in case that sheriff comes back." Cai bit her lower lip.

"Well, alright, then. Let's get these groceries over there. What's your address, Stevie?"

"I don't have an address. Actually, we live behind somebody's property. There's an old farmhouse back of their place. It ain't much, but we can rest there. You ain't got nothin' cold in them bags, right? We don't have 'lectric or water. Just an old well out back. Momma cleaned up the wood stove to cook on whenever I get us somethin'."

"What?!" Maive's shock threw her backward in her chair. "Hold on! Jaz, go get those girls!" She called.

"Yes, ma'am!" Jaz sprinted to the garage.

"Now, young man, how far away is that old farmhouse from any other places?"

"Oh, ain't nobody near. Nobody can know we're there. We ain't allowed to play outside when the tractors are on the place."

"Shame... m...m...m!" Maive cast a knowing glance toward the other boys.

"I know what you're thinking," Jaz smiled as he returned.

"Yessir, you sure do! You kids stay here. Cai and me and Stevie will go to the house. Get those groceries unloaded! And Nathan, I hate to do this to you, after all of your help yesterday..." Maive started.

"I got it covered, Maive. We'll have it up before you get back." He motioned at Jaz and Thad to follow him to the shed.

She patted his cheek as a grandmother would, "You're a good boy. Your grandparents would be proud of you, darlin'."

Cai helped Maive to the car, put Stevie in the backseat, and took her position in the driver's seat. She backed slowly out of the garage and down the driveway.

34

While the other teens set the bed up in the spare room, Cai drove past the house at the front of the property where the old farmhouse hid behind fields of oats, many yards away. Following the dirt road around, she tried to find a way to get Maive's car back to the house where Stevie lived. No driveway led to the old house.

"Sometimes, there's some roadway into those old fields. See which field it's nearest and find the entry. I'm sure there is one, isn't there Stevie?"

"Oh, yes ma'am. There's a drive-like around the field. Almost goes to the house. Look! Just passed those trees it is! It's been dry for a while, so we won't git stuck."

Cai directed the car into the rutty drive off the roadway. "Are you sure you want me to drive your car down there?"

"No other way. I wanna speak to this boy's mother. She'll be too proud to listen to you young'uns. You just get me there."

Cai slowed the car to a crawl as it bumped over the ruts created by truck tires and mud. Attempting to balance on the banks of the tracks caused the front end to scrape dirt; it made her cringe in her seat and stop.

"You just keep goin'. Don't worry 'bout that little scrape. It was just the bumper," Maive directed.

Cai tried to move over, again, away from the ruts, but the clotted mud was too dry and hard to ease over in a light vehicle. Driving on the rise at a slower pace was like trying to drive a car on railroad tracks. By the time she reached a smooth spot, her nerves were on edge. She made the curve, and there, hidden behind several old oak trees was a falling down farmhouse.

"Ain't no porch, Miss Maive. Let me get Momma to come outside to see you."

Stevie unbuckled his seat belt, slipped out of the car and climbed up the door threshold in the time that it took Cai to help Maive out of the car. When Cai and Maive reached the front of the house, Stevie's mom stood in the doorway scolding the young boy.

"Stevie, I told you, you can't be bringing anybody here. We ain't even s'posed to be here!" Tears of hopelessness dripped from her deep brown eyes, leaving shiny streaks on her smooth, cocoa cheeks as she shook her head at her young son. "Now what we gonna do, Stevie? We won't be able to stay here anymore. I told ya', son!"

"Now, there's no need to be angry with your boy. I made him bring me here! You taught him well to listen to his elders." Maive interrupted forcefully, overwhelming the woman's pride. "I have a proposition for you, Miss..."

"Burket."

Maive glanced at Cai and then back at the young mother. “I need someone to maintain my house and cook my meals. Gotta girl that drives me once a week to the store, but frankly, I’m gettin’ a bit too old for that, too. If ya’ drive, I could sure use that service, goin’ to the store, the laundry, all that mess.”

“Y… You’re offerin’ me a job?”

“Yes, I am. And a decent place to live. I am in desperate need of help as this ninety-seven-year old body grows more tired each day. I can give you a little spending money—and room and board a might better than this here gappin’, drafty house—for your help.”

“I don’t know. That’s too much. I couldn’t take your money and have you put us up…”

“I won’t take no for an answer. You cannot live in this broken down old house with those two beautiful children and no food. You are coming with me!” Maive ordered, her chin held high.

“Oh! Oh, yes ma’am!” Mrs. Burket stammered.

“Well, go get your things together. We ain’t got all night. We’ll wait here.”

“Ma’am, my two kids is all I have. Clarisse! Come on, Sweetheart!”

Stevie helped his little sister down from the threshold and passed her off to Cai. In true gentleman-of-the-house fashion, Stevie held his small hand up for his mother to take. Using him for support, she gingerly stepped her bare feet off the threshold and into the tall brown grass.

“Now, you get yourself into that backseat and we’ll be on our way!” Maive told the grateful woman as Cai took Maive's arm.

"Let me, please," Mrs. Burket stepped in to take Maive's arm, guiding and supporting her. "I really can't thank you enough, ma'am."

"Oh, don't you think about it, again. Cai, get that car goin'!" She winked at the young girl.

"Sure, thing, Maive!" Cai bounded to the car, strapped Stevie and his little sister into the backseat and opened the passenger door for Mrs. Burket to help Maive before taking her place in the driver's seat.

"She's not your granddaughter, then? Callin' you by name?" Mrs. Burket leaned in close to Maive's ear.

"Oh, no, but she might as well be. I've been all alone till those kids stepped into my backyard," the old eyes twinkled. "Hadn't been for them, I wouldn't be here askin' you for help, now."

"Kids? There's more than one? Do you have the room?"

"Oh, don't you worry. They'll be coming out to this old house a great deal, I suppose. They have a... project to work on."

"Would you like me to drive the car? I do have a license," Mrs. Burket offered.

"Oh, you comfort those youngsters. Your girl might be a little disjointed, movin' so suddenly. This young lady drives just fine."

"If you go out that way, it's a bit smoother. I walk that way lookin' for wood for the fire. I guess you didn't get us a rabbit, Stevie?"

"No, Momma."

"Wha'dya' do with Daddy's twenty-two?"

"It's safe, Momma. I left it on Miss Maive's back porch."

"You're a fine boy, my little man." She wrapped an arm around his frail shoulder and squeezed, patting his cheek with her other hand, and kissing the top of his head.

Cai teared up after glimpsing the exchange in the rearview mirror. Thoughts about her own parents, her life, filled her mind. She felt a comforting touch on her forearm and cast a bittersweet smile in Maive's direction. Maive nodded back reassuringly.

"So, how many are there, living with you?"

"You and yours will make nine and there's plenty of room. You'll see. Don't you worry."

When Cai turned into the driveway, she could just slip by the sheriff's car parked in the middle. The sheriff stood at the front door, rapping on the wood.

35

"What is it you want, now? Ain't it enough you woke me from sleep this morning?" Maive climbed out of the car, put both hands on her thin hips, and jutted her jaw toward the officer. Her gruff voice caused the young sheriff to move timidly toward her.

"You live here, ma'am?"

"You know I do! You're the same fella' came here before daylight!" Maive stood her ground.

"Well, actually, no, I don't know. I wasn't here this morning. We've had a report that these kids have been seen in this area. Would you take a look? See if you've seen them?"

"I would be happy to!" She grabbed the papers in his hand, flipped through the four pages quickly and reported, "No, no, no, and no! Now git off my property."

"There's no reason to be so hostile, ma'am. Are you sure? The report said they were seen in a car like this one here." He indicated her car with a nod.

"Sir, nobody's been in that car but me, Miss Maive, and my children." Mrs. Burket moved nearer to Maive, blocking the view of Cai, who slipped into the passenger seat, her head turned toward the window as far as possible looking into the back seat, cap pulled down.

"Those your children there?" Mrs. Burket glanced over her shoulder at Cai and her own two children, then nodded at the sheriff. "Well, have you seen these kids?" He shoved the papers in her direction. She could honestly answer no to all of the photos.

"M' kay. I just ask that you keep your eyes open and give us a call if you see them. It's very important that we speak to them. They're wanted for stealing, assaulting an elderly man..." he paused, taking in Maive's expression, then continued, "and evading a law enforcement officer when asked to stop. Please contact us immediately."

"Of course, we will!" Maive was not overly enthused by his request. "Now get off my place! I don't want to ever see another sheriff on my lawn 'less I've been robbed or killed. I ain't seen so many law in all my ninety-seven years!" Her gravelly voice pushed the sheriff back a few steps before Maive turned away and hobbled toward the house.

Cai remained in the car with Stevie and Clarisse until the sheriff drove away. She let Mrs. Burket pull the car into the garage, bring down the heavy door, and plug in the car before ducking out of the passenger side.

In the kitchen, Maive stood by the pantry wringing her hands. "Where'd you suppose they went?" She asked Cai as the young girl stepped through the kitchen door.

"They're not in the cellar?" Cai asked.

"No, and they're not in the house anywhere!"

Maive was truly worried.

"I'll go check the shed," Cai soothed.

"I'll go with ya'," Stevie offered.

"Me, too!" Young Clarisse grabbed her big brother's hand.

With the children outside, Mrs. Burket felt compelled to question the sheriff's words. "Is it true, do you think, what that sheriff said about those kids?"

"I don't know what kids he was talking about, but my kids wouldn't do none of that!"

"Good. I can't have my Stevie being influenced, you know? He's a good boy." Mrs. Burket's features turned solemn.

"Oh, if he were gonna be influenced by anybody, you'd want it to be these kids. I just hope they're okay. I hope that sheriff wasn't trying to fool me. Can't trust nary anyone these days, certainly not law!" Maive shook her head.

"Oh, but surely we can trust our law enforcement," Mrs. Burket assured.

"I wouldn't bet on that, Mrs. Burket, not one bit." Maive argued.

Cai burst into the house, "I can't find them anywhere!"

"What about their bags?" Maive moved into action.

Dark hair swung around Cai's ears as she hurried to the bedroom where they kept their things. The bed was back and made, but their bags were gone.

"No!" she almost yelled. "I can't believe they would leave without me! Where could they be? Their bags are gone! I don't even know where to look."

"Take the light, 'case it gets dark before you get back. Go check the woods, out there where you met Stevie!" Cai and Stevie left the back door standing open after hurrying through the kitchen.

Maive felt a tug on her shirttail and looked down at the tiny, drawn face staring up at her, "What is it, sweet?"

"Is that your san'ich?" Clarisse pointed to the counter where two small plates held two tuna sandwiches.

"Clarisse! Don't be rude!" Her mother scolded.

"Oh, she's not bein' rude, just hungry. Those sandwiches are for you and your momma. Go on, eat them. The best cook I know made them before he disappeared." Maive's eyes turned dark with her frown.

Cai sprinted to the wooded area where they practiced earlier, but the Gifted Ones were nowhere to be seen. She stood where Maive had stood and turned a circle, eyes searching, "Where are they?"

"I'll run ahead. Maybe they went to my old farmhouse?"

"Why? They don't have a reason to. They don't even know which house it is. Check that way, just a little ways, then come back."

"Okay!" Stevie ran as fast as he could. When Cai could no longer see him, she felt a pang of loss, loneliness, regret for having driven Maive.

Her shoulders sagged with worry. She could think of nothing but the fact that the five of them took off without her. Then there was the possibility that the sheriff had caught them and was using them to find her...

In mid thought, a hand covered her mouth from behind while an arm slipped around her waist and lifted her off her feet. She swung her elbows backward and kicked her feet to no avail.

36

"No, these children are special, Mrs. Burket. They're not our everyday teens, gettin' in trouble and all."

"Please, call me Deann. My family used to call me Dee. You can call me that if you like."

"Well, Dee. I can't tell you exactly what it is about these young'uns, but maybe you will see for yourself. Let me ask ya'. Did you ever hear a story in your youth about twelve princes and princesses?"

"Not that I recall." The younger woman shook her head.

"No, I wouldn't expect so. Very few have heard it." Maive puckered her lips.

"What is the story?" Dee prodded.

"Oh, don't you worry, I'll have time to share that story with you soon." Maive nodded solemnly.

"I want to hear a story! I like princess stories!" Clarisse's eyes lit up over the sandwich covering her lower lip and chin.

"Oh, I bet you do, and I know you would like this story!" Maive winked at her.

"Clarisse, honey, you be silent and eat. Drink up that milk, too," her mother ordered. "Been so long since that child's had milk."

"Oh, let 'er be, Dee. She's a fine young girl.

Reminds me of my own littlest girl."

"Do your children and grandchildren visit you?" Dee asked.

"Mhm, got none left."

"Oh, I'm sorry. My husband's gone on, too." Dee looked down at her empty plate.

"Yes, I know. That boy of yours is a talker," Maive nodded. "Well-disciplined lad. Wants to watch out for his momma."

"Yes, he's very disciplined. I hope they find the others, Maive. It's startin' to get dark."

"Momma, I'm tired," Clarisse yawned.

"Well, let me show you where the bath and bed are. Get that baby cleaned up and tucked in. No sleeping in the cold tonight, little one," Maive patted her head as she walked by her.

"Here's some towels. Right there is the room you'll stay in. Only one bed, but you're all very small. You should fit fine."

Dee's cheeks dampened as she stroked the soft towel, viewed the comfortable bed, "Thank you, Miss Maive, for takin' us in."

"Oh, you just go on now. Get your baths. I'ma see if I can find something clean for baby girl and you to wear."

Maive listened contentedly while Dee sang a quiet song of old while bathing her daughter. Out the kitchen window, the sun had taken its trip to the west and filtered through trees behind the house, adding to the shadows that Maive saw through her filmy eyes. What could she do to help find them?

What if that sheriff was lying to her and the law had the others locked up in a detention center—or worse, what if *he* had them now?

"What could this ninety-seven year old woman do to help them kids? Lord, please let them be okay," she whispered. She closed her near useless eyes and hummed along with the sweet song of the mother who's voice no longer carried worry for her children. Guilt flooded Maive's old heart, the guilt of making Cai leave the others to drive her. She had gone to fulfill a good deed and returned to a horrible unknown.

If she could do it over again, knowing what might happen, would she trade Dee and her kids for the Gifted Ones? Could she leave that poor woman, those babies, out there in that cold house with no food, the slow death of starvation filling their bodies?

She knew the answer to that. The Gifted Ones didn't belong to her in the first place. They belonged to a struggling world of Dees, a world of lost people trying to find their way in a society that no longer cared. They belonged to everyone who had no hope. They would be fine.

The Gifted Ones would be just fine.

37

Cai bit down on the fingers that covered her teeth.

"Ouch! You didn't have to do that! I didn't want you to scream out. A sheriff came to the house. He may still be here." Nathan let go of Cai, shaking his bitten hand.

"You scared the heck out of me! Where are the others?"

"You can't see them? Good!" Nathan's head jerked over his left shoulder.

"What do you mean?" One by one, beginning with Thad, the four others returned to themselves. "Wait a minute! You don't need me to do that?" Cai's mouth fell open.

"As long as we're connected, we can do it ourselves. Which means, we all have access to the powers. They transfer between us!"

"Okay... that's cool... so, now we know our powers have transferred. Let's try someone else's power." Cai glanced at Cheater, for the moment forgetting about the worried old woman at the house. Earlier, all six of them had changed with Cheater for Maive. Would it work without her?

Cheater stepped away from the group. With deep interest, she waited for their transformation. She had never seen her gift in action before.

Jaz was the first to change. The likeness of an older man took his place. "Is that your father, Jaz? My gosh!"

"No, that's my father! Daddy?" Stevie cried.

"Oh my, Stevie!" Cheater turned toward him, wanting to shield the boy from what was happening, afraid it would wound his tender emotions, but he wouldn't let her stand in his way. He wanted to talk to his father. When Cheater turned back, none of the Gifted Ones were there. Rebecca became Cheater's mother, Thad her brother, Nathan her father, Cai was Sadie. Cheater nearly passed out from the joy of seeing her mother again, her family.

"Mom?" Tears streamed down her cheeks, all those years, all those families, all the sadness, gone in one flash of time.

"Mom?" Stevie watched as Cheater moved closer to the group. Ducking into outstretched hands, she peered into the eyes of her mother.

"Sarah, honey, you've been alone for way too long. Not anymore!" The likeness of her mother smiled.

"I miss you so much, Mom!"

"I know, darling. But you are here for a much greater reason, a much greater love, and you have a wonderful gift that is going to return love to this world. Remember the story, Sarah. Remember the twelve. They will be your family now, until the end."

"She's right!" The jolly voice of Sadie called. Cheater spun on her heel.

"Sadie!"

"Honey, you know where I am, and I am happy. You be happy, too. You got a job to do, girl. Don't you let me down! Take care of that..." Cheater nodded.

"Now, Sadie, let me have a word," Cheater turned toward her dad. "I love you, my princess. You all need to get back to that house. You're keeping a very nice, old lady waiting and worrying," he smiled. Then Cheater realized that Stevey stood among them. Stevey, her Stevey, wasn't alive after all, no matter how much she had hoped to see him again. There he was.

Tommy wasn't Stevey.

Her heart rose and fell with lost hope.

Stevie Burket spoke to his dad, questioned his dad, yelled at his dad, drawing Cheater's attention to him. He said things he needed to say to him, and his dad listened with chastised solemnity.

Cheater turned back to her mother, who now began to fade into Rebecca. Tears stained Cheater's cheeks, and she moved to hug Rebecca.

"I don't know why you feel the urge to hug me, but okay!" Rebecca said, her hand still joined Jaz's hand. Cheater threw her arms around the quiet frame and squeezed.

"Sheez! Now I have to deal with all of you reading my mind. It's not bad enough that he does it!" Cheater joked wiping her eyes.

"Why are you crying?" Rebecca's confusion made Cheater remember her own confusion when the darkness took control.

"I just got the chance to talk to loved ones—my

mom, dad, Stevey, even Sadie—and I now know where my brother is. He's okay."

Stevie had thrown himself into Jaz, who now hugged the younger boy and let him cry out his frustration, though he didn't know why the boy had attached himself to his waist until he heard Cheater's words.

"We need to get back. Maive is worried. Daddy's orders!" Cheater stuck her lower lip out as she took in her five cohorts, and then she turned from the awestruck group and ran toward the house.

"I forgot! Oh my gosh! She's probably really worked up by now!" Cai ran to catch up with Cheater, the others following closely behind.

Jaz lifted Stevie up and set him on his shoulders, galloping to catch up to the others. Stevie's giggle filled the screen door as they approached the waiting women.

38

"Oh, heavens! There you all are!" Maive hugged each one as they entered the house, Jaz lifting Stevie and setting him on the patio before entering.

"We had to run, Maive. That sheriff pulled up; we went out the back door and into the woods. He followed us out that way, then came back to the house. We tricked him, though," Nathan said as she patted his cheeks with both hands.

"Where's my mom?" Stevie asked excitedly.

"Oh, darlin' they went straight to bed after their bath. They're already asleep in the room. Full bellies and hot water will do that to a tired body. Go see for yourself. Best you get your bath when you come back."

"Do I have to?" Stevie whined.

"Yes, and each of you others, too. We may run out of hot water tonight, but at least you'll be clean."

"Come on, kid. I'll show you where to go!" Jaz led Stevie with a hand on the back of his neck.

"I dug out some old pajamas and some old clothes and shoes and such from my children and grandchildren. Whenever they stayed here, they always seemed to leave some clothes. Whatever fits, you can have. I got enough of my husband's old tee shirts that should fit all of you like pajama gowns.

It's all in the living room. Help yourselves after you get your baths. There's plenty of soap, young man, so you better smell real good when you get out!" She called after Jaz and Stevie as they stepped into the bathroom.

"Will you stay with me?" Stevie pleaded with Jaz.

"Sure kid!" He smiled down at him and shrugged at the others.

One by one, hot or cold water, the six gifted teenagers showered after finding something fitting in the pile of clothes Maive shared. It seemed each found exactly what they needed and everything fit perfectly.

Stevie climbed into the bed with his mom and sister after his bath, quickly falling asleep on the edge of the bed.

Tuna sandwiches disappeared quickly upon their return. Full and clean bodies, they sat cross-legged in a circle in the living room laughing at how scared Cai looked when she ran through the woods searching for them.

"Hey, I thought you guys left me! I couldn't believe you would do that!" she defended.

"Why, 'cause you're so bossy?" Thad stuck his tongue out at her, and she pushed his shoulder.

"Yeah, I kinda noticed how she takes control of everything," Jaz nodded.

"Hey!" Cai slugged him in the arm.

"You're right, Jaz," Nathan teased. "She does take over."

"Unh!" Cai made fists and held them before her face.

Maive snickered, "Oh, you young people sure act like brothers and sisters."

"In a way, we are," Rebecca's voice filled their minds.

"Yeah," Jaz took Cheater's hand and nodded reassurance at her. Thad took her other hand, smiling meekly. Though they were the same age, he felt she was so much older than he.

Cai took Thad's other hand, the chain slowly closed beyond her. "Well, since I'm the oldest, I should be in charge!" She rolled her eyes at the rest. Glancing around at her new brothers and sisters, each different in their own way, each having suffered through their own tragedies, she began to see the greater purpose of her existence. She'd always known she was special; her mother made that connection from the beginning.

"Hey, speaking of when you were a baby, did you ever get lost outside?" Jaz asked.

"I see what you mean," Cai smiled at Cheater, who returned a huge grin. *"Nobody else seemed to want to get into my head, or at least say anything about it! To answer your question, no, I didn't start blending until I was a teenager."* She finished telepathically.

Nathan glanced at Maive who sat riveted on the edge of her seat, watching, listening with fascination, "Maive, you would have made a really great Gifted One."

"Ah! Now you're buttin' into people's heads! You kids are amazin'!" She cast a gaping smile their way.

"We do appreciate everything you're doing for us, Maive," Cai added.

"In spite of the danger, your choice to help us makes *you* the amazing one," Cheater smiled.

"Oh, stop it! I ain't done nothin'! You're just so dang easy to love. And knowin' who you are, what you're up against, well..." She shook her old gray head, tears forming in her filmy eyes.

"Group hug!" The teens shouted and dove to Maive's chair, surrounding the old woman with warm, happy arms. Tears of fear crawled down the cracks in her cheeks, fear for each one of them. Their mission would not be easy or safe. She might never see them again once they left her. It was the only way, though—the only way to change the world in which they lived. Maive knew that.

"Don't worry, Maive. Everything will work out as it's supposed to." Rebecca caught a tear on Maive's cheek with her index finger, then lay her head on the old woman's shoulder.

Maive's pointy old chin bounced near Rebecca's chin as the elder nodded agreement.

Their tender concern for their caretaker was brief. A knock on the front door and a frantic voice, "Maive! Maive! Are you still awake? Wake up, please!" forced the teens to scatter.

39

"What on earth is the matter?" Maive stood at the open door blocking the view into her living room. The middle-aged woman, housecoat hanging loosely about her body, worn slippers covering her thin ankles, glasses strewn crookedly upon her nose, took several deep breaths before continuing, "Please let me in! Please let me in! He's coming for me!"

"Who? What are you talkin' about, Polly?" Maive put a hand on the frantic woman's shoulder.

Polly pushed past Maive and leaned into the front door, closing it behind her. "He's coming! He's gonna kill me!" Olive eyes wide with fear, short, fast breaths falling harder on their ears, and skin so pale blue veins could be seen pulsing rapidly, Polly pleaded with Maive, disregarding the safety of those within her care.

"Who?" Maive repeated, shaking the slender, red-haired woman by the shoulders to draw her attention.

"Dave, he's out... Beatin' on the front door... I slipped out the back. I think he saw me run over here."

"Who's Dave?" Cai stepped forward. Jaz moved beside her. He knew that look. That look in Polly's eyes told him everything he needed to know about

Dave. Anger built within him, anger followed by years of memories.

"Dave is Polly's ex-husband. He's been in the pokey for about, oh... how long has it been, Polly?" Maive asked nonchalantly, the fear Polly felt not transferring through her tough hide.

Polly turned to the teenagers crowding around her, seeing them for the first time, "Oh, no! Oh, you innocent babies! I've put you in danger. No!" She reached for the doorknob with her right hand, putting space between her back and the wood behind her.

"Oh, these innocent babies can handle themselves. Don't panic." Maive closed her hand around the trembling hand of her neighbor, tugging her to the center of the room. Jaz pushed the door closed behind her, paused to consider locking it, and decided to leave it unlocked. The crazed man would likely break the door down if he locked the deadbolt. Maive didn't need that.

"Yes, we can. Come in here." Cai put her arm around the frightened woman's waist and led her to the living room where the teens crowded around the two women, three to the front, three to the back, each facing the front door, hands reaching for the next one.

An angry fist pounded on the screen door. "Get out here, whore! That old lady can't protect you! If you don't come out, I'm comin' in!" The door flung inward as the woman behind Jaz gasped and cried out. Jaz flinched from habit, then relaxed again, focusing on the mind of the man before him.

Cheater inhaled deeply, squeezing her friend's right hand, her vision beginning to grey and fade.

Jaz tightened his grip on Cai's right hand, alerting her to Cheater's response. Cai cued Nathan who signaled Rebecca. By the time Rebecca's hand tightened on Thad's the process had begun, the darkness enclosed them.

"Get away from my old lady! She's comin'..." The transformation of the teens halted the man's tirade. "What is this? Some kind of joke?" His dark eyes widened with fear as the transformation completed. His hands rose, opened and waved before him, protecting his face.

"Son, what are you afraid of? Why are you cowering like that? After all these years, after my death, you're still afraid? Put your hands down and face me."

Polly gasped, "He's lost his mind!" But Maive clutched her shoulder and pulled her closer.

Dave's large hands dropped to his thighs as his eyes cast downward.

"Look at me, son. I have something to tell you!" The deep voice ordered.

"Honey, please, your dad's speaking to you. It's okay. I promise," a woman's voice pleaded.

Dave's eyes followed the woman's voice upward, "Mom?" He searched the faces surrounding his estranged wife. His parents, his paternal grandparents and his maternal grandparents clasped hands around Polly and Maive.

"That's right." His phantom mother replied.

"Anger isn't the answer, son. I'm sorry you grew up with it. I'm sorry you saw me do those horrible things to your mother," the older man nodded.

"And if it hadn't been for me, your dad wouldn't have grown up that way, bein' like me. Your wife deserves better, grandson. Break the circle, David. You've done your time for it once. Don't let it end your life."

"Grandpa, I don't..."

"Your behavior, my behavior, your dad's behavior... it can't go on, David. Leave this woman alone, now. If you feel that angry when you're around her, then leave her alone. Don't you come back to her house. Go find yourself, figure out how to control what's inside you, what's eatin' you alive. Figure out how to leave your past behind you."

The man at the door stared at his grandfather, his father, "But, marriage is forever. That's what you said, Dad. Marriage is..."

"Not when it's like this son. If you can't respect her, leave her. Let go of the anger, son. Just let go."

Dave stared at Polly, his estranged wife quivering behind his mother and father. His face softened as her wide stare touched his heart, then his head dropped, and he turned and walked out the door.

"Dave, wait!" Polly ducked beneath clasped hands and followed him out the door as the teens returned to normal.

"My gosh, that was amazin'!" Dee stood in the

hallway entrance, a hand over her heart. "Miss Maive, I do believe you were right. These aren't no ordinary teens."

"No, Miss Dee, these here are The Gifted Ones. Well, six of them, anyway," Maive winked at Cheater.

"Do you think Polly will be okay with him, now, Maive?" Jaz whispered, memories bringing concern, filling his eyes and touching the old woman's heart.

Maive lay her wrinkled, old hand gently on his cheek, "Yes, Jaz. I think she'll be better than she ever has been. And David, too. You kids have that effect on people." She wiped at a tear slipping gently down the side of the young man's nose, a wispy, grandmotherly smile touching her lips.

"She'll be all right, Jaz." Nathan patted the taller boy's shoulder.

"Yeah." Cheater slipped her arm around his waist and squeezed. "We'll all be all right," she said. Her eyes closed to fight back her own tears.

"Yes, you will, darlin'." Maive stroked Cheater's damp hair, "Yes you will."

The floor quaked beneath their feet. "No! No! We can't let him win. The world, innocent people will die! Focus!" Cai reached out with her mind. Eyes closed, hands tightened, yet the fear began to build. Fire and earthquake? How would they stand their ground?

"It's not working!" A low, unfamiliar voice called through the roaring flames. "It's not working!"

Cai opened her eyes, and through the flames, she glimpsed a set of piercing eyes surrounded by chiseled features.

"Are you one of us?" She yelled back. He didn't speak telepathically.

"It's a trap! Don't listen to him!" Nathan pushed into her mind.

"Are you one of us?" Cai silently called.

The eyes stared back at her, pleadingly, "Yes, but I never wanted to be. And now, I'm wishing I wasn't." No words escaped his lips. "We can't win against him, against his evil. Good has never been with me, never on my side. We can't do this! We should just give up!" The blue eyes filled with hopelessness, then shame, as the earth shook harder.

Cai understood that look. She ran for so long from her uniqueness. Sometimes, she thought she was still running. "We can help you. We will help you. Where are you? What's your name? We'll find you."

"You can't find me. Nobody can find me. I'm in a place without visitors, a place where nobody will look for me, ever. I can't even find myself!" He rose through the flames, twisting with the wind that forced his body upward.

"No! Don't give up! Please! We need you!" Cai yelled above the torrent of rumbles and wind.

"Don't let go!" Nathan yelled, squeezing her hand with his, but it was too late. The connection was broken.

Cai rolled to her back, pulling her hand from Nathan's, ending the nightmare that filled their night.

Her eyes popped open in the silence and she fought to remember the features of the young man in the flames. He had to be one of them. "I can't even find myself?" She whispered into the darkness. She'd always loved a good puzzle, riddle, anything that made her think.

"I wonder where he could be?" Cheater's voice startled Cai from her thoughts, bringing her body upright. "Sorry, I didn't mean to scare you," Cheater whispered. "I'm not used to my dreams suddenly stopping like that... at least not until I try to see that horrible face."

"It's okay. I let go in the dream, and I guess I let go of Nathan's hand for real at the same time. I was just thinking the same as you. Where could he be? He must be one of us. Where could he be locked up?"

"Good question," Cheater nodded to the darkness, yawning her reply.

"Try to go back to sleep. We'll talk about it tomorrow. Maybe the others will have some ideas. One thing's for sure. We'll find him." Cai shuttered her eyes again, but sleep wouldn't come.

Cheater laid down, arms folded beneath her

head, worry filling her thoughts. The possibility of being caught was greater, now that they'd helped Polly and her husband. Too many people in this area knew about them. They had to move on, and the sooner the better. Besides, the longer they stayed, the closer they came to putting the household in danger.

She would speak to the rest of them in the morning.

40

"We have to leave, Maive. After last night, the sheriff is sure to come back here looking for us." Cheater reasoned with the elderly woman.

"Cheater's right. Word will spread," Cai added.

"You've already helped us so much. We can't put you or Miss Dee in danger, Maive." Nathan swallowed hard, "I know what they're capable of doing to others. I know what they did to my grandparents. We don't want anything to happen to you." Nathan hugged the elderly woman tightly around her shoulders, his cheek resting next to hers.

"You worry too much about this old lady! I can take care of myself! How do you think I got to be this old?" Maive gently patted Nathan's back and then pushed him away, sternly peering into his fear-filled eyes.

"But, what about them?" Jaz nodded toward the hallway.

"Well, all right, then, but you will eat first! And, you will take some food with you for later. I can't stand the thought of you six goin' hungry!"

They had risen early, with the sun, and discussed the dangers in staying too long. They had also decided to leave before breakfast, but Maive wouldn't let them.

"There are worse things than going hungry," Thad added.

"What?" Nathan and Cai almost gave themselves whiplash turning their surprised features on Thad.

"Very funny," Thad rolled his eyes.

Nathan moved to the kitchen to help Maive. "It is true, though. It would be much worse if we lost you, Maive."

"I don't care what you think, you ain't leavin' here without some food!"

"Okay, Maive, but we can't stay too long after. We'll be fine on our own. We've each been alone for a long time. That's what got us all here, to this place in time. Besides, once we take back my grandparents' place…"

"What?" The old woman stopped stirring the pancake batter. "You can't be thinking that! You can't go back there!"

"We have to. There's something about that place. It's important to their plan. I just know it. We know it! Besides, I have a feeling that's where the other six will turn up."

"Surely you don't think they're just gonna hand that place over!" Maive searched the eyes facing her.

"Of course not, but we have a plan. Sort of…" Nathan turned the sausage patties and pressed down on each to force the grease out.

"You 'sort of' got a plan? And, they sort of got guns. You told me that much. How are you going to protect yourself from that?" Maive beat the batter in the bowl with all the force of her anger and frustration.

"They have to be able to see what they shoot at." Cai offered, a slender hand resting on Maive's forearm, slowing the spoon.

"We'll come back, Maive. As soon as it's over, we'll come back. We can't risk your life, the Burkets' lives..." Rebecca, who'd been quiet all morning, softly spoke to the surrogate grandmother, confidence and assurance filling her words.

Maive searched Rebecca's expressionless face. "I know," she shook her head. "I know you will come back. I know you will be all right. That's the way of it. I can't help but worry that evil will win.

"I want you to take the car. We shouldn't need it."

"As sure as we do take it, you will need it. We can't. We've gotten this far walking. We're strong and full of energy. We'll walk." Cai argued.

A sharp knock cut their conversation short. Maive started, frowning at the early caller.

"It's Dave!" Jaz shot a smile of promise her way, reading the mind behind the door. "He wants to see if you need anything."

"Well, I'll be... There's a first time for everything. That young man's been nothing but a thug since he moved in! First time I know that he's ever thought of anyone but himself!"

Maive opened the door to a clean-cut face, new clothes perfectly covering a strong, tattooed body and the demeanor of a thoughtful man. He was not the man who barged into her home the previous night.

"Morning, Miss Maive!" The tall man nodded. "Before I leave to look for a job, I thought I might stop in and see if you needed any work done. I can do some plumbing, carpentry, drive ya' anywhere ya' like?" His humble words hardly louder than the frying sausage.

"Well, now, Mr. David, I have no need of any plumbing work or carpentry work, but if you and Polly would join us for breakfast, I might have a driving job for you."

"Thank you for the invitation, but Polly's sleepin' in. We were up late... talking." Dave glanced at the six snickering teens who quickly turned away and busied themselves with breakfast. "I'll go check with her. I'd be happy to drive you somewhere. It does smell good in there."

"Oh, not me. Them!" Maive turned toward the teens in the kitchen. "They need a ride to Paradise. Staying with a grandparent there for a few days..."

"Oh, sure! Let me get Polly. We'll be back!" Dave ducked away.

Maive left the inside door open and returned to the kitchen, instantly giving orders. "Well, we're gonna have a couple more for breakfast, Nathan. Jaz, reach up to that top cabinet and bring down those extra plates! Cai, get out some more forks. Thad, a couple more coffee cups, please."

"Got it covered!" Nathan smashed more sausage patties between his palm and slapped them in the pan.

"Plates coming through!"

"Two forks," Cai passed to the next in line, which was passed again until they made it through the kitchen to the table.

"Coffee cups," Thad tossed a cup to the waiting hands of Jaz, closest to the table, who set it next to the coffee pot.

"You're throwing my good coffee cups! You better not drop 'em!" Maive sounded.

Jaz juggled the second cup like a hot potato, pretending to let it fall.

"Oh, you horrible tease!" Maive waved her hand as she turned away to see about Dee and her family.

"We make a good team!" Jaz nodded at the others, a smile crossing his lips.

"Yes, we do," Rebecca agreed. "I wonder what the others are like?"

"We know what one is like. I just hope we can find him. It worries me," Cai frowned.

"From the dream? I don't know if we can. I mean, he seems to be as lost inside as he is to us."

"Wherever he is, visitors can't go," Cheater puckered her lips. "But if one of us were stuck somewhere, before we met each other, would we have visitors? None of us have any family who would visit. He probably doesn't, either."

"I can't believe I just heard those words!" Maive stormed into the conversation.

"Well, I mean, we didn't have any family before, and if we were locked up somewhere, before you, nobody would come to see us," Cheater stammered.

"I see. You're talkin' about that boy, in your dream. You know, he could be in a children's home, or maybe his memory's gone somehow, or possibly he's had some trauma he wants to forget. There's many options," Maive offered.

"Oh, we know too well about those," Cai raised her brows at Cheater who nodded.

"It seemed more like a place where he was locked up alone," Jaz added.

"Or... what if he's like me? Locked away... Doesn't get visitors... People steer clear of me all the time." Rebecca suggested.

"Maybe, because of his uniqueness, he's in an institution for the... unique," Maive offered with a nod to Rebecca.

"Like a home for people with mental disabilities?" Cai asked.

"More like a home for the..." Thad drew circles in the air with his index finger next to his temple.

"Hey! That could be it, too! I mean, if he exposed his gift to someone, they may have taken him for looney! I wonder if there are any state hospitals in the area?" Nathan snapped his fingers.

"Or his parents may have been scared and could have committed him when his gift matured!" Jaz offered.

"My father wanted my grandmother to do that to me," Rebecca fumed. Cheater put her arm around Rebecca and squeezed. "Well, you're stuck with us, now."

"Oh, I don't know about all of that, but let's get

breakfast going," Maive directed as Polly and Dave knocked on the screen door. Dee and her children came down the hall at the same time.

"Somethin' sure smells good!" Stevie moved through the crowd in the kitchen.

"I should be doin' that, Miss Maive!" Dee scrambled to help.

"Oh, not yet, Dee, not yet. Give these youngsters some room to work. You get the door," Maive gripped Dee's arm and turned her toward the front of the house.

"Hello, won't you come in?" Dee smiled, pushing the screen open.

"Thank you. My, it smells like pancakes in here!" Polly sniffed, "And sausage! Oh, my stomach is growling already! Thank you so much for inviting us, Maive!"

"Dee, whyn't you get some coffee poured for the four of us. We'll take a seat in the living room while they finish up in the kitchen. Cream or sugar?" Maive tilted her chin toward the neighbors.

"Neither for me," Dave answered.

"Oh, me either," Polly held out her hands to take the steaming cup from Dee, who quickly returned with another for Dave.

"Maive, I can't tell you how happy we are this morning. I still can't believe what happened last night!" Polly looked from Maive to Dee.

"We'd like you to come to our wedding," Dave stated hopefully.

"Well, our renewal wedding. As soon as we get

the money up for it. Dave is job hunting today." Polly's smile brightened the room.

"Isn't that nice, Dee? We will certainly be there!" Maive nodded.

"I remember my wedding day like it was yesterday," Dee's eyes clouded.

"Breakfast!" Cheater and Cai rounded the corner with two plates each, laying them on the table before the adults who were seating themselves at the folding table the teens had set up.

"Oh, my! This looks wonderful!"

"Smells even better!"

"Yum!"

"Oh, I better get the kids theirs," Dee stood.

"Sit," Cai pointed as to a training puppy. "We already got theirs. They're eating at the other table with us." She returned a moment later with the coffee pot, refilling their cups before sitting down to eat.

Quiet inundated the small house for the first time since the Gifted Ones arrived, and Maive saddened with the thought of the six leaving her home.

She would still have Dee and her children, of course—a family again. She smiled at Dee across the room, thinking of leaving Dee all of her worldly possessions upon her death. She had nobody else to whom she could leave her home and belongings. If she didn't leave it to Dee, the state would wind up with everything she owned, and who knew what the outcome would be with the fairytale? She certainly didn't want that monster getting hold of her worldly treasures!

She would speak to Dee about it later.

What of those laughing teens at the dining room table? They will need a place to stay, won't they? She glanced their way, watching their antics with each other, with Stevie and Clarisse. It was, to her, as if they had always been together, had grown up together, as if they were her own.

Maive longed to remain in their lives, be a part of their futures, but her time for this world was fading. She'd known that for a while.

A wispy smile touched her lips. She would tell them where they could find what they needed before they left. They could always return. Dee would welcome them as she had.

"We have to go, Maive. We'll be back, though." Nathan hugged the woman's neck. Rebecca was next, cautiously stepping up to Maive, fear of never seeing her again switching on her withdrawal. Maive knew this would be her final contact with them before she moved on to be with her own family.

When the teens showed up in her backyard, she was already having indicators of the final signs of her life. Their brief stay and the new boarders they brought to her made those problems insignificant and important at the same time.

"You can let go, Maive! You act like you won't ever see us again!" Cai laughed, placing her hands on Maive's shoulders and pushing back from her embrace.

No laughter escaped the elder's lips, though, only tears from her rheumy eyes as she held out her hands to the tallest boy's shoulders and pulled him into a tight hug. Jaz leaned into her without resistance, surprised by her need for such an embrace.

"Whew! You kids better get on, now! I don't have the energy for another round of huggin'!" Maive smoothed her cheeks with the backs of her hands wiping away final tears.

"We'll be okay, Maive." Cheater squeezed the old woman's hand one more time, concern filling her eyes.

"Okay, okay. You'd better be. You go find the others and you take care of that monster real good! Then you come back here and tell old Maive the end of the story!" She shooed them out with the wave of a hand.

Her pretend need for them to tell her what would happen vanished with a gulp. She already knew the end, and the thought of it gave her a heavy heart. At least she had this little time to get to know half of them, The Gifted Ones.

She wished for time to meet the other half. What a team this group of teens would make if the others were anything like these! "Dave, you take care of them. Make sure they get to their destination."

A slight nod of Dave's head and five of the six piled into the back of the old Dodge truck, hidden by a dented camper top. Nathan, as the navigator, climbed into the front seat next to Polly.

"They'll be alright, right Miss Maive?" Dee asked through her faux smile as she waved. Five heads peeked out the side window and waved in return, then disappeared as the truck started its motion down the driveway.

"Momma, anybody who can do what they do will be alright, but I'm sure gonna miss them. Now it's just me and Clarisse, again." Stevie looked down at his little sister who stuffed an index finger in her mouth and watched the truck disappear down the street.

"They'll be what they were born to be," Maive nodded.

"Well, I've got some cleaning up to do," Dee turned toward the front door. "Come on, children! You can help. Comin', Miss Maive?"

"In a bit." Though she couldn't see them anymore, her eyes followed the truck up the street until she could no longer hear the motor. When the door closed behind her, she turned, felt for her old rocking chair on the front porch, sat down and rocked her thoughts to calm. She'd done her part. She'd lived her purpose. In a short a while, it would be time. She needed to finalize things.

"You alright, Miss Maive?" Stevie returned.

"Yessir. You do me a favor and bring me that phone off the counter. I need to make a call."

"Yes'um!" Maive listened to the lively steps of the little boy as he raced through the house. A smile touched her lips just before she snapped her finger. Her heavy heart stole away the opportunity to tell the teens where to find the one thing they desperately needed, "Dang this old mind of mine!"

"Here ya' go Miss Maive!" Stevie returned with the phone.

"Thank you, young man. Now, can you write?"

"Yes'um, real good, too! Momma taught me,!" A proud smile lit his face.

"Good. Go get you some paper out of that old writing desk in the living room and a pen from the drawer above the paper. Then get an envelope from the shelf. I need you to write something down for me to give to those kids if they come back here."

"Yes'um!" He doubled back through the door and searched the desk while Maive made a call to her longtime friend's grandson, who had become her lawyer.

Stevie returned just as Maive finished her call. "Ready, Miss Maive!" He perched on the edge of the swing, envelope tucked between pages of a book, book in lap, paper on book, pen in hand.

Maive spoke slowly, sometimes spelling out words for the young boy. Stevie stopped twice, mouth hung open, eyes turned upward to Maive, and asked, "Are you sure, Miss Maive?"

"My mind is about me, son. Yes, I am sure." When she finished, she made Stevie read it back to her. "Good, now fold it up and seal it in that envelope. And don't you say a word to anyone else about this, ya' hear? Not even your dear, sweet momma in there."

"Yes'um. What if they don't come back to get the letter?" Stevie asked.

"Burn it."

"Burn it?"

"That's what I said."

Stevie solemnly turned to the envelope between his fingers, disappointed at the possibility of his hard work going up in flames."Okay, Miss Maive."

"It's very important that nobody else know about that letter, except you, me and those kids. Now, go hide it in a nice safe place in the cellar."

"Yes'um!" Stevie hung his head; his feet dragged across the front porch toward the front door.

Maive caught his arm as he passed her, "Young man, something else."

"Yes'um?" His sadness kept him from turning to her.

"Gonna be a friend of mine comin' by shortly with some papers for me and your momma to sign. Them papers will leave your momma and you this house and all I have. You take care of this place, your momma and that sister of yours, ya' hear?"

Stevie's face brightened as he looked up at Maive. "Our own place? Yes ma'am, Miss Maive!" He hugged Maive's neck before running into the house, screen door swinging closed behind him.

The old truck bounced over a dip in the road throwing the five teens upward. "Ouch!" Jaz rubbed the top of his head. The camper sat low enough that, with the crate he sat on, the slightest bounce was enough to close the three-inch gap between his head and the roof.

"Anybody else suspicious or is it just me?" Cheater frowned.

"Suspicious of what? You know what he's thinking." Jaz glanced over at her.

"I know, but it all seems too… I don't know."

"Rehearsed?" Cai finished. "Easy?"

"I think it's just that old man pulling one over on you. It'll be alright. Believe me, if he didn't do what Maive told him to do, I wouldn't want to be around when she found out!" Nathan added.

"Did Maive seem a little off to you guys? You know, more than just sad?" Rebecca sat facing the back window, hands in her lap, knees together.

"Yeah, I'm worried about her. What do you think is wrong?" Nathan asked.

"She's just worried about us, Nathan. After this is over, we need to come back and see her," Cai suggested.

"I'm just glad nothing happened to her while we were there." Cheater's fears relaxed. Was it the six of them being together that stopped Death from following her, or was Death just waiting for the twelve of them to find each other before taking them all? Were they that close to the end?

"That's not it," Cai intervened in Cheater's silent questioning. "Death has done the job of setting us on our mission. Think about it; if our families were still with us, we would not have come together to fulfill the mission our mothers set us on with the story. Now that we are focused on our mission, there's no need for others to die. Nobody stands in the way. Death has been a tool to guide us, to get us where we need to be, to bring us to this point in time. It's shaped us into who we are, who we need to be to follow through with the plan, the lives we were born to live." She paused, looking at each solemn face surrounding her. They seemed so much younger than she.

"We're not babies," Thad frowned.

"No, not anymore. Death is no longer our follower, either. We've lost all and survived. Death is our helper, our guide. Death fights with us now, not against us. It's time to stop worrying about ourselves and those near us, and time to believe in what we are capable of doing.

"Soon we will follow our helper Death into battle. We must let go of the past, and see the future. See what we can do for Maive, for Polly, for Dave, for Stevie and Clarisse. We are warriors and Death is on our side. Death has always been on our side." Cai inhaled deeply, exhaled slowly. "We must stay focused and prepare to embrace Death, the help it can give us."

Thad glanced at the back of Nathan's head. "Nathan?"

"Nathan already knows. He's been ready for some time. He's not worried about what has happened, or those near him. He's focused on the future." She smiled encouragingly at Thad.

"Oh," his eyes fell from her gaze to the hands in his lap. The stares of the others closed in on him. He could feel the looks before he even raised his head. He knew what they would say:

"You can do it, Thad!"

"We'll help you!"

"Just let go, Thad!"

"We trust you!"

But should they? Should they trust him? He didn't even trust his own actions. If it hadn't been for Cai finding him, stopping him from going back, would he have gone back? Would he be on the other side? One of them?

When Thad's eyes moved upward, his expression said it all... exactly what he expected.

None had read his thoughts.

None knew he didn't trust himself.

Why hadn't their faces changed?

Why didn't they speak to him through their minds?

Turning toward the back of Nathan's head, he caught Dave's over the shoulder glance, the smile of knowing in the rearview mirror, and the sly wink.

Thad's eyes widened again and he returned his

hands to his lap.

The truck bounced to a stop in front of the football field.

"Are you sure you want me to leave you here?" Dave eyed the old field house, the bleachers and the faded markings of the field.

"Uh... yeah, this is it!" Thad nodded a little too anxiously.

"Calm down, Thad! They're friends," Cai patted his shoulder.

The nervous tone in Thad's voice wasn't lost on Cheater. She recognized it immediately. She'd been in too many homes to not see it, but why didn't the others pick up on it?

Why wasn't she able to hear what Thad was thinking?

Jaz glanced at Cheater, followed by Cai and Nathan, but not Thad.

Cheater knew it was important for her to act normal and the others followed her lead as they waved at Dave and Polly.

With the truck out of sight, Cai turned toward Thad. All eyes followed her movements, but she only stated, "Okay, now that they're gone, we can head out. We should walk by twos so we don't draw attention to ourselves. Thad, you come with me."

"Well... why don't we just wait until dark, like before? We probably shouldn't separate, right?"

Nathan moved around to face Thad, drawing his lower lip between his teeth. He crossed his arms, his hands resting in the crook of his elbows. "I don't know," he contested. "We all know where we're going. We all know how to stay hidden. I think I should take Thad, though. After all, what would draw more attention, a boy and girl walking together, or two boys?"

"Actually, I'm afraid I would draw more attention." Rebecca turned away.

"See, Rebecca's right. So we should stay together and wait until d..." Thad swallowed the last of his shaky words.

"What's going on with you, Thad? You're not acting right," Cai cocked her head and frowned into his face.

"Not at all," Nathan scowled.

"Nothing, I just... I'm scared... about what's gonna happen," Thad's Adam's apple bounced before he checked out the toes of his shoes.

"My guess is, we better get outta here. Fast. I recognize the look of a traitor," Jaz nodded toward the youngest of them.

"I'm not a traitor!" Thad yelled, eyes flashing at the taller boy.

"Then how did you block your thoughts from us in the truck?" Cheater tilted her head, placed fisted hands on hips and moved closer.

"How do you know I did? I didn't even know I

did. Maybe I wasn't thinking anything."

"Sure, that's why Dave looked at you and smiled."

"What were you thinking, Thad? What's going on with you? Are you on the other side?" Cai's voice dropped to a whisper of disbelief. How could he? She took him in when he was alone and running from his father.

Her disappointed features guilted him, "I just... I don't know if you should trust me. I... I keep having doubts... I... want to go home, go back, the way it used to be!" His brown eyes filled with tears.

Cai placed sisterly hands on his shoulders and pulled him into a hug. "You're not going back. You can't. There's nothing left for you there, remember?"

"That's all you were thinking?" Cheater's skepticism rang through her words.

Thad pushed out of Cai's embrace and eyed his equal. "Yes, it is!"

"Then, how did you block it? Why?"

"I don't know."

"It doesn't matter. If he can, we can. If there's a chance they can read our thoughts, they won't even know we're coming."

"That puts us on equal terms!" Jaz's excitement flowed through the group.

"Only if we transfer the power when Thad does it," Nathan reminded. "How did you do it?"

"I don't know! I didn't know I could until we were in the back of the truck."

"We have so much to learn before we're ready

for battle. We need a safe place to reevaluate our plan," Cai searched Thad's face.

"The farm is safe, especially once we take it over. It's like five hundred acres, or something like that."

"Yes, Nathan, but they are on the farm; they know about it. I don't know if your farm is safe for us... not yet anyway." Cai's features expressed her deep level of thought.

"But, we have to take it over. The others will come there, I know!" Nathan pushed.

"How do we know for sure, Nathan?"

Quiet filled the air around the teens. A long moment passed before Nathan said, "The place in our dream, with the ring of fire, and the faceless man... It's on the farm. I've seen it. I've been there." It was Nathan's turn to feel shame in not sharing everything he knew with the Gifted Ones, his friends.

"Well, that does complicate matters," Cai nodded. "Then we need to find a place where we can plan, wait for the others. Standing out here on the side of the road is drawing attention."

Five sets of eyes followed Cai's as an approaching car slowed behind them. An elderly couple stared hard through the window.

"We need to get out of here," Jaz moved across the street alone after the car passed.

"It's not that far before we get out of town. We can keep in touch through thoughts." Cheater reminded, following him.

"True," Nathan took Rebecca's hand and

crossed the street, turning right toward the next block.

"Let's go, kid," Cai indicated the other side of the street with her head.

As Thad stepped onto the curb, a sheriff's car rounded the corner from the highway. All six teens still in view, he flashed his lights and bleeped his siren.

"Run!" Cai ordered.

41

The urge to abandon the cocoon of green leaves and branches that now hid Thad from the law enforcement officer quietly approaching was so strong Thad had to squeeze his eyes closed to maintain his blend. Although the officer couldn't see him now, he had seen him run this direction, heard his footsteps stop, and most likely could hear his breathing right now.

Sometimes, surrendering seemed the best choice, so much easier than this constant running, hiding, delving into dark places to avoid capture. Could the changes coming be so bad? Could it be so bad living that way, just letting go and being a kid again? Maybe he should go home to his dad, to his dad's family far away.

Maybe if he did, he would be safe. He could go back to school. He always loved school, especially science. Surely, the events taking place in this land would not affect his father's homeland.

Thad lifted his lids when the sound of the footsteps stopped. A scream caught in his throat!

The shiny, black boots rested right in front of his eyes.

"I know you came this way, kid. I know you're here somewhere. I don't know what game you're playing, but I'll find you... and your friends." The voice traveled upwards, a tall oak tree stretching its branches overhead. "You know, you could just come to the farm. Your dad will be there, waiting for you. You could just go home with him, and it will all be over for you. It has to be difficult, a kid your age on the run all the time. Wouldn't you like a good meal, now? Come on out to the farm. We'll fix you a feast, a send off for you and your dad."

Had he read Thad's thoughts? He'd figured out that he could block his thoughts from the others, but how? Had this officer heard what he was thinking?

"Give up your friends to us, and you'll be in high rank with him. We need your help, kid. Come on out. I'll make sure you're taken care of."

He'd had plenty of hot meals lately, but a home, a family, beckoned to Thad.

His eyes opened.

The guard chipped away within the shrubbery.

He almost let go of his blend and showed himself.

Then he thought of Cai. Cai had been his best friend, his big sister, his savior, when he first ran away. She rescued him from the world he now knew, from the bullies crowding him that day before the wind came, from the hunger that found him crying in an alleyway.

Cai magically took the place of his mother, providing more concern for his well-being than for her own, more concern than his father had ever offered him.

Could he do that to Cai? Just give up?

She trusted him. Even though he gave her every reason to doubt him, she showed him trust.

She believed in him.

Fear-filled eyes glimpsed the khaki clad legs, again, and his lids pinched together into tight darkness.

Just blend and ignore, he told himself.

Cai let go of Thad's hand in an effort to make the sheriff choose a direction.

She'd hoped he would follow her, but he hadn't.

From her blended spot among the trees, she could hear the officer's whispers, tempting Thad. Trying to focus on Thad's own thoughts, she hoped to acquire nothing but a block, that he kept his thoughts private as he had in the truck.

Rebecca had shared the information about her father being a sheriff, and Cai wondered now if this officer was Rebecca's estranged father. Who was he that he knew about Thad's father? How did he know so much about Thad's needs?

Her jaw clenched with the thought it might be Rebecca's father.

First, he'd been so cruel to such a wonderful girl like Rebecca, and now... now he stood there tempting Thad.

Anger built within her.

She wanted to jump on his creepy back and tighten her arm around his neck.

Visions of rubbing his face in the dirt increased her anger.

Cai considered the possibility that Thad wasn't blocking his thoughts from everyone, but instead communicated with the sheriff now.

If he were, she'd rip his little head off his shoulders like an annoying grasshopper in a blooming garden!

She wondered if it was safe to contact Thad.

Would it be safe to speak silently to the others?

Could the sheriff, obviously part of the other side, hear them when they telepathically talked?

Cai trembled while the tumultuous questions tumbled through her mind. What would happen if all of them were apprehended by the other side? What would those people, those followers, due to the Gifted Ones? *Could they catch all of us?* She wondered.

Were they already holding the other six somewhere else on the farm?

Cai wanted so badly to encourage Thad to stick to the blend. She wanted to protect him, but if he was...

Taking a deep breath, she let herself dare.

Rebecca squeezed Nathan's hand tighter. They'd run east of Thad and Cai, but somehow she felt the fear now filling their bodies, knew her father closed in on at least one of them.

How had he found me? She thought.

Fear gripped her heart, memories of his cruel words filling the back of her eyelids. She resisted the urge to run.

He'd been the first to notice her difference, and he had never acknowledged her talent. He could have helped her, helped her become what her heart led her to become. He could have sent her to that Art School for Children with Special Needs.

The memory of his abuses, his careless destruction of the beautiful images she'd drawn him for his early visits, fueled her anger now. He'd shredded the very likeness of her hugging his neck as he gently kissed her three-year-old cheek.

He'd shredded her life that day.

He'd shown her what he could do, would do, if anyone ever spoke of her being his daughter.

He'd destroyed the image and any possibility of love for him.

She was three years old, and drew miraculous images almost as well as she did now.

She was three years old, living with her grandmother because he had taken her mom's life for trying to tell everyone about her.

She was three years old when she had to learn to curb her hatred.

She was three years old when she lost everything, yet gained even more.

She wanted to communicate that to Thad and Cai right now, but her fear of him choked her desire, though she knew he couldn't hear them.

Nathan slipped his strong arm around her shoulder, squeezing ever so slightly.

Now he knew.

Her anger spread like fire through him.

His teeth clenched.

Now he knew what he would do to this man if ever he had the chance.

But right now, he needed calm.

A deep breath forced his lungs against his rib cage.

Jaz pinched his lips together in frustration. He'd take abuse from the Beast, just to survive. He didn't have to take it anymore.

The Beast was gone, but tugging at Nathan's insecurities was another like him.

The heat of rage flowed up his neck, burned his cheeks, and tightened his grip on Cheater's delicate hand.

They'd managed to stay together when they reached the woods. Turning west to create indecision for the officer, Cheater had kept up with the long stride of Jaz who pulled her along, their hands firmly clasped.

Fury built within Jaz, and he struggled to remain crouched against the fallen tree, his features a blend with its rough bark.

Old feelings of inadequacy fired his emotions as Rebecca remembered the destruction of her childhood masterpiece.

Every limb shivered with the desire to release Cheater's hand and fly head first into the belly of the officer who tormented Thad now with his words.

The man had known exactly which of the six to pick on, to follow, to lead on with temptations of a normal life.

Cheater's tightened her grip on Jaz's hand when he rose, forcing him to remain in place.

She'd thought her life was so bad, losing all of those she loved, who loved her, but now she considered the severities of the lives the others had lived.

Wouldn't it be worse to have a parent who didn't care than to have none at all?

Her arm muscles tensed when Jaz attempted to release her grip again and show himself.

Certain he would return to himself while on the run, she couldn't allow him to give himself over to anger. They had to maintain control.

There had to be a way to help Thad. He was the weakest of the six, that was clear to her, but he could block their thoughts, block his own thoughts from them. It seemed Dave had known what Thad thought in the truck. If he knew, would this man know, too?

She couldn't trust their communications now. This officer of the law was obviously one of the many minions Jag's mom had spoken of in the hospital, which meant he might be able to block his true plans from the Gifted Ones, as the imposter at the farm had done.

No, they couldn't help Thad.

If he gave in, though, it would be his end.

Whatever he decided, Cheater could not let Jaz give himself up by following through with the immediate plan his body indicated.

Thad quivered, thankful for the slight autumn breeze twirling the leaves of the bush where he now blended, a hushed sound rustling through his eardrums. He focused on the whistling sound, avoiding the tempting offer of the sheriff whose words moved away from the young man.

Every muscle in Thad's body clenched with fear and indecision. Did the others know of his traitorous thoughts?

Cai tuned in on Jaz's thoughts of attack. They made sense to her. They had to do something to protect Thad. Though she couldn't pick up on what Thad was thinking, she had been with him long enough to know that he felt confused, indecisive. Slowly she straightened from her crouch.

Nathan rose to his feet after a brief pat on Rebecca's shoulder. He couldn't let Thad suffer with the verbal temptation that man offered. He had to act. He sensed Cai's need to defend the younger boy.

Nathan was ready.

He would be by Cai's side until the end, for Thad, for Rebecca, for the newest ones, Cheater and Jaz, and for the ones unmet.

Nathan would do what was needed.

Death did not frighten him.

"It could be a trap!" Cheater ventured a

thought, reaching through space toward the others.

"She's right! Don't do it! What if my father's not alone?" A silent tear streaked the side of Rebecca's nose.

"I know you're here. I can feel you, boy. I know the others are here, too." He turned his body to the west, then to the east, straining to hear the thoughts passing between them.

Thad watched as the officer spun, afraid Cheater and Rebecca had given up their location.

Thad had heard them clearly.

Maybe it was a trap.

Maybe there were others waiting.

Unaware of the plan being formed around him, he forced his mind to block his thoughts from the others so he could speak only to the man standing a few feet away from him. He had to do something to draw the attention back to himself.

He had to protect Rebecca, Cheater.

The world swam in grief before Rebecca's eyes.

She feared the man who tried to lure Thad from hiding.

She knew her friends were planning to protect Thad, protect her, protect each other.

She had to do her part to remove this threat from their mission. After all, it was her threat, her problem, her father.

Another tear escaped her eye as she glimpsed from its corner the man moving in her direction. The gun at his side glinted ominously in the speckling sunshine.

He could shoot her, get his wish.

She couldn't let the rest of them take the chance they were taking to protect her from her father.

It was her fight.

She stood, uncoiling her fingers from Nathan's.

They'd come too far to separate now. Cheater wasn't about to let Jaz take on Rebecca's father alone.

Although she knew from looking at the officer that her power was useless—there was nothing left for him to believe in except the power that he had over others—she hoped she could remain blended until just before she ran her full force into the larger man, helping Jaz take him to the ground.

Rebecca let go of the blend.

Her figure wavered, flickered, returned until she stood full to the right of her father as he turned.

"I'm the one you're looking for... father."

The tilt of her head just allowed her to glimpse the officer's face as the features contorted insanely.

He spun toward her, lunging, drawing his gun from its harness. "I am not your father, you little twit!"

Sunlight bounced off the shining weapon as he wielded it at her, his lips snarling like a rabid dog.

A breeze touched her face, but all she saw was the gun barrel growing closer, the dark hole getting bigger, as he approached, and then...

He toppled, the gun leaving his hand and flying straight upward as though hit by an invisible hand; miraculously the bullet remained in the chamber as the gun stopped midair.

"What the..." He started as his body thudded upon the ground, face in the dirt. He lay in full view of Rebecca's downturned eyes.

The gun floated, remaining stably pointed toward his head, moving closer, until Jaz appeared behind it.

"You think you'll get away with it, go ahead!" The man laughed as he rolled to his back. "So, you're one of them? Let me guess; you can blend. We know all about you. Only thing is, we thought the blender was a girl. He won't be happy about that intel." He huffed again, cutting his eyes toward Jaz.

"Don't move! Who's we?" Jaz prodded, jabbing the gun at him.

"You don't know? Now that's interesting. So, let's see, you hooked up with this stupid kid here. She's one of you, too. I already knew that. She's not as dumb as she looks. They told me. I wanted to kill her when I did away with her grandmother. Killing one of you is as good as killing all of you. You won't be able to function without one. That's what *he* says. But for some reason, he doesn't want us to do anything to you, except catch you, bring you together.

"That's why I had to let her go runnin' out the back door. I thought she had left with that other boy, though. Interesting. She's just like her mother, runnin' with every Tom, Dick, and Harry." His head created a crinkling sound as it bounced into the dry leaves beneath it and up again as he turned his smirk toward Rebecca and back.

"Who's *he*?" Jaz demanded.

"You don't even know who you're up against. Do you know where the others are? Where's the one that escaped with you? The other girl?"

"I asked first. Who's he?"

"Boy, you are in for the biggest surprise of your life. You and your friends would be better off to just give up now."

"That will never happen!" Cai glared at the man

on the ground, fists clenched at her sides. “We need to make him talk. Shoot him in the leg!” She ordered.

The gun shook slightly as Jaz turned to look at her. “Uh, yeah. Okay.”

“Give it to me! I’ll gladly do it!” Nathan appeared next to Jaz, taking the gun from his hand and firing a bullet into the ground right between the man’s knees.

“Shit! Stop, kid!” The man scooted back on his elbows, face red with shame at being bested by teenagers.

Nathan fired again.

42

"Thanks, kid. You'll have every person in the neighborhood calling the law about gunshots."

"Nathan!" Cai turned on him.

"We gotta get outta here. Fast!" Jaz began pacing.

"Calm down. That's not going to happen. It's deer season." Nathan produced an ear-to-ear grin, never taking his eyes off the sheriff.

"You attempted to murder an officer of the law, boy. You'll be in jail for the rest of your life." The man rose from the ground, straightening his knocking knees.

"Nope." He didn't scare Nathan. A sense more powerful than fear had filled him.

"Here!" Thad produced a backpack drawstring from Cai's bag, thrusting it at Cai.

"I got it!" Jaz pulled the string free of Thad's grasp. "Put your hands behind your back!" He ordered.

"Seriously?" The man laughed. "I will take you down so fast!"

Nathan fired another shot between his feet then moved the pistol upward. "My grandpa taught me how to shoot accurately. You're one of *them.* Maybe he won't be able to function without you. We'll take that chance."

"Okay, okay!" The man crossed his wrists behind him, Jaz tied the string, wrapping it several times in a figure eight and finishing it off with a tight knot that would have to be cut out.

"Make sure it's good and tight." Thad thrust his head at Jaz, adrenaline coursing through his veins.

"I know how to tie a knot. I spent a couple of years in the scouts before my dad..." Jaz cut his answer short.

"What are we gonna do with him?" Cheater moved closer, Rebecca stepped around to view his face.

"Take him with us. There's a perfect spot for him on the farm," Nathan added.

"Are you kidding? He'll create nothing but problems for us on the way there," Cai shook her head.

Rebecca moved closer to the man who had fathered her.

"We could leave him here if we had something to tie his feet. The coyotes would take care of him." Nathan watched Rebecca move into his line of sight. "He could run off if we don't tie his feet."

"That would slow him down," Jaz suggested.

"I'll slow him down!" Rebecca moved closer, lifted her foot, and then forced it down, planting her right shoe onto the sheriff's left shin. Unable to pull his shin into his hands and rub at the pain, he hopped up to get away, balancing on one leg. Rebecca kicked the other shin, bringing him to the ground.

Nathan choked on a laugh.

Cheater pulled Rebecca away from the jumping feet, and the others laughed aloud, jeering Rebecca on.

"Get up!" Nathan ordered.

"I can't. Jeez! She kicked me!" The man rolled on the ground.

"I could just shoot him," Nathan shrugged.

"You couldn't!" Cheater frowned.

"I will if he doesn't get up."

"I think we can use him for leverage somehow. Or, maybe he knows where the other kid is, the one in our dream? Let's take him to the farm," Cai pursed her lips.

"Get... up!" Nathan cocked his head at the man who still rolled pain that he could comfort. "Well, that's definitely gonna slow him down... us too." He nodded as the man limped and hobbled in front of them.

"Wait! What about the car?" Jaz stopped.

"Right. Better go check on that. Hurry up!" Cai glanced over her shoulder as Thad and Jaz sprinted back in the direction of the road. "We'll catch up!" Jaz yelled over his shoulder.

"Alright, Mr. Lawman, lead on," Nathan swung his leg, pretending to boot the injured man in the seat of his pants, bringing a giggle from the usually silent Rebecca.

Feeling their shocked stares, she thought, *"Well, it was funny."*

Realizing the importance of the situation, and the need to break the shocked silence, Cai laughed again, a deep, contagious, belly laugh that fell like dominoes to each of the others until they were all chuckling. The limping sheriff brought more laughter as they watched him. When Jaz and Thad caught up with them, they sent a strange glance toward each other.

Cheater tried to fill them in, but every time she began, fits of giggles took over.

Cai tried, too, without success.

Soon, all six of them laughed, unspent adrenaline leaking from the corners of their eyes, though not all of them understood the relief.

"So, what about the car?" Cai wiped her cheekbones with her sleeves.

"Let's just say, it won't be discovered for a while."

"Yeah, probably a really long while," Thad added.

"Are you sure?" Cheater questioned.

"Oh, yeah. Remember that tank we passed on the run?" Jaz smiled.

"No! You didn't!" Cheater stopped, staring at Jaz.

"We shouldn't have?" Jaz froze. "We had to hide it."

"You sunk my car?" The limping man whirled around, jaw hanging, knees bent to adjust for pain.

"Uh, oh!" Thad mouthed.

"Did you check it out first, like, I mean, the

trunk?" Cai prodded.

"Uhm... no? Do you think there might have been something in it we could use?"

"Yeah, there was something in it, all right! You idiot kids. You just got me killed. You might as well shoot me now!' The man leaned into a nearby tree, his head shaking.

"What was in the trunk?" Nathan jabbed the pistol toward him.

"Go ahead, shoot. It doesn't matter what was in the trunk. It's gone now. You kids would be best to just take me out. I'm tellin' ya'. You can't take him down without that other..." His head shook, eyes cast to the ground.

Dawning twisted Cai's face as she figured it out. "Go back! Fast! The best swimmers. What did you do with the keys? Tell me you didn't throw them in the water."

"No, I thought we might need them... handcuffs?" Jaz produced the keys and cuffs he found on the seat.

Thad caught onto her impatient requests, grabbed the keys and sprinted back to the pond where the car had begun its descent into the water. Cheater followed, flashes of swimming lessons playing in her mind. Jaz bounced in indecision a few times before tearing off after them.

The water was cold, but fortunately, though hidden, the tan sedan had not coasted too deeply below the surface. The three stood staring at the top of the trunk lift, just a few inches below the water.

Puddled footprints pressed into the black dirt of the bank, grew farther apart in the browning grass, and disappeared into the fallen leaves leading toward the woods.

"I wonder who it was?" Cheater bit her lower lip, staring in the direction of the invisible prints.

"I don't know," Thad pinched the keys between thumb and forefinger, "but I'm glad they got out. The way Cai acted, he... she must be one of us."

"If that's a girl, she's humongous!" Jaz set his foot next to the fullest, clear print on the bank and it overhung his all the way around, twice as long as it was wide. "Sure hope that person isn't mad!"

"We better get back. At least whoever it was got out." Cheater turned away from the prints.

"Well?" Cai's brows rose in expectation.

Jaz shrugged, "Whoever was in the trunk is gone now."

"Gone?" The sheriff's head jerked upward, eyes wide.

Nathan returned his attention to the man

leaning against the tree. "Who was in the trunk?" The pistol in his hand jerked, punctuating the question.

Shifty eyes moved from one to the other, then looked away in fear. "One of you!" He winced in expectation.

"Another one of us? They're already coming, just like us. They're already searching for the rest of us!" Rebecca couldn't contain her excitement.

"He'll find us, too," Cai nodded.

"Don't be so sure. This one is..." The sheriff glanced over his shoulder.

"What? What is *'this one'*?" Cai prodded.

The sheriff's head turned toward the group, "Well, different. I wouldn't trust the person that was in that trunk if I were you. You better be really careful around that one."

"Why?" Nathan pushed, fear cracking his angry voice.

"Don't let him get to you. He's just trying to scare us. He wants us to suspect any of the others we encounter. That's how he is, always bringing fear and suspicion!" Rebecca moved into Nathan's view, drawing his vision from the man.

"Rebecca's right. Don't listen to him, Nathan." Jaz could tell by the man's voice that he was playing them against each other.

"Fine! Don't believe me! I don't care. You'll see for yourself. Just remember where you didn't find that one!" The sheriff's shoulders rose and fell.

"Well, he's right about that. He or she wasn't in the trunk, like we thought. And the trunk was open.

How could that happen?" Cheater searched their eyes for an answer.

"One of us, right? There's no telling what power's the others have."

"That's true, could have some serious kind of power, or..." Cai paused. "The trunk has a latch?"

"You wouldn't believe the power if I told you! And I'm not gonna tell you." The sheriff jerked his head from side to side. "I just hope someone can control that one."

Six pairs of eyes slid from one to another passing a deeply curious look of concern.

"What're we gonna do with this guy when we get to my farm?" Nathan whispered to Cai, leaves crackling beneath his feet, the sound just loud enough to cover his question from the stumbling man before him.

"Maybe we'll hook him up with a room at Chez Jaz and Cheater?" She rolled her eyes toward Jaz.

"I don't think so. That's where all the food is hidden!" He answered playfully. "That is, if it's not tainted by the smell of death by now."

"You don't think that guy is still down in the cellar?" Cheater turned her head.

"My grandma canned some good peaches, didn't she?" Nathan's mouth watered at the thought of his grandmother's cooking.

"I hope he's not still down there. I hope they got him out." Thad couldn't stand the thought of all that food going to waste.

The view of the back acreage of the farm filtered between the trees, and the teens stopped. Nathan ordered the sheriff to sit down. "Okay, we can't just walk up to the house. We need a plan." The five huddled behind Nathan so he could hear.

"We have a hostage." Jaz pointed to the man struggling to free his hands from the binding.

"He won't do any good. They don't care about each other like we do." Cai pushed her lower lip out in thought.

"We can't be sure of that. I mean, the old guy was the only one living there when he brought us here. This guy's just another dirty cop like the imposter's cousin. What about all of those cars that were here yesterday?

"And the fact that the farm seems to hold the truth about the end of the fairytale," Cheater added.

"Yeah, this is where it's going down, the fire, the faceless guy. I don't know exactly where, but that dream takes place here. I felt like I was losing my home, again," Nathan whispered over his shoulder.

"Well, we should check out the house. And somebody needs to stay here with a gun on this guy."

"I would be more than happy to take care of that," Rebecca held her hand out.

"No! No, you can't give that gun to her! She'll shoot me!" the sheriff pressed his back into the scratchy bark of the oak tree behind him.

Nathan glanced at Rebecca's emotionless face. "Would you? Could you?" He thought he saw a wisp of a smile as she rolled her head toward the man to her right.

"I don't like the idea of splitting up. Maybe we should just throw him down in the cellar, anyway?" Jaz offered.

"We have his cuffs. Too bad we don't have something to tie him to a tree or at least tie his feet and hands together."

Nathan turned, pressed the gun into Cai's hands and sprinted toward the barn. The others cringed as he entered the clearing. Faces turned toward his shrinking back.

The crunch of leaves, a low rumble behind them and the whispered word, "No," of the sheriff turned their attention back to the man by the tree.

43

"Splash!" Rebecca moved toward the dogs surrounding the sheriff.

Cai's breath escaped in a whoosh, and she steadied the gun on the man before her.

Jaz returned his attention to the barn, where Nathan had disappeared, then reappeared with rope in hand. "Sweet!" He nodded, just before a loud shot sounded, pushing up dirt between Nathan's striding feet. "Oh, crap! Nathan's in trouble. Come on, man!" He yelled before another piercing boom rang out.

Nathan's stride grew longer, quicker, and twenty feet from safety a shot, a stumble, then silence as the teen lay on the ground just out of reach.

"No!" Rebecca moved toward the clearing, but Cheater reached for her arm, pulled her back.

"We gotta go get him!" Cai's harsh whisper filled their minds.

"I'll do it," Jaz volunteered. "I've been dodging bullets for the past couple of years!"

Cai moved forward. "I'll fire some shots toward the house. Maybe that will keep them from firing again so soon."

Searching the immobile Nathan, Jaz watched as the bloodstain on the leg of his jeans seemed to grow right before his eyes. He shook away the blur, before preparing himself to run.

"No! Don't do it! Stay there. Don't fire a shot. Save the bullets."

"Nathan?" Rebecca replied.

"Yes. I'll be fine." Don't come after me.

The bloodstain told a different story.

"Ha! There you are! He's going to die now and you won't stand a chance against ..."

A low growl followed by a snap cut off the cruel words.

Nathan pulled himself toward them, sliding on his stomach, the dry grass poking through his shirt, scratching his stomach with each inch of movement. He hoped the shooter didn't notice from that distance, hadn't seen him bend his arms. If the shooter was as old as the imposter, his eyes couldn't be that good. The only problem was that with each inch he pulled himself closer, the more his consciousness waned.

"We have to do something!" Rebecca tried to free her arm from Cheater's grasp.

"Wait, someone's coming!" Cheater told her.

"So, tryin' to sneak back onto the farm, are ya' kid? Where's those other two, the two you let loose?"

Footsteps grew closer, but Nathan lay still on the ground, the hand he pulled with stretched out over the ground above his head.

"Ah, I know you can't be dead, kid. It's only a leg shot. Git up!" The poke of the rifle in Nathan's side made it difficult for him to lie still.

Cai glanced at the sheriff, who had a low snarling Splash half an inch from his nose. The look on the sheriff's face told her he wasn't about to breathe, let alone speak. She glanced at Jaz, but he wasn't there. Neither were the others. Smiling to herself, she blended and watched as one of the border collies, Nathan's own dog, ripped through the trees, around the teens, and blasted his body into the back legs of the older man at Nathan's side. As he fell back cursing, another round erupted from the rifle, its whistle trailing upward into the white clouds. The dog turned back into the wooded area, giving Nathan just enough time to blend.

The large man gained his balance and turned back to Nathan, "Damn dogs! I'd shoot 'em if I could keep aim on them! Now, let's finish you... what... where..." The bearded face searched the clearing near the barn, a few drops of blood leading to nothing. His eyes turned to the wooded area. He pointed the rifle into the trees and moved slowly toward Rebecca.

As he left the clearing, he noticed the khaki clad legs stretched out on the ground. He glanced left, right. Those damn kids had to be somewhere. Another step revealed the sheriff back pressed against a tree trunk, afraid to move for losing his nose.

"I bin lookin' for you, too, dog!" The old man growled, raising the rifle.

The sheriff's eyes grew wide with surprise as they took in the imposter

Splash saw the man, the gun, from the corner

of his eye and whirled, just as Jaz unblended, moving quickly to stiff-arm the old man in the back. Stumbling forward, the barrel of the gun fell away as the other border collie ran into the unbalanced feet, tripping the imposter, sending him face first into the dry leaves and dirt.

"Don't move! Hand cuffs!" A shaky voice above the old man's head ordered as the bearded face, bits of leaves stuck in the disorderly hairs, rolled onto his back, hands beneath him, and looked into the barrel of the rifle.

Cai held the pistol on the sheriff, the three dogs standing guard.

"Nathan!" Rebecca cried running toward him.

"No!" Cheater screamed.

But Rebecca, already kneeling by her wounded friend, hadn't thought about others on the property.

Another shot rang out from the direction of the house.

The teens watched in horror as Rebecca fell to her knees. Her delicate hands gripped the motionless Nathan and rolled him to his back, seeking the hole in his leg.

As though a bubble protected them from one bullet after another, Rebecca worked quickly without fear. She tied the rope as tightly as her hands would allow, just above the growing patch of dark red to stop the flow.

She stood, bending forward to grip Nathan's armpits, and tugged, but could barely budge the dead weight at her fingertips.

"I'm coming!" Jaz rushed out of the safety of the trees, replaced Rebecca's tiny hands with his own, and began to pull Nathan to safety as the shots whizzed past them.

Once again hidden in the safety of the thicket, Cai dropped to her knee and planted the pistol's barrel at the base of his skull. She shouted, "How many are there? How many more are in the house?"

A deep chuckle filtered through the leaves and into the open air around them. "I guess you'll find out."

Cai had never shot a gun before. Though anger took over at times, she wasn't violent. Her anger was taking over now, and it told her to pull the trigger.

"If that boy dies, Will, we die." The sheriff whispered slowly through gritted teeth trying not to annoy the dog at his face.

"*He* doesn't need that one. That boy has no power!" The man snarled. "He's the one that ran off!"

"That's not what *he* said. He has..."

"Shut up!" The old man grumbled. "There's only one more person in the house. Just one. We're posted here to wait for the twelve of you, to keep you contained, but not to hurt you."

"He's coming!" Cheater threw the words over her shoulder as she peeked around the tree.

Rebecca and Jaz remained over Nathan, who moaned with pain in a semiconscious state. Nathan lifted his hands to them, the strain of blending having drained his energy. "Help me." He spoke weakly.

The crunching steps of the third man neared them, just at the edge of the clearing to the barn.

Thad raised the rifle, cocked it, and took aim, following the man in the sights.

"No!" Cai sent the warning toward Thad, who glanced her way in reply watching her disappear into leaves.

Cheater didn't blend. Cheater felt the familiar sense of darkness overwhelming her as she found herself face to face with the armed man.

"Get your hands up!" He ordered, and her hands rose, turning into the tips of wings. Her face faded into that of his own young daughter who he'd believed lost at the hands of faith. "Daddy, why are you aiming that gun at me?" The girl asked as the wings folded behind her back.

The man released the trigger, set the safety, laid the gun on the ground, "Charlotte? Baby?"

"Don't fall for that you idiot! It's the girl, the one who can change..." Cai planted her invisible knee on the old man's throat gargling the rest of his words.

The man hadn't been listening to the comment anyway. He was moving toward his daughter, his arms open to embrace her. Tears of joy dripped from his chin. "Daddy, it wasn't the Gifted Ones who killed me. *He's* wrong, Daddy. He's lying to you. It was *him.* I know you're hurting, Daddy, especially now that Mama's left you, but you can't blame these kids. They're the good ones, not *him. He's* misleading you."

"What is that girl telling you? Turn away from h..." The sheriff pressed his head against the bark.

Grrrrrr Ruf! Splash pressed bared teeth against the sheriff's throat.

"Charlotte? My baby, my girl, what are you saying?" The man asked Cheater.

"Help them, Daddy, don't harm them. You have to find a way to help them, please. For me!" Charlotte began to fade as Cheater returned, her brown eyes still bearing the pleading look of the young girl she had become.

The gun lay behind him on the ground.

Cheater was completely vulnerable to the man's actions and somewhat dazed from the change.

She recalled the words her mother and father had spoken to her, the words Sadie had spoken.

The man's face changed, the smile faded, but the anger had left his eyes. He surveyed the situation, the two men taken over by the six teens, the one young boy on the ground, bleeding, the look in the face of the young girl who moments earlier had been his daughter. "That boy's gonna need a doctor, and it looks like you kids need some help." Leaving the gun on the ground, he pulled out a pocketknife and knelt to cut the rope next to Rebecca's knot above Nathan's knee. "Mhm, that bullet nicked an artery."

The man took the rope in hand, picked up his rifle, and took aim at the other two men in warning.

The teens gathered around Nathan, Rebecca on the ground still clinging to Nathan's hand. He winced in pain as he reached upward with his other hand. Each gathered another's hand, Cheater, Jaz, Cai and

Thad, completing the circle of six, connecting their energies with Nathan's weakening body, hoping for some way, some power, that would help him.

Nathan's immobile body began to glow; a fine yellow light radiated from his torso, his hands, and spread to the rest of the group, a half circle of light working its way around to connect in the oldest of them, Cai.

The light brightened, intensified, changed course and returned, circling among them and back to Nathan's hands. It trickled through his arms, down his waist, outlining his body until the two trails met at the bullet hole in his left thigh where they joined, disappeared, and burst from the hole in a radiant, sparkling, spiral reaching up into the clouds.

Nathan blinked his eyelids, opening them to Rebecca's broad smile, the first smile she'd given to anyone.

"My name's Joseph." The man told the six. "I have to say, I've never in my life seen anything like what just happened here. When he said you kids were powerful, he wasn't fibbin'. I guess that was the only thing he told us that wasn't a lie." Joseph threw an angry glare at the two on the ground. Cheater let go of Nathan's hand.

Frowns passed between the Gifted Ones. "*He* who?" Cai questioned. Finally, they might get some answers.

Joseph viewed each of them, his own brows drawing down. "Our soon to be leader. You kids don't see the news too much I take it." He frowned at them.

"Uhm, no, we've been a little busy," Jaz nodded.

"Of course. Right now, he's one of the greatest organizational leaders in the world. Followers all over listen to him every week. He talks about you, the twelve of you, and the evil you cast around... Sorry, I know now that's not the truth." Joseph shook his head.

"Shut up, you moron!" The bearded man yelled trying to kick at him. "You jis' signed your death certificate!"

"Only if he finds out. And where I'm taking you, he'll never see you again." Joseph turned back to the teens. "Now that I think about it, all of his speeches, I think he plans on..." Joseph bit his lower lip, "...well, I don't really know what his plans are because I can't take anything he's said for truth. I'll take care of these two. If you'll stay here a minute, I'll go get my car, and you can help me put them into it."

"What are you gonna do with them?" Nathan asked.

Joseph glanced at him and shook his head. "First, I'm gonna go find my wife. She'll know where to put them." He disappeared for a few minutes, driving back as far as he could.

"What did you mean your wife would know what to do with them?" Cheater asked him after the two men were loaded into the backseat.

"I didn't believe her. She kept telling me there was some kind of faction against him. Some group of people trying to help you, take him down. I was so lost after my daughter died. I believed in him, but I would never hurt my wife. She left me. I would bet, to join the faction." He pulled out his wallet and handed Cheater a card. "Call that number on the top, but don't leave a message if I don't answer. Just to be safe."

"Will somebody check in with these two?" Nathan asked.

"I'll take care of that, too. I have the radios, cell phones, in case somebody calls."

"Thank you, Joseph!" Jaz stuck his hand out to the older man.

"Hm, I should be thanking you." He glanced back at Cheater. "I haven't felt this sure of myself in years, ever since Charlotte..." His lips tightened to dam the tears; he nodded and slipped behind the steering wheel, closing the door to his thoughts. They watched his car bounce over the uneven terrain and disappear around the side of the house.

The three dogs mingled among the teens for scratches, rubs and licks. Rebecca squatted, hugging Splash's neck.

"Well, let me show you around my house," Nathan smiled at them.

"I already know my way around," Jaz nodded.

"Me, too," Cheater returned the grin.

"Can we be sure he's telling the truth, about nobody else being in there?" Thad peered warily at the house looming before them.

"True. We got played once before by that sheriff and the old man. Thought the sheriff had left, but he didn't," Jaz nodded.

"Well, we're out here in the open, he just drove away with those two men, and nobody's shooting at us? We probably should check it out, though."

"They could just be waiting for all of us to enter the house together. It could be a trap," Cai added.

"I guess so. Maybe we should be on the lookout for something suspicious. Do you think we can really trust Joseph?"

"Yeah, I think so," Cheater nodded. "He acted just like all of the others I helped before I knew what I was doing."

"Yeah, and we all know what he was thinking when he left, right?" Jaz added.

"Yeah. He was going to find his wife and take care of the sheriff and the imposter," Nathan added. "He was thinking about calling her from his other cell phone. His thoughts were happy, peaceful."

"Well, did you get any readings from the imposter? The sheriff?" Jaz pointed out.

"No," each answered.

"Then, there you are. Joseph was a changed man."

"I hope so. I've never been tricked by someone I've changed."

The teens moved slowly toward the back porch, the dogs in tow.

"The dogs don't seem afraid to go up there. They're smiling," Cheater suggested. "They were afraid before."

"You're right. We know we can trust them.

Here's a plan, though. We'll all enter at the same time, let the door slam, and then blend until we're sure nobody comes at us."

"Yeah, that's a good idea. And the dogs can come in too?"

"But, I've never blended inside before. I don't know if we can," Cai stopped them.

"Of course we can. We can do anything! We can even go to the cellar and get some of those peaches! I'm starving!" Thad rubbed his stomach as it gurgled in response.

Laughter filled the chilly afternoon air.

"We'll come back for those when we know we're safe." Cai put her arm across Thad's shoulder and squeezed.

"Do you think we'll be able to turn *him*, I mean, when the time comes?" Rebecca wondered.

"It doesn't work on everyone," Cheater replied. "I tried with those other two, when Jaz and I were caught. There has to be some hope for good. Some people have no hope left, I guess."

"Maybe all of us together?" Cai wondered.

Cheater shrugged.

"Well, at least now we know we have a healer among us." Cai patted Nathan's shoulder.

"Hey, I don't know if that was me or all of us. I've never done anything before unless it had something to do with food."

"He can feed us and heal us! Now that sounds like the beginnings of a good restaurant!" Jaz chuckled.

"A healer, hmm?" Rebecca nodded at Nathan.

"Yeah, I'm pretty sure it wasn't *just* me," his head bobbed.

"Well, however you did it, we'll probably find ourselves in another situation that will require it, so I hope it's easy for us to do it, again."

Splash stepped lightly next to Rebecca, licking her dangling fingers, happy she was back.

A determined, wary eye peered through the rifle scope, between the trees, watching the six teens approach the house. The eye squinted, twisted the scope for magnification, and panned between each one as the six walked onward.

Any other viewer wouldn't believe those kids were anything special by looking at them, but the person eyeing them through the scope had seen everything and knew who those kids were.

The hooded person watched as each of the kids passed through the backdoor, holding it open for the next. The smack of the screen door as it bounced against the doorjamb echoed through the still woods.

The scope scanned the surrounding buildings, the trees lining the property, and returned to view the barn. If the watcher was right, those six kids were so focused on the house that they wouldn't notice outside movement at all. To be sure, the watcher remained in the trees before trekking a slow half circle around the back of the property where the barn stood between the watcher and the house.

Now the barn was an easy walk, but not knowing if any others might be lurking in the woods, the viewer had no time to waste, so the person ran, crouched low, until the watcher's large frame was safely protected within the walls of the old wood barn.

Review Time of Dreams on Goodreads.com and any of the stores listed here books2read.com/u/bwdZ0y to help other readers determine if they want to read this book.

Continue to the next page for an excerpt of book three in this trilogy, The Lost Prince.

Enjoy this first chapter of the final book in this trilogy,

THE LOST PRINCE

1

Crouched deep in the closet corner, black spandex clad knees shook with anticipation beneath his calloused hands. He couldn't believe he was hiding in a closet dressed in his Comic Con costume. If one of his friends saw him dressed this way now... he shook his head at the thought.

Only she could talk him into wearing this costume on a normal day. Of course, she was the only one who knew the truth about him.

She thought he was a real superhero.

Hmpf!

What did she know? She was only seven years old.

He could hear her soft footsteps approaching.

He'd grown to love her so much this past six months. She was so innocent, so delicate, so happy— and in need of a big brother to protect her from the woes of this world. She'd become the little sister he never had the chance to know. Being her big brother made him feel strong, responsible, loved— in control. Nothing in his life had allowed him those feelings before his new foster parents brought him here.

As he squatted there, waiting for his sister to pull the door open, listening to her last few approaching steps, her high-pitched scream startled him from his hiding place. He burst from the closet, panic hidden beneath his masked face.

No!

No!

Not now!

His body shook with rage; his jaw muscles swelled as his teeth clenched. Every step became the longest sprint of his life, yet his stride seemed to slow down.

Her scream muffled, grew distant, silenced.

Noooooooooo!

The word flourished deeply within and then rose in crescendo.

He wasn't going to make it.

Not this time.

By the time he made it to the other room, she would be dead, just like all of the other times.

He couldn't save her.

His sense of control was false.

He couldn't stop her death.

She thought he was a superhero.

The door creaked under his forceful push on the brass knob. She lay there, on the floor of her room, motionless, breathless, colorless. Flames licked the walls, circled the room, and concealed her from his view. From the center of the flames, he heard it, the laughter, the taunting, the voice of the faceless man.

Tears blurred the roaring flames as he relented to his grief. He couldn't fight it any longer. He wanted to give up.

When he finally consigned himself to the thought, another voice called to him, the voice of a girl, "Unite, Gifted Ones!" He peered through the watery flames for her face, for some hope, and there she was across from him in the hot spiraling whirlwind.

The constant drumming grew louder as Jamie woke from the nightmare, the Juniper tree he curled beneath little protection from the heavy drops bouncing and splashing into the already muddy ground. A puddle formed beneath his left side. Water trickled into his right ear through the needled branches above, a tiny waterfall winding its way over his auricle into the ear canal. He could feel the cool December rain building, seeping through the black spandex covering his body. The cape served well to protect him from the cold wind, but did nothing to keep the water away from his skin.

What Jamie wouldn't give for his own clothes and a rain slicker— better yet, a room with a warm bed.

Jamie's conspicuous costume drew too much attention when wandering the crowded streets, especially in small towns like this. He cringed at his foolish decision to flee his home without clothes and supplies.

On the plus side, the raindrops masked the hot tears trailing over the bridge of his nose.

Some hero!

Whenever the recurring nightmare brought him to the ledge of lunacy, a face loomed before him, her face. That sincere, hopeful look was the only image that refocused his thoughts.

Thinking about her, he rolled out from under the evergreen and sat upright, allowing the hard rain to wash dirt, leaves and wet needles from his costume.

Through the curtains of rushing water dripping down either side of his forward bent face, lightning flashed, followed by a roll of thunder so near him the ground vibrated his crossed ankles.

He squinted into the pouring rain and silently wished the seeking arms of lightning would find him, strike him, end this nightmare, but he knew that wasn't possible. He could never escape the endlessness of his lonely world, his life.

He'd tried.

In spite of the raindrops racing over his cheeks, he wiped at his hot tears.

They had left him in charge of her.

They had trusted him with her life.

Worse, he had trusted them... both of them... his foster parents who said they loved him, wanted to adopt him. Ha!

He closed his eyes to the images of the last time he'd seen the only other people he'd loved since his own family.

Never again would he trust anyone, love anyone.

Long strands of soft, brown hair framed a floating face full of hope. The wavering image pushed through his depression, grief, anger, warning him of his self-pity. "Don't give up, Jamie!" Her voice fell softly into his thoughts through the heavy drops. It was like she was there, right next to him, speaking directly to him. "You are a hero." Her translucent image smiled, a bittersweet lift at the corners of her mouth, the pain and loneliness in her eyes so familiar to him.

He scoffed, a harsh, ironic chuckle escaping his throat as he scanned the Comic Con costume he donned.

"Who are you?" Jamie begged of the brown-haired girl before sobs disarmed his sanity. He gritted his teeth against the drenching rain, then he released a thunderous scream.

When Jamie lowered his eyes from the gray, branch parted sky, he noticed a hooded figure in the distance dodging from one tree to another. Jamie squinted through sheets of rain as the figure moved closer, hiding and running. The rain gear looked like the ones he'd seen cops wear in the movies, but it was much shorter. Curling himself into a ball, he rolled beneath the Juniper, drew his cape around his body and tugged down a lower limb for camouflage.

"Shut up! Are you trying to get us killed?" Neka whispered harshly into the darkness. "You and that incessant whistling! Sheez!"

"I can't help it. I'm bored. How much longer do we have to wait here? I'm starving, too."

"Ugh! You're not the only one who's hungry! Just be quiet." She mouthed, turning an ear toward the barn door, listening intently for the gruff voice, trying to discern the muffled conversation through cracks in the old wood.

Steps.

Mumbles.

Deep voices.

A clearly stated fact, "I know I saw them over here, but there's no way into this old barn, as far as I can see. Boarded up all the way around." A young man's voice, probably not much older than two hiding in the barn.

He sounded so nice. And cute...

Neka wondered what he looked like. Her back pressed against the stall wall, she closed her eyes imagining his face.

Wouldn't it be nice to have a normal life? Date someone? Someone with a voice like that? She wondered, the face she created hovering in the darkness behind closed lids.

Her life had never been normal, but then, considering all she'd seen since her parents' disappearance, maybe normal wasn't such a great thing. Slowly she opened her eyes as if the one behind the muted steps on the other side of the wall might catch sight of her slight movement; her muscles stiffened as his shadow passed over a sunlit crack in the wood next to her.

An eye, the sliver of an eye. "Too dark to see

anything in there. I tell ya', there's no way in. Been around it three times."

"A'ight. Let's call it in and get outta here. He ain't gonna be happy."

Who? Who's not going to be happy? The man who tore apart my family, maybe? Neka frowned.

Two car doors, a quiet engine, and tires crunching on gravel eased the tension in her muscles.

"Is it safe now?" The boy next to her whispered. There were days when his ignorance and arrogance made her want to punch him.

"Shh!" She peered angrily in his direction. She'd learned the silence seeming to wrap her in safety was the furthest from safe. Staying low, she crawled to a crack in the wall facing the gravel drive. She couldn't see the car, but something felt off. Intuition screamed from within, telling her to stay put, someone lurked beyond the wall, waiting for the two of them to slip up.

Was it intuition, or paranoia?

Following her intuition brought mistakes along the way and those mistakes cost her everything. One had cost her her parents. Her eyes stung with unshed tears as she returned to her spot through musty, dirty, dried hay— each swish surrounding her with the scent of old horse manure. Doubts filled her.

As annoying as the boy next to her was, she

didn't want anything to happen to him. He was all that was left of her past— of her life.

She had to hold on to her brother, keep him safe.

She closed her eyes, inhaled the horse smell, and reached a calming, protective hand toward his knee but felt only dirt. Swearing out a sigh, she searched the darkness for his silhouette before rising to follow him.

"Stop!" She raced toward the worn wooden wall of the barn and reached for his arm, but the connection brought an electrically charged pain to her hand, up her forearm, her shoulder, her neck, her brain, then nothing... darkness... her body ripped into tiny pieces, atoms of charged energy exploding into the atmosphere. When she opened her eyes, she stood outside the barn facing wild, overgrown woods. Pressing her back against the barn wall, she shifted her eyes cautiously before breaking the stillness with motion.

What if that boy on the outside could still be lurking? Hmm! Might not be a bad thing. Wishful thinking!

Nothing happened.

The view over her left shoulder revealed nothing but cracks in the old barn wall, a rusting tin roof, empty bird nests in the eves, yet she shivered from head to toe.

Her extremities tingled with the anticipation of being caught.

She hated when Nashota became uncontrollable!

Her parents should have switched their names, but he was born after she was. No matter, to her the name Neka—meaning "wild goose"—fit his personality better!

Ugh!

She slipped along the barn wall, side stepped to the corner, and peeked around it.

Nothing.

Hopeful, anxious lungs deflated like an unknotted balloon. If only she had been correct. If only the one with that voice had remained behind. She would like to see his face. Scanning her torn shirt, worn jeans, and tattered, fringed boots, she combed her fingers through the long dark snarls of waist-length hair and shrugged away the discouraged feeling. She would not want to meet a boy looking like she crawled straight out of a dumpster anyway. Still she wondered about his face, his personality, that one kind eye peering through the crack, the deep sapphire shielded by darkness that blocked daylight.

Absently, she stepped away from the barn, her brother yards ahead, whistling like he didn't have a care in the world.

Idiot! He had no fear of anything!

Dry grass crackled beneath her feet as she followed the whistling bird toward the woods. Absently her fingertips continued the grooming of her long dark hair and she let her guard down.

Snap!

The noise followed her; she froze, every muscle ready to run like a startled deer.

"Stop right there... Don't take another step... Turn around."

It was him— the voice from beyond the wall, the eye peeking through the crack, harshly whispered words like a wild breeze blowing into her ears.

Joyful mischief filled her; a slight smile touched her lips as she turned coyly.

She would see his face.

"What are you doing?" Carmen fisted her hands and pressed them to her hips. The force of her motions swung long, dark corn rows over her left shoulder. Anger deepened her delicate, caramel complexion as she prepared to fight for her belongings. "I said, what are you doing?" Her voice intimidated the thief into glancing over his shoulder.

She was tiny for having such a dominant

voice... and beautiful beneath the anger. Too bad she's so young, he thought as he pivoted, empty turned-up palms facing her. "I was looking for something to eat, okay? I haven't eaten in two days. There's nothing out there... nobody's willing to help me."

Her dark eyes squinted and scanned. Was he telling the truth, or was he just another homeless thief looking for valuables to sell for drugs or alcohol? He didn't look homeless. His clothes were too new to the streets. No matter, this bag wasn't her real bag. This bag was a decoy to catch the thief who stole her mother's teardrop pendant— worth more sentimentally than monetarily as they would learn when they went to pawn it.

"Please, I'm really dizzy. I need food, water. Do you know where I can find some?" he pleaded. Carmen almost felt sorry for him, but she'd lived on the streets long enough that her nerves steeled her emotions. Nobody would take her belongings, again. Everything in her bag was all she had left of her parents, her family, her home.

As she eyed the young man before her, his knees buckled beneath him and he crumbled to a heap in the dirty alley.

"Hey! Hey, are you messin' with me? You better not be fakin' it!"

No answer.

No movement.

Carmen tentatively moved toward him. She pushed his shoulder with her worn boot. "Hey, you okay?"

No response.

He must have been telling the truth.

She felt his neck for a pulse, found one.

Lifting his hair, she rested her palm on his forehead. She lightly pinched the skin on his arm and counted to three.

Definitely dehydrated.

Compassion overpowered her own self-preservation code; she would have to share her food before it was too late for him. In spite of the horror in her world, Carmen wanted to believe that everyone still had a good side she could coax out, but dark, muddy green filled the world. Yet, when she first glimpsed this guy, she'd seen gray, splotches of dark gray. Even so, she knew she couldn't trust the colors anymore.

Gripping the young man at his armpits, she began dragging him toward her temporary home. He wasn't light for his size, but she had strength beyond her size. Once inside the mass of pallets, crates, and cardboard, she shrugged loose the bag on her back, unzipped it, and removed a can of chicken broth. It was her last can, one of the many items she'd taken the night she left.

"It's all I got, but it will be the best thing for him." She told herself, propping his head on a mildew scented, worm eaten blanket. Using the church key on her mother's keyring, she punched two holes in the can, one larger, one smaller. She caressed the old house key between thumb and forefinger, forcing the brief thought of loss from her mind.

She lifted his head with one hand and slacked his jaw with the other, then poured a bit of cold, fatty broth into his mouth— not enough to drown him, but enough to stimulate his taste buds, hopefully wake him from his faint. A yellow blob of fat escaped the corner of his mouth, traveled down his chin.

His mouth closed; his tongue and throat worked together to bring the liquid downward. His eyes flickered, opened, stared warily at the cardboard above him.

"Where am I?" His unfocused eyes found her pretty, deep, dark gaze shrouded by long curling lashes, the smooth caramel face of a young girl, the can of chicken broth. "Thank you!" He managed a weak smile, his lids falling closed, again.

"Yeah, just don't get any ideas. You're not stayin'. This is my dive. Took me a long time to put these crates together, find enough plastic to keep the rain out." Her eyes warmly scanned the interior, then coldly returned to his face. She offered more broth. He forced open his eyes and drank it slowly. Elbows bent to push his torso upward as he scooted to lean into the exterior wall of the building serving as one side or her shelter; he took the can from her as he straightened against the brick wall.

"Hey, I can't argue. It's a great place for a pretty, little girl to hide from the masses of bad people out there!" He joked weakly.

"Don't you be gettin' any ideas! And I ain't little. I'm fourteen!" She argued.

"Well, it's nice to meet you, fourteen. I'm," he frowned, confusion filling him, "lost." Leaning into the brick wall behind him, he stuck his right hand out to her. She refused it.

"Just drink your broth— slowly— then get out." She sat back, watching his every move.

"Yes, ma'am!" He saluted. Tipping the can to his lips, he tilted his head back... and fumbled the half empty can when his eyes viewed the makeshift ceiling. The map, or flowchart, or whatever she would name it, reflected a memory, and there was little need to study it.

"Who are you?" He lowered the rescued can to his leg, but his eyes never left the ceiling.

"N-O-Y-B! And stop lookin' at my stuff!" She raised her hands to block his view.

"N-O... oh, your business, yeah, okay— no, you don't understand." Rolling onto his left hip, he dug a finger and thumb into his back pocket to remove a folded, heavily worn paper. After setting the can of broth aside, he pulled the delicate corners apart with care. Holding the paper corners gently, he crossed his forearms flipping the drawing toward her.

Finish the quest for answers! Read the final book in trilogy, The Lost Prince. Just scan the QR code below.

ABOUT THE AUTHOR

P. G. SHRIVER lives in Texas with her family of two and four legged beings.

She has been writing since the age of seven and was first published in a local newspaper. Some of her hobbies include gardening, reading, sewing and cooking.

She is a retired Developmental Education Instructor and 4-8 teacher. She enjoys writing, traveling and presenting at schools and festivals.

Visit her website today at pgshriver.com! Follow her on Goodreads.

www.ingramcontent.com/pod-product-compliance
Lightning Source LLC
Chambersburg PA
CBHW011653010726
47499CB00010B/3238
* 9 7 8 1 9 5 2 7 2 6 0 2 6 *